Golden Boys

PHIL STAMPER

BLOOMSBURY
LONDON OXFORD NEW YORK NEW DELHI SYDNEY

BLOOMSBURY YA
Bloomsbury Publishing Plc
50 Bedford Square, London WC1B 3DP, UK
29 Earlsfort Terrace, Dublin 2, Ireland

BLOOMSBURY, BLOOMSBURY YA and the Diana logo
are trademarks of Bloomsbury Publishing Plc

First published in the United States of America in 2022 by Bloomsbury YA
First published in Great Britain in 2022 by Bloomsbury Publishing Plc

Text copyright © Phil Stamper, 2022
Illustrations by Brett Wright

Phil Stamper has asserted his right under the Copyright, Designs and Patents Act, 1988,
to be identified as Author of this work

A catalogue record for this book is available from the British Library

ISBN: PB: 978-1-5266-4384-1; eBook: 978-1-5266-4383-4

2 4 6 8 10 9 7 5 3 1

Book design by John Candell
Typeset by Westchester Publishing Services

Printed and bound in Great Britain by CPI Group (UK) Ltd, Croydon CR0 4YY

To find out more about our authors and books visit www.bloomsbury.com
and sign up for our newsletters

To teenage Phil, who was always looking for himself on the shelves. A little late, but you're here now.

CHAPTER ONE

GABRIEL

BEING THE BIG SPOON is such a chore. Don't get me wrong, it's nice having Sal curl into me. The warmth coming off his body is calming. My heartbeat thrums through my chest, but I feel my heart rate slow.

Breathing is a bit awkward, though. First, his lightly tousled blond hair keeps getting in my mouth. Second, it's like I can see my hot breath curl around his neck—is it uncomfortable for him? How fresh *is* my breath, exactly? And how does Sal not worry about all this when our roles are flipped.

Mentally, my body's suspended in this kind of light, peaceful state. Physically, I'm *sweating*. We've kicked off the blankets, but not even the constantly running air-conditioning his mom insists on can combat this heat wave. My left arm is fully asleep, and I'm not sure where to put my other one. Right now, it's draped awkwardly around him, rising and falling slowly with his breath.

Every time I shift my body, my skin peels lightly away from his. Normally, this is when I'd call it quits and roll over, but if this is the last time . . .

I can't think about it. So I think about him.

He seems comfortable and safe in my arms, in his bed, in his house. His confidence claims ownership over everything in his sphere, and sometimes I feel like I'm pulled into that, even if we're not actually, officially a thing.

Something in the way he softly presses his hips into mine and arches his neck back reminds me he's in control of this situation, even as the little spoon.

I place my lips on his neck, then give it a playful bite. He laughs and jerks his head away from mine.

Sometimes it feels good to remind him that, of all the things that are his, I am not one of them.

"What's up?" Sal asks, rolling over to meet my gaze. Our foreheads touch, and a smile pulls at my lips. My breaths grow longer, smoother. "You're stiff today."

I arch a brow, which prompts him to say, "Ugh, not like that. I mean it, though. Are you worried?" he asks. "About this summer?"

"I'm worried about a lot of things," I admit. But it doesn't exactly take a mind reader to figure out what worry is at the top of my list. "Don't get me wrong, I'm excited to volunteer with them. And it'll look great on my transcript. And I'll help save the trees, which is cool."

Sal pulls me in for a kiss. "Are you worried you'll miss me too much?"

"Right," I say with a laugh. As much as I do love this thing we've had going on for years, I don't love *him* like that. "We could probably use the time apart anyway. Give me a chance to find a boy who doesn't consider political commentary to be pillow talk."

"Ah. I see. You want the good stuff." He pulls closer to me, and the chills fly up my back and settle uneasily into my shoulders. "Don't make me use my secret weapon."

"Oh my god, don't!" I shout, slapping him away while holding in a laugh. But he leans into me. His voice drops to a whisper, and his breath on my ear sends shivers down my whole body. I pull up the blanket, despite the heat. "*Où se trouve la station de métro la plus proche?*"

My heart plummets into my stomach, and I hate myself for being so basic. I mean, he's saying nonsense he picked up from French III, I know this. *But.* He says it so directly, so boldly, that I almost see myself falling for him in a real way.

"*God*, why didn't I end up taking French?" I say. "What the hell are you even saying?"

"Oh, you know, romantic stuff." He clears his throat. "*Je voudrais acheter un billet.*"

Despite myself, I shudder. "Sounds pretty romantic," I say dryly.

"Ms. Brashear always said I had the best accent of the whole junior class. Reese hated that, but maybe he'll pick up the accent after living there this summer. A few of us might get to go on a trip to Paris next year for French IV, so I've got to keep practicing. Wouldn't that be freaking awesome?"

"Wow. The Village of Gracemont, Ohio. Taking over Paris." I pause. "I kind of feel sorry for them."

He laughs, and I do too. But when the laughter stops, an unsettling silence replaces it. Without thinking much of it, I roll away and stare at Sal's room. It's so tidy you'd think he doesn't have any stuff. But there's hints of his personality throughout the space. A ring light and a selection of makeup in one corner. A tie rack filled with bright bow ties, most with price tags still attached. A large desk with a spinning chair and laptop, adorned with academic medals, trophies, and one term paper. He's got his good grades pinned to a corkboard like he's his own proud parent.

"I'm excited to go to DC this summer," Sal says. "But I'm almost more excited for you to go to Boston. For Reese's design school in Paris. Heck, even for Heath to get to Daytona."

"Heck?"

"An upstanding young gentleman never curses."

Simultaneously, we roll our eyes. He's quoting his mom right now—she was bad before, but she pivoted to full helicopter mode the moment he got the call about his summer internship with Senator Wright.

He reaches around and pulls me into him, and a rush of calmness floods my body. He never wants to be big spoon, so I savor every moment. "I mean it, about all of us. We've been inseparable for years, but . . . there's only so much we can do here, you know? Mom's always pushed me to do this kind of stuff. She was always making time to take me away from here, to show me what life is like outside Gracemont. She even opened this particular door for me, by helping me get this internship. I know I can pick up where

4

she's left off and turn this into my life." A darkness fills the silence. "We need to get out of here."

"That's so easy for you to say." I push back. "You're comfortable in big cities, you fit in everywhere. Nothing scares you." I don't mention that he also has the money to do these things, while my parents are eating into their savings to send me to Boston. "But it's hard for me to even think about. I want your confidence, you know?"

"You still *did it*, Gabe. You have to be confident and brave to make these plans—to apply, to tell your parents, to actually commit to this bonkers save-the-trees passion. You saw the opportunity, and you said yes. That's brave. Don't let your anxiety overshadow everything you've already done."

I sigh, long and slow, as he holds me tighter. "I keep thinking of all the people I need to impress, all the crowds I have to deal with. I'm going to hate Boston, I know it. Seriously, what the 'heck' did I get myself into?"

He laughs, then mumbles something about how I'm going to do great. He's so casual with how he holds me right now. His sticky body is pressed to mine, and he's not even doing anything, but his intensity still radiates. It's addictive . . . his energy, his confidence, his drive.

He's always striving for more: better grades, more accolades for his desk, but he's somehow as content with me as I am with him. I can't help but think we both deserve better than content, though. So, maybe this summer apart will be good for us.

He holds me close, and I breathe him in. I ignore the part of me that never wants him to let go.

CHAPTER TWO

SAL

I DON'T KNOW WHY, but something hits me when Gabriel and I step onto the porch. Something other than the heat wave, that is. A wave of longing, maybe? Remorse? *Fear?* But I smile and push through it. Those feelings will just hold me back, so I can't let myself think too hard on it.

We're already running much later than we planned. Reese wanted us at his goodbye party early to help set up, and if Gabe doesn't leave now, we don't have a chance of getting ready, picking up supplies, and making it to Reese's on time. But something's stopping him from going.

"So," he says. "With how Reese's family is, his goodbye party's bound to go on all night. You've got family stuff Wednesday; I've got family stuff Thursday."

"On Friday, the four of us will be together all night," I say, catching on to what he's saying.

"And we leave Saturday."

"We leave Saturday," I echo.

He shifts uncomfortably, and the longing settles in my chest again. "Which means, this is it for us, in a way?" he says.

"It'll never be *it* for us." I wink. "But yeah, we won't have alone time for a while."

Our friendship is unconventional, to say the least. We've always been able to talk through it, though. Even if Gabriel's anxiety sometimes gets in the way and makes it hard for him to express his thoughts. But today is different. It's never felt clipped like this. He's never seemed so guarded.

I reach out to him, and he pulls back at the last second.

"I . . . don't know why I'm thinking so much about it," he says. "Three months is a long time, I guess. And we finally have our first chance to date other people."

"And you've suddenly realized you love me."

Our eyes meet, but he busts out laughing first.

I know I love him. It's not *that* kind of love. But it's not nothing. There's something there, and it's just that everything around us moves so quickly. I'm freaking busy, Mom's always breathing down my neck, and everything is hard.

But this isn't. In fact, sinking into his lips is easy.

"I'll miss this, though." I admit it with a gentle smile on my face. "And if we never get to hook up again because we're off falling in *real* love with our cosmopolitan boyfriends, then good for us. Right?"

The silence after I ask is full of emotion. We knew there was an expiration date on this, but I didn't think I'd be staring it in the face so soon.

"Right." His voice is quiet, but it doesn't reveal much of anything. "And if this is it for us, just know I've appreciated it, Sal. Even if you are just *awful* in bed."

I scoff and pretend to turn away, but he grabs my arm and spins me toward him.

"Joking," he says. "I really will miss us."

With Gabe, I always have to be the strong one. The confident one. And I *like* that dynamic. I like feeling in control, taking the lead, but right now I don't feel so confident.

He turns to go, but he stops when I let out a whimper.

"Did you say something?"

I bite my lip. "No. It's nothing."

It's not nothing, of course. I'm stressed about moving to DC, about our friendship, about the other guys. About my mom's three hundredth lecture on "college strategy" last night. I'm *scared*. I want to say that, and I need him to hear it. But I can't cling to this dynamic we have. This *whatever*ship that we've been in, off and on, for years. I need to move forward, and he does too, and this summer is the perfect time to do it.

He must sense my hesitation, because he comes back onto the porch and wraps me in a hug. We break apart, just briefly, and I bring my mouth to his. We have a million unspoken rules to our hookups; the most obvious one is that we never do it in public. But here he is, biting my lip and pressing his tongue into mine. We kiss, and we kiss, and we kiss.

But I'm still scared.

• Golden Boys •

GABRIEL + HEATH + REESE + SAL

Earth to Sal

Earth to Gabriel

What exactly is the point
of a group chat if no one
responds to me

I respond!!

Don't text and drive

We're at a stop sign and you're
in the passenger seat??

Shut up and drive.

Guys, whenever you're done doing whatever it is you're...doing

S, can you still pick up ice? And G, you're bringing your dad's cookies right?

Don't be late 😡

CHAPTER THREE

REESE

"I CAN'T BELIEVE THEY'RE doing . . . *it* again."

I've sent four messages in a row, and I know a fifth would be too much, but they're supposed to help us set up the party. A sigh escapes my lips as I swipe from our group chat to Find My Friends, where the *S* circle and the *G* circle are practically on top of each other at Sal's house. Fitting, as they're probably literally on top of each other right now.

Gross.

"Still bothers you, huh?" Heath says from the driver's seat. I want to snap back and tell him what bothers me more is his erratic driving, or the fact that his truck's shocks needed to be replaced about two decades ago. That usually stops him from prying. But I don't do that.

Because that's not exactly true. Sitting shotgun with Heath is like this. Like a thrill ride at Cedar Point—the feeling of danger in a safe, contained space. We bounce along the roads, and I take a second to collect myself.

I'm flustered, yes, but I have good reason to be. My goodbye party starts promptly at six. I asked Gabriel and Sal to be there on time so they can help set up tables and chairs, put up decorations, set out the chafing dishes, and so on.

It's how every party goes. My moms spend the full day in the kitchen making party food, and they expect us to set up the rest of the house. Which is cool in theory, because setting things up wouldn't take long with four people . . . but it gets a lot more stressful when two of us are late.

And they're late again, like always, because they're *obviously* hooking up right now.

"It's not the first time we've had to do this alone," Heath says, and a grin smacks me across the face. "And it probably won't be the last."

I groan. "Well, if they're more than fifteen minutes late, this time *will* be their last. I'll make sure of that."

"Sure, sure, we've all been friends since preschool, but today's the day you take a stand."

He laughs, and it's such an aggravating laugh in its sincerity. Heath gives me a hard time; that's always been the case. But of all the people who put pressure on me, who critique me—from my moms to my graphic design tutors and everyone in between—he's the only one who does it in a way I *know* he's joking.

"They do this shit." His voice is a bit more serious now. "I mean, they can't even make it to one of my games before the fifth inning, and Gabriel's backyard literally touches the park."

He releases a dry laugh, but it doesn't seem particularly sad. Maybe it doesn't affect him as much as it does me, though he was quick to find a very specific, personal anecdote.

"Everyone's flaky," he says.

"You're not," I reply.

Instinctually, my mind reaches for anything to lighten the sincerity—for a witty remark, or anything clever—but I come up dry. Because he's not flaky. He just isn't. Some days it's like he's the only one I can depend on.

"Neither are you." A smile crosses his face, and butterflies invade my stomach. "Last row of the bleachers. Sketchbook in one hand, hot dog in the other. Every game."

"That's different. See, I just like baseball."

He chuckles. "Tell me again what a full count is?"

"Three balls, two strikes. Don't test me. Though you're correct that I'm only there for the concessions stand."

He turns to me briefly, but I break eye contact. We both know I'm only there for one reason. Him. Or, maybe he doesn't know.

We hit a bump, and the shock sends me flying up off my seat. My stomach flutters.

"Sorry," he says, and I don't know if he's sorry about giving me a hard time or making my head hit the roof of his car.

I respond to both. "It's okay."

My gaze falls on the window, and there's a sort of comfort that takes over me as I watch the blur of fields and country houses fly by. The sameness of it all can be beautiful, but the charm's kind of lost on me. My heart needs something I can't find here: an art scene, a city with a complex history. Part of me is already in Paris, though my flight doesn't leave for a few more days. But so much of me is here.

Heath changes the topic. "Okay, so I think I've finally got your family memorized. All fifteen cousins, even the ones with the identical-sounding names. Elena, Isabella, Gabriella, and . . ."

"Wait, really?" I turn to him in shock. "*I* can barely keep them straight."

"Gabriella"—he overpronounces the *G*—"is the one with *guh*-lasses. *Elena* looks *eleven* even though she's, like, our age. Want me to keep going?"

"Save the magic trick for the party," I laugh, and then we settle into an easy silence. I study his face for a moment as I take a sip of one of the cappuccinos we got from the gas station. The sweetness of the drink matches the satisfied smirk on his face. "I can't believe you memorized my extended family. You only see them like once or twice a year."

We pull up to a stop sign, and he turns to me gently. His cheeks redden, I think, as he runs a hand through the wavy peaks of his new haircut. I've read nonexistent signs way too many times; it's hard to tell what's real and what I'm making up as they happen.

But this feels like something. Or rather, it feels like we're close to something.

"I love your family," he says plainly. His gaze drops. "I don't get big parties, I don't have eighty-five cousins, and I love that you could so easily take it all for granted . . . but you don't. It's so clear how much you love them. Even—what's his name?—that kid who's kind of a dick."

14

"Ryan?"

"Ryan!" he exclaims at the same time, then laughs. "I knew that, I swear."

He looks up and hits the gas, and we're suddenly flying down country roads again, the wind tearing up our hair.

"Anyway, they're important to you, so they're important to me. I can at least learn their names, even if those girls' identical Italian names make it *impossible*."

My phone buzzes, and I see Gabriel thumbs-up my most recent message. Helpful. And suddenly, my mind's thinking of Sal and Gabriel again. I go quiet, thinking of their easy relationship, even though they don't call it a relationship. "Friends with benefits!" they announced when we were, like, thirteen. *Thirteen!* Back then, the "benefits" were a few stolen kisses when me and Heath left the room, but god only knows what that means now.

How can they keep it so uncomplicated? How can they make it look so damn easy?

But I look to Heath, and my complicated feelings all attack me at the same time. I *want* that easy love, but . . .

"Try to give them a break," Heath says after peeking at his phone and noticing my sudden quietness. "They'll be on time. They know how important all this is to you."

For one bright, hopeful second, I think he's going to place his hand on my knee, but he grips the gear shift and kicks us into third gear.

Benefits or not, I don't want to be just friends with Heath.

• PB Allergy •

GABRIEL + HEATH + SAL

> I made the chat name peanut butter allergy since theres no reese in it

> No reese's

> lol get it? (H)

(G) What's up H?

> Reese is getting more frozen apps from the store for the party (H)

(G) And?

> Typing! Hold on (H)

(S) ...

Ok, so: Reese is worried you two won't make it on time. Y'all do have a tendency to, um, come after the expected start time, as it were. So, I was hoping you could not do that this time? He's really flustered about all of us leaving, and idk, having some time together before his family whisks him away for awkward conversations is important to him....

Can you do that?

Sorry

CHAPTER FOUR

HEATH

I TUCK MY PHONE under my thigh and drum nervously on the steering wheel.

Isabella is a *Belle* and likes *books*.

Elena has *eyewear*. Wait, no, Gabriella has *guh*-lasses; Elena looks eleven.

Arianna can sing, and Lucia is *lucky* to be the youngest because she doesn't have to know all these freaking identical names.

I love his dumb family, but Reese's older cousins need to stop having girls. Or, I guess they could just pick names that don't consist primarily of *L*s and *A*s.

In better news, I did just put on a good show for him, revealing my secret mnemonic device, but I know as soon as we get to his house and that van of girls starts unloading, that's all going right out the window.

I should have made flash cards for this.

From my parking spot, I have a good view of the whole shopping center. There's not much here besides the grocery store, a pharmacy, and the local dentist. I have to admit that I don't like the area much.

There's no "charming downtown" like you see in rural towns on TV shows; there's just this. A wannabe shopping center, plus a few gas stations for people passing through. The stores never change, and the buildings are in the same sad state of disrepair they've been in since I was a kid.

I wonder if that's why I like the country roads so much. The crops grow and change, the trees turn from green to red to bare. But this shit just stays the same. Dad says we might have to move into the apartments down the street from here if we end up selling the farmhouse, and that thought alone makes me want to hurl.

Reese unloads a few bags of groceries into the back of the truck and hops into the passenger seat. I put my phone away completely, as he'd probably be pissed if he knew I was texting the guys without him. Once he's buckled in, I ease out of the parking spot.

As we pull back onto Main Street, I glance back at the bags in the truck and notice a bag of ice peeking out of the top of one of them.

"Wait, isn't Sal picking up ice? Should I tell him not to? That might save him some time."

Reese shakes his head, and his cheeks burn red for a moment. "No, it's just a backup plan. I don't know how long they'll be . . . occupied. That bag will last until he can get the rest here."

"Maybe they're on their way already?" I sigh, lightly. "They frustrate me sometimes too, but you've got to trust them a bit more, Reese. They know how important—"

"So, what about *your* family?" he says, cutting me off. He's shifting uncomfortably in the passenger seat, which he does from time to time, but I can't really spot why. He seems furious with the other guys. Which, fair. But it's almost like he's more annoyed with them for hooking up, which, is just not a new thing. "The ones you're living with in Daytona."

I grip the steering wheel tighter as I punch the clutch and shift into fourth gear. Crops fly by my window, and it starts to sink in that this time next week I'll be on a beach. *Daytona* Beach.

"Okay, sure. I don't know them well myself, since my aunt Jeanie and Mom had this big falling-out when I was younger. But I'm staying with her and my cousin Diana. She's around our age. You've probably seen her on my Instagram—she comments on about everything I post."

"Is your family from Daytona?" he asks weakly, and I wonder if he feels weird that I haven't shared all of this with him by now. I mean, he *is* my closest friend. It doesn't compare, though. Reese has got, like, fifty cousins, and they have all these structured family gatherings and traditions, and I've always just had my parents.

And I don't even know if I have them, after all this.

"Here's what I know: Aunt Jeanie left Ohio for Daytona when she was really young. She owns an arcade on the boardwalk that sounds pretty cool. We don't talk much, but she always makes sure to call me on my birthday, when she always ends up complaining about the first wave of spring breakers making their way to her arcade." I laugh as I say, "I guess we'll be complaining about drunk frat bros together this year."

We hit another bump, and I flinch as Reese's slight body gets tossed around in the passenger seat. He never complains, but it's got to bother him. But it's hard to find the cash to replace the shocks, especially when most of the money from my part-time job has been going to groceries.

"It sounds fun, though," he finally says. "I know it feels like you're being shipped there while your parents sort out the divorce, but you'll have fun. I mean, it's the beach. It's not here, at least."

"Yeah, true."

I didn't get any choice in the summer move, and the guys know that. They don't know how tight money's been for us, though. They don't know that I'm going to be working the boardwalk, right next to Diana, serving beer to college kids all summer, and holding on to every penny in case it helps us keep the house.

It might be fun, but it's not a vacation.

We pull up to a stop sign, and a growing squeal comes from the brakes. I cringe with the sound, and I start to worry about how I'll even make the drive to Florida with it in this state.

I silently pray for Reese not to bring it up, to point out our obvious differences. Our friendship is so good, so stable, but where will we be once he's back from Paris, and I'm back from *Florida*?

CHAPTER FIVE

SAL

WE'RE CUTTING IT REALLY close. How I ended my *intimate hangout* with Gabe was kind of bizarre, and it's left me with an icky feeling. Our time apart really only lasted about twenty minutes, though, while I took a shower and got dressed in one of my many crisp white button-ups in record time. Then I was on the road, stopping by his house to pick him up on the way to the school.

I have Gabe lug the giant cooler from the trunk of my car as I set off to unlock the front doors of our high school. In summer evenings, there's never anyone in the office, and it's always a bit unsettling to see the halls so empty.

"This cooler is heavy," he says as we walk inside the lobby, so I take one handle and we split the load, though it's about to get a whole lot heavier. Soft emergency lighting illuminates the halls, but it's nothing compared to the fluorescents that we normally see.

"The perks of having your mom as the vice principal," Gabe says.

"The *only* perk," I snap back. "And I would say free ice from the kitchen's ice maker is hardly a perk."

"She can order from the kitchen's food catalog, though. Remember that time in middle school when you had, like, hundreds of rectangle pizzas in your freezer?"

My stomach turns. "Don't remind me. I ate those for an entire summer. I went through an entire bottle of ranch every week. It was not my finest moment."

Gabe stops suddenly, and I'm pulled back by the handle of the cooler.

The steps down into our cafeteria-slash-auditorium are just off to our right, but I avoid looking. I feel the anxiety rising in my chest.

"We can't be late," I say, wiping my brow with the back of my hand. "Come on—the back of the kitchen is this way."

Sweat prickles at my skin, and I feel an itch to bail on all this.

"Or we could walk through the front," he says coolly.

He takes the cooler from me and jerks his head toward the cafeteria. I know he's testing me, so I lead the way. Each step I take echoes through the halls, and maybe it's just my brain short-circuiting, but I can smell the fried chicken they served that day.

There are no tables in the cafeteria right now, which makes sense—why would they keep them out all summer when they have no bodies to fill them? I tell myself not to look, but I do. There's an unassuming corner, just by the auditorium stage, where student council sets up all their lunch events: prom ticket sales, fundraisers.

Fundraisers like the one we threw on the last day of school.

Being the student treasurer, I was there to take donations. Reese was next to me, because he was the one who brought up the idea in one of our last meetings—an end-of-year fundraising drive for The Trevor Project, an organization focused on suicide prevention among LGBTQ youth. We're not the most progressive school, but there was unanimous support from the rest of the student council. It was an early celebration of Pride Month, a way to show support for queer students, and everyone thought our school was ready for it.

We weren't.

A tear slips down my cheek, and it's only then that I realize how rigid my body's gone. Shoulders pulled in so tightly it hurts, stilted breath. So much sweat. Gabe wraps me up in a hug from behind, and I flinch.

"It's okay. He graduated."

"He absolutely did," I say. "He walked across the stage at graduation, decked with honors' cords, and got hugs from every single teacher. And no one gave one shit about what he put me through every single year. No one cared about what he said that day. Not even Mom."

We fill the cooler with ice, then leave, barely saying a word. On the way out, I don't give the cafeteria another look, I don't give *him* another thought, and as we step out of the doors of the school, my core steels and a smirk comes on my face.

In a few days, I'm getting the heck out of here. I'll be in DC, working on Capitol Hill, wearing a suit every day, somewhere where no hometown bully can follow me.

• iMessage •

GABRIEL + HEATH

Hey, we're leaving
the school now

Only 10 min late! That's gotta
be a record for y'all

Yeah, about that.... Sal had
an unfortunate moment in
the cafeteria when we got
the ice. I know Reese will
be annoyed we're late but
maybe give him a heads-up

Shit, didn't even think of that…. Reese was there too though so he'll understand

Fuck

Now R will feel bad that he sent S into there

I mean, he had to go back sometime. Probs good it was just the two of us

True true

See u in a bit R's ma is making me hang up banners bc I'm tall 🙁

Ha, right. You love when people take advantage of your tallness, don't lie 🙁 🙁 🙁

CHAPTER SIX

GABRIEL

ONE TIME, IN SIXTH grade science, we had to give presentations to the whole school during an Earth Day assembly. The auditorium was packed with clusters of students, each grade taking up a section of the seating, and within the sections there were defined groups of people. I wanted to map out the entire auditorium—choir boys in one cluster, the girls' basketball team in another. I could see the groups forming, connecting with one another as the teacher tried to get my PowerPoint on trees to show up.

In all the teen movies I'd seen, there were definite cliques. Jocks, nerds, band geeks—but that's just not how it was here. Our school was too small, and it was messy. I spotted slick and fashionable Sal make his way toward a couple of Agriculture Club girls in denim dungarees, while artsy Reese was up in a corner with Heath and the baseball team. Everyone seemed to fit in everywhere, and I . . . didn't. If I wasn't in a class with Sal, Heath, or

Reese, I usually didn't talk. Maybe it was the added pressure of public speaking, but that's when it really clicked: I don't know how to make friends.

My presentation wouldn't work. Actually, the whole projection system was down, and the teachers didn't know what to do. So there I was, dealing with the fact that I had no backup friend group, nor the capacity to *make* friends, when the teacher whispered into my ear:

"Do you think you can give the presentation without your slides? Looks like you have it all printed out here, so maybe you can just relay some of the facts without the visuals. You'll still get full credit, of course."

A knife of anxiety slashed my chest, and I again looked out in the crowd. Their chattering had gotten louder, it seemed. In the halls, I could just put my head down and push through to my locker, then get to class. At baseball games or birthday parties, I could just cling to Sal. But here, I had no one, and I'd never felt so vulnerable in my entire life.

I'd had many awkward moments in the years since, but nothing's brought up that memory quite like this upcoming trip. I can't make friends in Boston. I don't even know *how*. The anxiety's been building all week, all month really. Combine that with the mini-breakdown Sal just had, and I can feel a knot in my stomach twisting so tightly it's like it's sucking me inside out.

When we get to Reese's house, Sal pulls his car off the driveway to park in the grass. We sit in the car for a few minutes, and I don't think either of us wants to do anything. To move. To say anything.

A part of me wishes I'd have been there when that guy went up to Reese and Sal, but my lunch period had already ended. I don't know what I would have done. Probably just stare in disbelief, then follow Sal out of the building.

I reach out to grab his hand, and our fingers lace together. It pulls us away from the past, back into this moment. Hand holding is against our rules, technically, and this feels like we're crossing into the not-just-friends territory. But I want to be there for him like I wasn't able to that day.

"Don't tell them I freaked out back there," he says. "Just pretend nothing happened."

My cheeks flush, knowing I've already told them. "Sure," I say. Because that's what he needs to hear to save face.

We get out of the car just as Heath busts out the front door, Reese tagging along behind him. Sal comes to my side, and we lean against the car as they approach. He loops his pinky through mine, and I feel a warmth, a rightness of having us all together again.

"Hey, Reese," Sal says, forcing a cheery tone into his voice. "Sorry we're late—"

Reese cuts him off with a hug. It's not a boastful one, not one with arms spread wide, but it's full of emotion nonetheless. Reese buries his head in Sal's chest and holds the fabric of his shirt a little too tightly. My gaze meets Heath's, and he gives me a sympathetic nod.

Reese doesn't seem to be letting go anytime soon, so I wrap my arms around them both and press my forehead to theirs.

Reese is an ember, smoldering and furious and full of tears. Sal still seems caught off guard. His breathing is irregular, and my heart aches for him. For what he and Reese went through that day. As expected, Heath joins the fray and uses his lengthy wingspan to pull us all into him. We're a little off balance, and it's not even comfortable anymore, but it feels so safe and so right.

I know they'll all be here when I get back. I know twelve weeks is nothing. A tiny part of me wonders what will change, how I'll change. But then a darker thought enters my mind . . . what if I'm the only one who doesn't?

CHAPTER SEVEN

REESE

AFTER WE ALL BREAK apart and awkwardly shuffle to the door—
Heath last because he insisted on bringing in the cooler of ice all
on his own—I feel a brush of heat hit my cheeks. See, I don't
show emotion. I have emotions, but I don't get why people feel
the need to show them all the time. Like how, by the time we've
hit fourth period, Gabriel's blown up the group chat with four
different anxiety spirals, or how it only takes one good "unlikely
animal friends" video on YouTube to make Heath cry.

But Sal and I aren't usually like that. I like to think we have a
good head on our shoulders, or something, but that's probably
ages of toxic masculinity radiating up from the farmlands. Even
after that guy hurled abuse at us, I don't think either of us really
reacted. Sal technically flipped the table on his way out, but that
was more a matter of convenience. At that point, nothing could
have stopped him from getting to the door. Meanwhile, I was

frozen in place and burning with rage, replaying that jackass's words in my head until one of Heath's baseball friends stepped in and put an end to it.

While Gabriel and Heath head around back to fill up the other coolers, I lead Sal to the kitchen and peek in on my parents. Mom's carefully stirring something on the stove in a big pot, while Mamma's at the table forming what looks like a few hundred meatballs.

"Hi, dear." Mamma turns her head around, wrist deep in raw meat and onions for her meatballs. "Oh, Sal! Thank you for helping out. It'll be a crazy one."

Mom laughs. "You know how it is by now. Is Gabriel coming too?"

"He's out back with Heath. I told them to start setting up the coolers and tables. We're going to take care of the living room."

"Sounds good," Mamma says. "Your cousins should be here soon—don't dawdle."

"Oh, they're always late," Mom says. "How are things going, Sal? Are you as excited for DC as Reese is for Paris?"

"Things are good," Sal says. "Honestly, I can't wait to get out of here."

Mamma points a spoon at him. "I hear that. I felt the same, and that's why I went to London."

"That's right," Sal says. "You studied abroad too. Have you figured out where you're going on your trip?"

My parents look at me, and I feel my cheeks turn red.

"They're coming to Paris at the end of my term," I tell Sal, "and then we'll be in London. They want me to pick one more city on our big European trip, but I don't know where I want to go yet."

"Clock's ticking," Mamma says. "You two go set up the living room. When you're done, tell him how nice Lisbon is in the summer. Or Barcelona. Or—"

"We said we wouldn't push him," Mom says while rolling her eyes. "Though I've heard Prague is nice."

I hurry Sal out of the kitchen. "Sorry about that. They're never going to let it go."

"Where *do* you want to go?" Sal asks.

I shrug. "No clue. I'll figure it out eventually, after they stop giving me endless suggestions."

Once we get to the living room, Sal instinctually starts opening up one of the folding tables. The jealousy starts to settle in again, just seeing him, and I curse myself for being so damn resentful of what he and Gabriel have. I take a few deep, cleansing breaths, hoping that'll calm me down a bit, because I know I'm fully in the wrong here. It's their bodies, their lives; they can do whatever makes them happy.

But how do they do it? *How* can they be so confident?

"You okay?" Sal says when he realizes that I'm clearly not. "Your face is all scrunched—really, the cafeteria thing was fine. It's good I went. We can even go there before school starts just to make sure there's no, you know. Bad feelings."

"No, it's not that," I say, even though I should probably take him up on that offer. "Actually, put that table down for a second, I want to get your opinion on something."

"Yeah?" he replies, then starts to follow me upstairs.

"It's just that you're not really one to mince words—if you thought, say, a special going-away gift I made for the crew was bad, you'd totally say so."

"I'm actually a great liar when it comes to bad gifts," he says. "Mom just got me this engraved pen for the summer. It literally says *Intern to Senator Wright* on it."

We take the final steps, and I open the door to my room. My somewhat barren gray-blue walls greet me. I spent the last week taking down the pictures I had taped to the walls—so many pictures of the four of us, plus a few of my friends from summer camp, of logos and other design inspiration I liked. I'm bringing them all to Paris for this graphic design program, so I have a little bit of home with me.

"Intern to Senator Wright," I repeat. "That's cringey."

"I acted like it was the best thing I'd ever seen. But for this, I will be honest. Promise."

Reaching underneath the bed, I clasp a tiny cardboard box. We sit on the bed, and I go to open it . . . but then I stop.

"I've never done anything like this before." I try to mask my anxieties with a stern tone. "So, yeah. Just keep that in mind."

Another sigh, then I open the box. One by one, I pull out the copper wire bracelets hiding inside. Each bracelet is made from the same thick wire, but each is adorned slightly differently.

"Oh, whoa. You made these?"

"It's a bit crafty, and I've never made jewelry, but I think they came out okay. It's mostly twisted wire, with a metal clasp here, then I pressed the copper really thin to make the charm and painted them, which is how I tinted the metal into four different colors."

"Is mine the green one?" he asks.

"Naturally. It's engraved; sorry if that's a trigger for you after your fancy pen gift."

"You engraved a little *bow tie* into this? I'm dying, this is so sweet."

"You really think so?"

"No, seriously. I was going to crap on whatever you were pulling out as a joke, but I couldn't even do that. You really made these? With tools?"

A bit of pride creeps into my chest at the compliment. I did this. It's such a step outside my normal art, which consists fully of illustration or designs. But working on something I could physically touch was a new experience.

"I did," I say. "We've got plenty of tools around here, plus I had an old engraver that Mamma bought to put my name onto my TI calculator. It was fun."

He takes another bracelet. "Let's see, the bracelet with the red charm has got to be Gabe's."

"Yep. His charm's a sapling. Felt like it worked on multiple levels: he's volunteering with a nonprofit that deals with trees; he gardens for *fun*."

"But it's also brand-new," he says, running a thumb across the etching. "I get the feeling he wants to reinvent himself this summer."

I nod. "You don't?"

"Is it conceited if I say no?" He chuckles. "I really like who I am now. I feel like DC will help me be *more* myself, if that makes any sense."

He offers a smirk, and I wonder what it would be like to be so sure of yourself. It's no wonder someone like Gabriel would find comfort in him.

"The other two are blank," he says, holding two bracelets. One has a metal charm tinted blue, and one a pale yellow.

"I don't think I know who I am yet. Or what this summer is going to mean to me. And Heath," I say with a sigh. "Nothing seems good enough for him, you know?"

CHAPTER EIGHT

HEATH

THIS IS TOO COMPLICATED. A nondescript white van just birthed dozens of identical children like one of those pregnant spiders, and I'm standing on the porch, fully unprepared for this quiz. Even though I literally studied for this.

"You've got this!" Gabriel says, a hint of laughter in his voice.

I wave to the group, and Reese's older cousins come up to give us hugs. Four girls from ages three to sixteen tag along, holding various dishes for the potluck, family games, and all the other essentials for a big family party.

"Here, Gabriella, let me take that from you," I say, reaching for the large bowl of pasta salad in her hands. "Are those glasses new?"

She gives me a funny look, and just beyond her, I see a clone pop up.

"Oh god, you're Isabella. I didn't realize you got glasses too.

Wow, now you two look identical. Sorry. And sorry, Gabriella." I shake my head. "You know what, let's just go inside."

I turn from them, the embarrassment eating me from the inside out. It's bad enough all these girls look the same, but now they all have to be nearsighted too?

"Heath," Gabriel says as we walk into the kitchen, "it's okay. They might as well be twins—don't get flustered about it."

"You don't understand," I say.

Once Reese comes into the living room, he's suddenly the star of the show, and my embarrassing mishap seems to be gone from everyone's memories. More of his family arrive, plus members of their church and other family friends. His house is huge compared to mine, but once it's packed with forty people, even it seems tiny. Some people spill out into the backyard; others start to play cornhole in the front.

I mostly stay in the same place all night, talking to his family. Lucia hops onto my lap, and I make the point to call her the *correct* name, as a three-year-old would be much less forgiving.

Reese's family does this thing where a big group of them all gather in one room, and they'll play a party game that's obviously meant for smaller groups. None of them have difficult rules— usually, *guess what I'm describing, quick!* or *guess what I'm drawing, quick!*—but we still have to repeatedly go over how the game works.

We finally split the group up into teams, but then Isabella gets bored and leaves the room, and we have to count off again. At this point, no one knows what team they're on or what game they're playing, but they're all shouting answers. Even when the timer runs out. Even after Reese's aunt yells, "God, stop saying 'seahorse'—it's not a seahorse!" over the whole group.

It's . . . pure chaos.

It's perfect.

It reminds me that I don't have a family like this. I don't know how *not* to be jealous about it, either. Sure, Diana and Jeanie might be great, but having a handful of family members spread out across the country, while the only traditions you did have are being ripped out from under you, will never be the same. It'll never feel like this.

And . . . tears are running down my face. Thankfully, no one seems to notice—honestly, no one can really notice anything in the chaos that's happening. I lift Lucia off my lap and place her on my seat, then quietly leave the room. I survey my options: Sal and Reese are in the backyard, and I don't want them to see me like this. The cigar smokers are in the front, and they always trap me in a convo about baseball I don't really care to have. Which leaves me nowhere to go but up.

I take the stairs two at a time and crack open Reese's bedroom door. The dim walls welcome me, protecting me from everything that's happening down there. I can still hear everyone, but it's muted. And I can breathe.

I don't want to be a jealous person. Seeing his family, even hearing them now—"*it's not a fucking seahorse!*"—floods my body with warmth. I feel so welcome here, and I know they'd easily take me as one of their own. But they're not mine. I'm not theirs. I'm a welcome visitor here, but I'll always be a visitor.

I sit on the floor and lean against the side of his bed. His bed is neatly made, his comforter draped perfectly. Everything in the room smells distinctly of him—of wildflowers and leather. And, for some reason I can't place, a metallic smell that reminds me of Dad's old welding gear in our garage.

I pull out my phone, and when I go into my messages, I see an unfinished message I had drafted. Seeing his cousins hug Reese and support him and talk about how jealous they were—it reminded me that I do have a family of my own, and I care about them. Even if I don't know them.

Hey cuz, it's Heath!! How are the spring breakers???? I'm heading down there in a few days, can't wait! 😋

"Everything okay?"

I look up as Gabriel peeks into the room. I scramble to stand, but he places a hand on my shoulder and sits next to me.

"No shame in crying, you know?" he says with a laugh. "What's got you upset this time?"

"I assume you wouldn't believe me if I told you it was just a video of a goat and a horse becoming friends?"

"No, I wouldn't believe it." He rolls his eyes. "Because I distinctly remember you crying about that last week in the group chat."

I laugh. "Shut up. Just because I sent a few crying emojis doesn't mean I was literally crying."

"No, I remember, you sent like eleven crying emojis and said, 'I'm literally crying, what's wrong with me.'"

I'm silent for a bit as the memory comes back to me. I absolutely cried at that, fuck.

"Well, I guess I'm just thinking about it again. They're *friends*." I realize the joke's run dry, so I sigh. "Don't think poorly of me, okay? But I was just watching his family and it reminded me that even the few traditions my parents had are basically gone. It's hard enough being an only child with no cousins around, but who's going to throw a party for me now? How did I not know my last Christmas with my parents would be our *last* Christmas together? Fuck, Gabriel, this is hard."

He leans his head on my shoulder, and I rest my head on his.

"I know Mom and Dad didn't get along all the time. But Christmas morning? That always felt perfect, no matter how old I got. Dad would make biscuits and gravy; Mom and I would spend hours baking little Christmas tree cookies. I knew I wouldn't have many years left, what with college and everything coming up, but I didn't think we were just . . . done. You know? Why didn't they warn me?"

"I'm sorry," he says. "I can only imagine what that's like."

We sit for a while, with no awkwardness to our silence, which is something I can always count on Gabriel for. Reese has this frantic energy where I feel like I always need to fill the silence, and Sal acts like he doesn't have the time to waste on a pause in the conversation.

After a while, Gabriel continues, "But it's great Reese's family is so welcoming. I know we're not really a part of the family, but it sure feels like it sometimes. I think I can even tell the difference between Lucia and Isabella now."

"Lucia is three."

"And I remember that! Give me some credit." He laughs. "For what it's worth, Sal told me that Reese really appreciated you learning all their names."

In my mind's eye, I can so clearly see Reese in his design school in Paris. I can see Sal taking DC by storm. I can see Gabriel saving Boston parks.

I look down at my phone, with my message to Diana still queued up. I still can't see myself working on the boardwalk in Daytona, living just off the beach with my cousin and aunt. But it's happening, and I can't avoid it any longer. I take in a long breath and hit send.

This is my family, and it's time I get to know them.

• Golden Boys •

GABRIEL + HEATH + REESE + SAL

> Who's got family stuff today? **R**

Not me lol I barely have one

Too real? Sorry

H Continue

Can't you ever combine all your thoughts into one text, H? Anyway, family dinner with Congresswoman Caudill tonight. Big night. Want to help me pick a bow tie? **S**

Harsh

The green one

H

H Green bow tie

S You know what? If you spend the rest of the day typing entire sentences, I will wear the green one.

H Sir, I'm perfectly capable of writing a complete sentence, which is why I got a 98 in English and you got a 94. Regardless, I will take your challenge, out of respect for the congresswoman.

S Ok rude.

R Good luck!

G You'll do great!

H Wishing you the absolute best of luck with the congresswoman, Sal. Good day, pip-pip, cheerio, and other proper-sounding things. Ta-ta!

CHAPTER NINE

SAL

I BROWSE MY SELECTION of bow ties, thinking about who I want to be for my dinner with Betty Caudill, the Democratic congresswoman from our district. She's an old family friend who put my name out to Senator Wright, a friend of hers, who was looking for teen interns to help with a special project over the summer. I don't know exactly what the project is. I'd love to think it's some supersecret plan that's too sensitive to explain over email, but more likely they don't have the details finalized yet. I get the feeling we're to be guinea pigs for this high school internship program, which is exciting, but also a little unnerving.

For dinner, I want to wear a bow tie. *Really* dress the part, to prove to her and my parents that I was the right choice. But I also just like wearing them, which the guys never seem to understand. My tie rack is overflowing, which is silly considering I never wear them to school.

I've got linen ones that go with my short-sleeved button-ups when I'm hanging out with the boys during the summer. I've got black silk ones I really only put on for weddings or funerals. I start to wonder if there will be black-tie functions this summer, but I doubt it.

And then I have these semiformal patterned ones that my hands always automatically drift toward. Except, my mom really doesn't like them. "We don't own a boat," she always says with a scoff. Which, yeah, it's a preppy, boaty look. But to me, it's also fashionable and unexpected. Who knows, maybe one day I will own a boat—I mean, Lake Erie isn't that far. I would look *good* on that boat. I'm attracted to the greens and blues, but I've also gotten away with a more muted gray one. I'm trying to figure out which one would get my point of view across while not starting a fight with Mom. Ultimately, I pluck the gray linen bow tie, because the thought of wearing a loud patterned shirt under my coat jacket feels right.

I feel so ready for DC. Capitol Hill could use some younger blood, someone with a vision, with all the political turmoil that's been wrecking those halls over the past decade. I imagine it's not too different from how Gabriel feels when he's joining environmental rallies—I know I can make a change for the better.

This summer isn't just a fun opportunity; it's a necessary one. The start of a career path.

"Are you sure you want to wear the gray one?" Mom asks, peeking in the doorway.

I sigh. It's one of those suggestions that isn't really a suggestion, but I pretend it is anyway.

"I think I'm going to wear that one paisley button-up, so something muted makes more sense with that."

"Ah." A pause. "That's a little loud, don't you think?"

Loud. Any guesses to what that word really means?

"Please, Mom?" I hate how whiny my voice sounds, but I'm desperate. "I leave so soon. I don't want to fight. This will look really nice under the jacket. Just . . . please?"

I turn and see her grip the doorknob a bit tighter. She's torn, and I can hear her inner monologue from here—*the paisley shirt is too flamboyant, can't go wrong with something simple, don't want to stand out for the wrong reasons.*

She's not outwardly homophobic or anything, but she has this rigid idea of who I am in her mind, and she always wants me to fit that picture perfectly. To fit in a box she's designed and that she's comfortable with.

But haven't I already? I'm about to start working with a senator. I wear ties for fun. I don't really curse. I've had my list of dream colleges set for years. I've fit into that box so long that I don't even know where her ideas stop and mine begin.

"I'm going to wear this," I say. The words are resolute, but my tone is not. I don't like to challenge her, but I won't give this one up. It's just a freaking shirt for a three-person dinner party.

She releases the doorknob, and a click echoes through the room. I see her give up, and I hope it's a sign of growth. A sign of something.

"Fine, you're right. Betty will like the shirt, I'm sure."

"She will," I say.

I begin the process of undressing, and dressing, and think again about how this opportunity, and living in DC, it's where I need to be. Forget seeking Mom's approval—there are times I can barely look at her after last month, and I know she knows it.

I apply a light layer of foundation and thicken my brows with an eyebrow pencil. As I cover up a small pimple with concealer and blend it in with the rest of the foundation, I consider doing a quick coat of paint on my nails, but decide I've pushed it enough with Mom today. Plus, I don't have enough time to dry it anyway.

Before I go downstairs, I check myself in the mirror one last time. The suit jacket fits snugly over my dress shirt, which is speckled with a small paisley print—all greens and blues with a touch of bright pink. My gray bow tie brings the look together just as expected. I sweep my hair back one last time, and the blond strands fall nicely in place.

Polished, thoughtful, with a touch of flair.

• • •

Congresswoman Betty Caudill must be under five feet tall, but she commands a room like she's the world's tallest woman. She's in her second year, and she made quite a name for herself by standing up for a number of issues in her first few months. Conservative media labeled her a nuisance, but that soon faded when everyone realized she was actually getting stuff done.

Her start was mainly grassroots. Our district had been red for years—gerrymandered to death—but she brought a fresh voice, and she went county to county to convince the people that she had the right vision for Ohio. Mom helped with her campaign, becoming a press secretary of sorts. People needed someone to look to as COVID-19 tore through the district, so while the incumbent shared Instagram photos of him eating at restaurants near his vacation home in Florida, she went to work.

"Sal, my boy!" As I come down the stairs, she wraps me in a tight hug. She's basically family at this point, so it feels natural to be squished within her grip. She turns to my mother. "Rachel, so good to see you. I brought some wine—it's local, and it's not great, but I have to support these Ohio vineyards. Here in a few years the wine won't be as sweet, that's what I'm told, and our district will be the new Napa Valley."

She pauses, and it's like her own facade breaks. "I'm not holding my breath, but it's good to shoot for the stars."

"Sal," Mom says, "why don't you set the table?"

I set all the fancy china out, crystal glasses, fabric napkins, the works. Apparently, all things Mom and Dad registered for, for their wedding. I sometimes wonder if bringing this out makes her sad, or if she likes to look back on this time. Going through catalogs with Dad and picking out the exact style of fork they thought represented their new home together.

It's monotonous work, but there's always a bit of comfort in seeing the table looking perfect and ready for company. While I set the table, I think of Betty, breaking character to make a joke about Ohio wine. As she stepped through the doorway, I could see the walls she'd built up for the public come tumbling down. In a way, I guess we all do that. I have guards up for my teachers, my parents, my friends. Everyone, it seems, but Gabe. I want to be more myself when I move to DC, but is that even possible? Won't I have to present a certain way—less flamboyant? more serious?—there too?

We take our seats at the dinner table, and Mom brings out a salad tossed in a rustic wooden bowl. It doesn't exactly go with the fancy china, but Mom sets her own rules here about what fits in, what feels right.

"You always set a lovely table," Betty says. "Some days I'm so exhausted I can barely open whatever plastic container our take-out's come in, let alone find a plate."

"Thank you, ma'am," I say, and I get a slight nod from my mom.

Her guard may be down, but mine sure isn't.

"Still on the 'ma'am' thing, huh? Well, I appreciate your commitment to flattery. With a cute face like that, a little bit of politeness goes a long way. As long as you don't let anyone take advantage of you."

Chills run down my spine, and I take a small bite of lettuce. The tang of the dressing hits my lips as I wonder what exactly she means.

"Oh, no, don't mean to worry you. The high school program Senator Wright has set up, it's very selective, very well done I think. We usually wait until kids are twenty, twenty-one before bringing them on for internships, and we only pick these poli-sci majors"—she looks to me—"political science, that is. And they all come in so bright-eyed and excited, drink the whole summer, then leave with five hundred business cards, and we never hear from them again. The experience isn't engaging, you know?"

"I was thinking about studying political science," I say after Mom gives me a look. "Maybe tacking on a minor in history."

"I'm trying to get him to minor in communications," Mom cuts in. "See, public relations applies broadly to every field; you never know what opportunities will come up."

The congresswoman looks to both of us. "I do not miss being sixteen," she finally says. "It's good to think about all of this, of course. You have to. But, if I can be honest, do you know what I want to see in a future politician? Someone who's clever and educated, sure, but I want to see someone with passions outside of politics. You should be invested in this field, but it can't be everything. I want to see musicians or playwrights, geologists or biologists, environmentalists, waitresses, whoever. Give me someone who is fully in the world they want to change."

I pause. We've had career and life conversations before, of course, but she's never been so frank. Could I study something else, while still pursuing politics? And then the lingering idea claws at me—could I even decide *not* to go to college?

Mom sets down her fork, and the frustration sinks into her expression. "But politics is his passion. His only passion, as far as I'm concerned. It's always been the case. We'll just have to work on what'll make his résumé stand out—this summer experience should certainly help."

I go to object to the idea that politics is my only passion, but I can't. I like to read, but I read political or historical biographies. If

I can't work in politics, what could I do? What would I even want to do? I'm not saying I need to be POTUS, but coming in as an outsider seems irresponsible.

"I enjoy French class?" I say, but it comes out as a question. "It's interesting learning about new languages and cultures and all that."

"Oh dear, you'll be fine. You're whip smart and tenacious—and a snappy dresser if I may say so—and if I still get to serve in Congress by the time you're out of college, know I will do my best to make room for you. But you are so young, Sal, and I want you to know that while history and politics are important— In this world? Getting to connect with people, being an authentic and relatable person will always mean more than any of that."

"When we were in college," Mom jumps in, lightening the mood with a cheeky tone, "we had quite a few interests."

"And speaking of," Betty replies, "time for some wine?"

The conversation settles after that. And their topics of conversation drift from college to the boys they dated, the mistakes they made, and how important everything seemed when they were my age.

My mind keeps drifting to Gabe. Years from now, will I call him a mistake? The thought of our perfectly casual relationship falling apart over one summer has me paralyzed right now. But in the future, will it just be a joke between us? This feels important.

If he's the only one I can be around with my guard fully down, and we fizzle out, who does that leave? Who would I turn to? I don't want our relationship to progress any further, and I don't think he does either, but I'm not ready for it to stop.

"You'd like my friend Gabe," I say. "He's super passionate about everything. He got this internship with Boston's Save the Trees Foundation, and he's ready to go off and save the environment this summer."

Looking up, I see my mom's face sort of freeze. I realize I've interrupted a conversation about their early crushes to talk about a "friend"—and I see that panic come across her face whenever she's afraid people will know more about me.

"He certainly sounds like someone I'd like to meet!" Betty says cheerfully. "I always say we have the country's finest people in this district, and I see it every time I get to visit schools in the area."

"The feeling is much different when you work *in* the school," Mom says, then covers her mouth. They both start laughing. I think the wine is making her loosen up a bit, but I get why she said it. My classmates give her hell, and until last month, I'd have backed her up on this.

"Gabriel is a nice boy. Actually, Sal's surrounded himself with a great group of kids. They're all at the top of their class."

"Very impressive."

I check my phone, and I see a text from Gabe: I can't pack anymore. I took down everything from my walls, and I just keep crying. I know I have to do this, I want to do this. But I'm so scared.

"Everything okay, Sal?" the congresswoman asks with a gentle tone.

"No phones at the table." Mom snaps so quickly from tipsy college friend to strict parent in one second flat.

"Oh please, I'm sure he's got a lot going on. He's got a big move coming up. I remember leaving for summer camp in high school, and I just couldn't stand to be away from my friends. I couldn't focus on anything that whole week before I left. I know that expression well, my boy."

Despite myself, I smile. She's perceptive and understanding, which is probably how she got the job.

"It's my friend, the one who's trying to save the world. He's packing, and it's stressing him out."

"Poor thing," the congresswoman says, looking to my mom.

"Right," she says. "Well, I'm not sure we need dessert after this wine, but I have a pavlova in the oven that won't be ready for a while. Sal, maybe while you do some of these dishes you can give Gabriel a call." She looks to the congresswoman. "His friends always look to him for advice and guidance—it's really sweet."

I slowly back up and stand from the seat. Truthfully, that's not the case. But I see how she'd think that. Gabe and Heath wear their emotions, their issues on their sleeves, but I keep everything under wraps.

Mom and the congresswoman head to the dining room to finish the bottle of wine, while I put in my AirPods and start a call with Gabe. The warm water rushes over my hands as I scrub the plates, but nothing provides that perfect, full-body warmth of when he picks up the phone and says, simply,

"Hey, Sal."

CHAPTER TEN

GABRIEL

"LITERALLY, WHAT HAVE I gotten myself into?" I ask Sal through the phone, knowing this is not my finest moment. "Wait, is your dinner over? It can't be. Oh god, your mom is going to be so pissed if she hears you talking to me. Never mind, hang up, hang—"

"Gabe," he says, and I feel my shoulder muscles loosen. "It's fine, I'm doing the dishes. She said we could chat for a few minutes before dessert. They're getting a little tipsy and are in full college-reminiscent mode. I feel like I'm talking with your dad."

"Yikes," I say, and he laughs. My dad talks about college like he just graduated from Ohio State last year. He really needs to let it go, but I don't think Mom or I have the heart to tell him to stop.

I hear the clink of what I'm sure is expensive china, and the splash of water. We listen to each other's breathing for a bit, and I'm not sure where to start. Even with this conversation, I feel like I need his guidance.

"Okay, so let's get into it. What's freaking you out? Give me a list."

"Right, a list," I echo.

Sal's not the most sentimental person in the world, and I'm sure a big part of that is his relationship with his mom. It's good, I know that. There's a lot of love in their two-person household, and he's got the kind of confidence a gay kid only gets by growing up surrounded by emphatic support and seemingly endless resources from day one. But it's not like they're the Gilmore Girls.

How he approaches his emotions has always been helpful for me, though. He's practical and methodical, and he loves lists. See, Heath and I are not known to be the most organized people, while Reese and Sal both rely on lists and planners to get by. But where Reese brings artful design to his dot journals, Sal is a little more straightforward. A calendar, lists, phone reminders, Post-it notes of all sizes and colors.

I get how you'd use that for day-to-day life, but to use it for your emotional well-being? Your breakdowns? It's counterintuitive, but it's not a bad plan. So I list:

"Let's see, okay. My fears are: airports, COVID, suitcases getting lost, Boston, roommates, volunteering, new people—what if they don't like me?"

"Your boss or the other interns?"

"All of the above. Am I likable?"

He hesitates. "I mean, I like you."

"You didn't at first," I say.

"That's true. But that was, like, ten years ago. And you were throwing a fit because we only had string cheese for snack time. I'm going to hate anyone who loudly declares that they don't like string cheese, that's just a fact."

"So I should keep that hidden, is what you're saying?"

He laughs. "Don't let them see your flaws right away."

I roll my eyes, but then I do realize what he's saying *is* true. It's how he gets through high school—though I would be pretty guarded about my flaws in school if my mom was the vice principal too.

"I might actually take that advice," I say, even though my flaws might be too large to cover. Especially when one big ol' flaw is literally a mental illness. And okay, my therapist would be upset if I called my anxiety a flaw. But it certainly doesn't feel like a strength.

"I'm joking, if that wasn't clear," Sal says quickly. And I wonder if he's a bit of a mind reader. "You are flawless."

"Ha, right."

"I mean it."

"Back to my list."

He stops me. "Maybe scrap the list. What does your therapist always say when you get overwhelmed with school stuff? 'Focus on one thing at a time, and you've got this.' You know it's pretty special, all this stuff you're doing, right?"

"I do," I admit. "The parks in Boston are huge and sprawling and interconnected, and it's going to be so cool to help raise money for them. I think I can make a change."

I hear a sound on the other end, and I know my time is running short.

"Mom's calling me back to the table. Are you gonna be okay?"

"Of course," I say. "Just needed to talk it out. Thanks, Sal."

"Anytime. Love you."

We hang up, and for once, I believe him. Maybe I *am* flawless.

HEATH + REESE

hiiiiiiiiiii

You're such an obnoxious texter, you know that right?

Autocorrect is supposed to help you, H....why did you disable it???

are you in a bad mood or are these just your normal thoughts

i cant tell sometimes

Just normal thoughts. Sorry

It's fine, I can type normal if you want it's just going to take much longer.

No, don't do that for me

I was being snooty
like Sal... sorry.

If it bothers you I'll stop, really.

No don't I was being an ass

...I mean, I won't disagree.

hiiiiiiii whats up

Oh now you're
making fun of me?

no!!! just turned
off autocorrext

this is pure chaos

that's more like it

Ok it's back on, I couldn't do
it. But seriously, type however
you want. I don't care, I just
like getting texts from you.

I like getting texts
from you too.

CHAPTER ELEVEN

REESE

IT'S NOT LIKE THIS has to be perfect.

I hold the four bracelets in my hand, trying to ignore the fact that two of them are still unmarked. It was so easy to come up with an emblem for Sal: the green bow tie that represents so much about how he presents himself to the world. Who he wants to be, and who he gets to be this summer. Confident, flashy, precise.

Gabe's sapling makes sense on every level. A young tree, something with a ton of potential but still delicate. He isn't sure who he wants to be, but he keeps growing anyway in hopes that he'll figure it out one day.

I tap the back end of my pencil on my planner. The left side has a concise list of bullet points featuring my daily to-dos. It's orderly and straight, and there's nothing quite as satisfying as crossing off part of the list.

I don't know how I would survive without the daily to-do

list, but the right side is just as necessary. A classic dot journal where I illustrate meticulous designs alongside quotes that resonated with me that day. In a way, this is my journal as well as my planner, and somewhere between these two sides of the page is my life.

I zone out a bit, staring at an illustration of the Louvre that I'm trying to finish up before the week. Before I turn that page and set foot in France for the first time ever. I get distracted and start to sketch the bracelets in another one of the corners. The way it's set up, the four dots that make a square fit perfectly inside the first charm I draw, and I see myself in that.

After grabbing my engraver, I take a deep breath. The blue charm stares back at me, and I think I've just stumbled across a representation of myself that feels right. An empty piece of the dot journal, a perfect square ready to be filled in.

I turn on the engraver and press on four dots, aligned in a perfect square in the center of the charm. The square is empty and bursting with potential, and it signals to me that there are so many days ahead. The artistic opportunity of design paired with the structure of the dots is a perfect fit, and I ignore the impulse to put the bracelet on right there.

As the metallic smell dissipates from the room, I'm left with three engraved charms and one empty. It's almost mocking, how easily so many of these came to mind, but the one I really want to impress someone with, the one I want to mean the most, remains empty.

So I make a list.

What Heath's charm needs to say:

1. You have a lot of varied interests. You find time for sports and a part-time job, you study harder than any of us, and you always, *always*, make time for me.

2. You're the only one of us who's being forced into this summer trip, but I know your summer will still be special.

3. Even if it isn't, we'll be here when you come back. All of us. Especially me.

4. You mean a lot to me.

I distractedly underline point number four. Over, and over, and over again.

This is why it's impossible to pick something. I'm going to tell him I love him with this. Maybe not in those exact words . . . or maybe I will. What's the harm anyway? If he doesn't feel the same way, then I can spend the summer getting over him, and I'll start my senior year as a brand-new guy. It's a flawless plan, really.

I sigh and stare up at the ceiling.

This is going to be impossible.

| MON | ○ START PACKING! |
| | ○ ENGRAVE CHARMS |

| TUES | ○ PICK UP SNACKS W/HEATH |
| | ○ FAMILY GOODBYE PARTY |

| WED | ○ KEEP PACKING |
| | ○ FINISH BRACELETS |

| THUR | ○ REVIEW CHECKLIST ✳ |

| FRI | ○ GOODBYE TOUR W/THE BOYS |

| SAT & SUN | PARIS |

FOR H?

Mbraghi

5

66 I AM NOT THE SAME,
HAVING SEEN THE MOON SHINE
ON THE OTHER SIDE OF THE WORLD. 99

— MARY ANNE
RADMACHER

FOR H?

FOR H?

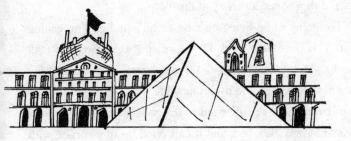

CHAPTER TWELVE

HEATH

Just packing, I type into the group chat when Gabriel checks in with all of us to see what we're doing.

I try to sound casual, and I hope they let it slide. As they all pack their suitcases and travel bags for their trips, I'm packing my entire life up, on the off chance that Dad's able to sell the house this summer. I've stacked the last of the boxes in the corner of my room, and I'm left with so little. I have my suitcase with enough clothes to work with through the summer—mostly tank tops, shirts and shorts, and a variety of flip-flops.

If I'm going to be living on a beach all summer, I'm leaning into it. This time next week I'll be wearing an airbrushed tank and a shark-tooth necklace with my sunglasses on the back of my head. I'm fully committed to this new life.

But I wonder if I really need to say goodbye to my old one. I disassembled my Ikea bed, and it's all piled up in a corner, with just the mattress left on the floor, so I can roll out of bed and get in the car tomorrow morning. And I know it's possible that this house won't be there for me when I get back, but that's so far beyond my comprehension right now.

I'm all alone today, since my parents had a meeting with their divorce lawyers in town, so I take my time walking through the house. My parents' bedroom, the spare room, and as I step down the stairs, through the back door, and into our expansive yard, I see glimpses of my past. Even if we don't move, it'll still never be the same here.

We used to have a swing set right here, I think as I walk into a particularly dead patch of grass. *And I learned to play baseball right here.* Dad and I would be out for hours just practicing my swing or perfecting my curveball. When it got too late, a few bats would fly around us as the stars dotted the sky. If you threw the ball up at just the right time, the bats would catch it with their echolocation and follow the ball as it fell for a few seconds. I always thought that was cool.

I sit on the tailgate of my truck and think about going to the field early, but something keeps me tethered to this place. What if, when I come back, someone else owns this place? Dad and I could be living in one of those apartments on Main Street, pretending everything's just fine. It would be fine, I guess, just not the same. It especially won't be the same without Mom there.

I think again about Reese's family, and I can't stop myself from being jealous.

Where do I fit in? Where's my family? Maybe I'll find what I'm looking for in Daytona.

My phone buzzes, and I see that Gabriel's already staked out our usual spot on the baseball diamond. I laugh, knowing how stunned Reese will be that he got there first. On cue, Reese texts me, Hey, I'm ready for you to pick me up whenever you are.

Or, maybe I'll find my family right here waiting for me, when I get back.

CHAPTER THIRTEEN

SAL

I GET TO GABE'S house, and when the door opens, I jump back in surprise when Katie peeks her head through, and we both laugh. I haven't seen his sister since she started college in the fall, now that I think about it. But I get to see glimpses of her life on social media, or through Gabe's stories.

"Sal, hey. How are you?" she asks with a sweet but cautious question mark at the end of it. "Are you ready for DC? I know it can be stressful."

"It is," I say. "But I'm ready. I think it'll be good for me to get away from here for a bit and see what life will be like after I graduate."

She sighs, and a smile comes across her face. "Yeah. I mean, you'll have a blast in college. Do you know where you're going yet?"

The question stops me, for once, and I'm not sure how to

respond. Every line I usually respond with doesn't feel like my own, and that's because it's not: I'm just parroting what my mom says.

It's like there's a whisper inside me that I can't let go of. One that's been growing and growing since I watched my mom shake that homophobe's hand at graduation.

"I'm not sure I even want to go to college," I say. "I'm feeling a little lost right now?"

She gives me a quizzical look, and the ache of vulnerability hits me in the gut. I scramble to cover it up.

"That didn't come out right. I guess, I still don't know what I want to do, but I'm hoping this summer will clear it up." I pause. "Don't tell Gabe I said that."

"Oh yeah, of course. I bet you know I didn't like college at *all* when I started this year. I was down on myself because college wasn't everything I expected, everything our college-obsessed dad told me to expect. So I didn't try for a while. But I found my group, eventually."

She drops her voice to a whisper. "Don't tell Dad this, but college is *not* for everyone. I had a friend drop out this year, and she's never been happier. To each their own."

I breathe a bit easier after that line. I picked a hell of a time to say that out loud for the first time ever, but at least it wasn't to anyone important, really. My mom would have a heart attack; even Gabe and the other boys would be confused. Having my shit together is basically my whole brand, and really, could I even get away with not going to college?

This is probably just a phase. Momentary cold feet about signing my life away for four whole years.

She clears her throat. "Anyway, Gabriel went out back already. Mom sent pretty much all the snacks we have out with him."

"Oh, okay. Sorry, I thought he'd be here. Can I go out your back door?"

She lets me inside, and I quickly slip through the house without getting noticed by his parents. Clearly, I can't be trusted with my own mouth right now, so I better move on before I tell more people I might not have my future as set as everyone thinks.

Gabe's house backs up against our school's baseball diamond. There's a fence, but it's always unlocked. As I slip through the gate, I see that he's the first one here. He's spread a bedsheet over a patch of sand and has claimed one of the corners for himself.

The smell of freshly cut grass and dirt hits my nose as I approach, and it's one of those perfectly Ohio smells that I might even miss when I'm gone. Though I guess they have grass and dirt in DC, so maybe I'm just feeling sentimental.

"So much for us always being the late ones," I say with a scoff. I take a seat across from him and survey the snack collection in front of me—trail mix, grocery-store frosted cookies, pita chips and hummus, and a tote bag that likely has even more goodies inside.

"Hungry? Mom gave me enough food for the whole school."

"I see that," I say.

He's far away from me, but a part of me wants to close the distance and give him a kiss. But this is kind of our tradition.

73

The four of us do this. We take a seat on each of the four corners of the sheet and catch up. It's something we started doing back when COVID swept through here. Which meant we had to all stay six feet apart when we hung out. We'd slip off our masks and talk in person, sharing some snacks but otherwise staying inside our quadrant.

"I like that we still do this," I say. "It's like a picnic now."

"I like remembering that we all had to go through that," he replies. "I mean, it was so scary. Still is, kinda."

A dry laugh escapes my lips. "Everything's scary."

"Not to you," Gabe says. "God, I wish I had some of your confidence right now. How can I feel so passionate about something but so terrified at the same time?"

"You seem to think I can't be confident *and* scared. We're humans; we're capable of all sorts of emotions at one time." The words aren't coming out right, but I let them go anyway. "They're not opposites, is what I'm saying. Being scared is *normal*. I don't know how many times I can tell you that."

An awkward silence settles across us, and I avoid eye contact, pretending to find something really captivating on the bottom of my shoes. He doesn't speak up; of *course* he doesn't speak up.

He's so trapped inside his mind, and I just need him to, for once, let it out.

But he won't, so I continue. "I don't know what you want me to say. I can't hype you up anymore. If I keep doing this, then you're just going to flop when you're on your own."

"That's harsh," he says, and I'm immediately hit with a pang of regret.

"I'm sorry." I take a long, cleansing breath. "That was unfair. I think I'm scared too. And I don't know what to do about it."

His eyes flicker just past me, and I know that Heath and Reese must be approaching. I build walls up around me again and feel confidence, or something like it, flood into my body. My shoulders pull back; my lips perk up into a smirk. I've got this. I've *always* got this.

Something about this summer is throwing me off, I guess. But I know I'll feel way better once I'm there, suited up and strutting into the Capitol.

"What are we talking about?" Heath says, placing his large palm on my shoulder and giving it a light squeeze.

CHAPTER FOURTEEN

REESE

THE VIBE'S OFF WHEN we show up, so I'm guessing we just interrupted some sort of lovers' quarrel. As Heath smooths things over with his natural charm (or blissful unawareness?) I set the box of bracelets down in the middle of our spots.

"Actually," Sal says, looking to the box, "I was, um, telling Gabe how Reesey has some gifts for us."

Heat rushes to my cheeks. The thing is, they're just bracelets. Nothing fancy, nothing special. I've known these boys long enough to know when I've given them a present they don't like, and I get the distinct feeling I'd be crushed if one of them wasn't impressed by the bracelet, or the charm.

One specific person, that is.

I realize people are expecting me to say something or, at the very least, open the box. I do, slowly, and I see the four copper bracelets rattling around. Heath's charm looks back at me, and the true nature of the hesitation hits me:

I've put so many of my unsaid feelings into this, and now I'm just going to hand it to him. In that way, it feels like I'm showing him how I feel.

"Ooh! What are they?" Heath asks.

"I made something for us. Ever since we started bingeing *RuPaul's Drag Race* and *Project Runway*, I've always wanted to try designing some clothing or jewelry, so I came up with the idea to do these twisted copper bracelets."

I pull in a deep, slow breath, savoring the last moment when I get to keep this project to myself. Then, like ripping off a bandage, I take mine out. Heath and Gabriel instinctively crawl forward to see what it is.

"This is amazing, Reese," Heath says as he takes it in his hands, and I see a flicker of joy and awe light his face. "How did you brush this with color? That blue is really cool."

"Wow," Gabriel says. "It looks like something you'd order off Etsy. What made you want to do bracelets?"

"I tried to think of something we could each take with us, something that would work with pretty much any outfit, whether you were at the beach or in the Capitol. Something that I could personalize too. There's one for each of us, each a different color, each with a different charm."

I slip the bracelet on my wrist, and the blue charm flips, so that the four dots stare back at me. It brings out this sort of melancholy feeling in me, and the dots blur in my vision as my mind reels.

"I have an idea," I say. "Remember when we played Truth or Dare during our first sleepover, like, ages ago? And how no one would pick dare, so it just became this string of confessions?"

Heath snorts. "By the end of the night, we all just started listing our biggest fears. That's how we found out Sal was afraid of ketchup."

"I'm not afraid of ketchup." Sal crosses his arms as we all laugh. "Well, not *anymore*."

I look to each of them, remembering the laundry list of fears—tornadoes, fire, spiders—but I don't recall exactly which fear belonged to which person.

"Can we do that now?" I ask. "Get all our fears about this summer off our chests?"

"Well, you just put on your bracelet." Sal gestures to me. "We yield the floor. What's on your mind?"

Immediately, I think about how overwhelming tomorrow's international flight will be, but there's a part of me that's excited and ready for it. It's what happens next that stresses me out more.

"It all happened so fast," I say. "My graphic design tutor mentioned this program, Mamma immediately fell in love with it on my behalf, and next thing I know, I'm filling out an application, I'm accepted, and flights are *booked*."

I pause, and try not to meet anyone's eyes. "I can't complain about going to France, I know that. I'm excited. But when I was trying to list all my goals for the summer in my journal, I couldn't come up with anything. I love graphic design, but do I need to go to France for that? Compared to how I usually am at school, feeling goalless is new for me."

Heath laughs. "Not every experience has to have a list of goals, you know?"

78

"Or maybe you can just pick something really broad," Gabriel says. "Like, I don't know, 'My goal is to have fun'?"

"Ooh, or to eat a lot of French pastry," Heath adds.

There's a pause in conversation, and that's when I lock eyes with Sal. When it comes to this stuff, we're usually on the same wavelength. In a way. I plan out my days to the *T*, but I don't know what my future looks like. Sal has exact goals for the next ten years of his life, but he doesn't know what he's doing day to day.

"Not to get meta here, but I think your goal should be to spend the summer figuring out your goal," he finally says. "Yeah, it sounds so cliché to spend a summer in Europe to *find yourself*, but it's what you're doing, right? There's a reason it's a cliché."

"The fact that I have a dot journal filled with all my plans, dreams, and designs makes me seem precious enough," I say. "Do you really think I should write 'find myself' in there?"

Sal crawls over to me and pulls my journal out of my bag. "Absolutely. Be that precious; make us absolutely sick with your idealism."

The others laugh, but I admit to myself that it's not exactly bad advice. I flip to my "summer goals" page, which is completely empty save for a few illustrations around the sides.

I make a few notes, then close the journal with a sense of finality. My single goal for this trip is to figure out my goals as I go along.

"If there's one thing Paris has in excess, it's inspiration, right? I'll figure it out. Thanks, guys."

I look to Heath, and he gives me a soft smile. Truthfully, there is one more fear I don't say: I'll be four thousand four hundred thirty-nine miles from Daytona Beach. And something about that hurts.

But I brush it off, then I reach into the box and pull out a random bracelet.

"All right, let's see who's next."

CHAPTER FIFTEEN

SAL

WHEN HE PULLS OUT the bracelet, I squint, looking for the familiar green tint. I'm not big on sharing my feelings in this pseudo-group-therapy session, but I do like hearing that I'm not the only one apprehensive about the upcoming move.

Reese feels like he doesn't have a goal. I can't relate. If anything, I'm worried I have *too many* goals for my short time in DC. My brain goes into overdrive trying to find the best "fear" to reveal here.

But when I see a flash of red on the charm, I exhale. Gabe seems to know it's for him without Reese even saying anything, and when I see the smile cross his face, the edges of my lips perk up.

Heath leans over to inspect the charm. "A twig?"

"Sapling," Gabe replies with a laugh.

Reese cuts in. "Right, so on each charm I etched something

personal. Don't read too deeply into it, or anything, it's just something that reminds me of you."

I give him a sharp glance, because I *know* there's a lot of meaning behind them. Maybe he was able to find the perfect emblem for Heath, after all.

"God, this is like therapy," Gabe finally says, before launching into the fears I know all about from our chats this week. A big city, crowded planes, an unclear job description, and so on. But then his tone shifts, just slightly. It's softer, more vulnerable, so much that I feel myself leaning into the pull of his story.

"I'll miss you guys. We'll have our group chat, and we can all FaceTime, but it won't be the same. And I'll miss this." He gestures to our picnic spread. "This is our last summer, and we'll be thousands of miles away from each other."

This is a new fear. And I think it's one we all are feeling right about now.

"That's it." he says, and though I know there are more worried thoughts rattling around in his brain, we all let it go. In the lull, I check my phone just long enough to send a heart emoji to Gabe. Reese clears his throat, and I see that he's pulled out the next bracelet: mine.

"Here you go, Sal." Reese tosses it to me, and I put it on immediately. It looks even more spectacular in the bright sunlight. "What are you most freaked about?"

"Can I choose Dare?" I ask, but he just rolls his eyes.

Can I tell them I don't know if I want to go to college? If I don't go, then what the heck has all of this been for? Near-perfect grades, sleepless nights, hours and hours spent on projects and studying and flash cards and essays. It was all to get into a good college, right?

"Sal?" Gabe asks, but I still can't figure out what to say. All my rehearsed fears go out the window.

I decide then that I can't bring this up with them. What if this is just a weird phase and my brain's all jumbled? What if they don't take me seriously and I eventually flip on this, proving them right?

Student council president, honors society, peer counselor. There are only so many things we can do to stand out at our tiny school. What if they start to resent me for putting in so much work and taking opportunities from them?

I clear my throat. "I guess I'm worried I'll make a bad impression."

"Not to minimize that fear," Heath starts, "but are you sure that's it? You always make a good first impression. It's kind of your thing."

He adjusts an imaginary bow tie to get the point across.

Gabe narrows his eyes. "Yeah, there's something else going on."

"Are you . . . turning Republican?" Reese jokes, and I dart a glare toward him.

I laugh, breaking the tension. "No, I can safely say I have not flipped values in the last twenty-four hours."

"But something *has* happened, right?" Gabe looks at me hard when he says it, and I have to fight to keep eye contact. I don't know what my face is giving away. Everything? Probably.

But I'm not ready.

"Nothing's happened." I drop a dramatic eye roll, covering up the weird tension thrumming throughout my body. I want to talk freely about my fears and the pressures that are being put on me, but I also want to keep them inside. To resolve them myself.

"I'm going to run to the restroom," I say. "Anyone need anything while I'm in there?"

"I'll take some of the snacks back inside," Gabe says. "After we hear Heath's deepest, darkest fears, we should head out."

On the walk inside, I feel Gabe's eyes on me. He doesn't ask anything, though, and that makes me feel better. He puts his hand on my shoulder when we reach the edge of his backyard.

"Really, it's okay," I say. "I'm going to crush this DC internship, just like you'll do with your volunteer thing in Boston. It's going to be a good summer, I know it."

"It will," he says.

I'm still not sure what's going on in my own brain, but I know one thing: I don't need their help with this.

CHAPTER SIXTEEN

HEATH

THOUGH THE OTHER BOYS have gone, we still sit across from each other. It seems so far for us, and there's a part of me that wants to inch closer. If this feels far apart, how will we last being on separate continents?

Reese tosses the bracelet my way, and as it hits the grass by my blanket, it snaps me out of my throughs.

"Finally!" I say with a hint of a laugh in my voice. "Every time you pulled one out, I was hoping it'd be mine."

"You're that eager to get your worries off your chest?"

"That? Oh, no. I don't want y'all to worry about me."

I inspect the yellow-tinted copper charm. Etched into it is a flame. But no, it's more than just a flame—it's got kindling at the bottom with logs blocking the fire's path.

"You want to know something that worries me?" Reese asks. "Something I didn't tell everyone? There's a lot of deeper meaning in all these charms. I felt weird telling that to the others, but as silly as these bracelets are, they mean a lot to me."

I slip it around my wrist, and the glint of the fire reflects back to me. I know it must mean so much, but I wonder vaguely, *What message is he sending me?*

"I liked the double meaning of these," I say. "Gabriel's little tree because he'll be saving and planting trees this summer, but how he's also a sapling himself. Sal's bow tie because he loves wearing them, but also because of how perfectly he tries to present himself to the world, even to the point where he can't tell us—*us*—what's bothering him in case we'll think less of him. Your little planner dots, how you love scheduling your life with those dot journals, but how, with this summer, those dots aren't filled in."

"Shit," Reese says. "You got all that?"

"I've proofed almost every English essay you've ever written," I say with a laugh. "You look for complexity in everything. I've tried to be more analytical, like you, but everything you say and do always has added layers, multiple meanings. That said . . . I'm a bit stumped with this one."

Reese's cheeks turn red. "Not the charm you'd have picked?"

"No, I honestly thought it'd just be a truck. Capturing my love for that little piece of shit, but also giving it the sense of movement, of going somewhere. But this is a bonfire."

"It is. You're the only one who knows how to throw a proper bonfire. I wanted to show you that your bonfire will always bring us together. I get the feeling you're worried about us all moving on without you, but that's just not true. You're the fire of our group. You keep us together."

My heart swells with his words, so much that I stand and take a few short steps over to him before wrapping him into a tight hug. The top of his head rests just under my chin, and I'm struck by how easy it would be to kiss his forehead right now.

"It also means a lot to me personally," he says. "You threw that bonfire after that asshole hurt me and Sal. And I know neither of us wanted to leave our bedrooms, but you just sent that photo of the giant stack of wood to the group chat, and you said . . ."

"Let's burn this shit to the ground." I laugh and lessen my grip on him. He looks up to me, though we're still slightly entangled in an embrace.

"When I see you, I see fire," he says. "Not a flickering candle, but this huge, warm, beautiful . . ."

He trails off and pulls away from me, just slightly. Almost like he said too much.

I've read into these signs before, but I don't think he knows how destructive fires can be if they're not contained. If he's asking, which I don't think he is, he doesn't know what he's asking for.

Sure, my fire may be what brings this group together, but I could just as easily be the one holding them back. Besides, all fires go out eventually.

CHAPTER SEVENTEEN

REESE

"HEATH, IT'S YOUR TURN," Sal says once he and Gabriel finally come back. "And after that's done, let's agree not to freak out any more today. It's our last day, and we should get the most out of it. I will not let you all taint our last diner dinner and drive-in movie of the summer with your angst."

He smirks, so we know he's joking. But I know he's not, really.

We stuff our blankets into our backpacks and walk toward Heath's truck, waiting patiently for him to spill it.

"I feel kind of numb," he says. Clouds pass over the sun, casting a shadow over Gabriel's driveway. "It just doesn't feel real. My parents' whole 'divorce-in-progress' thing, Dad trying to sell the house. I'm trying to stay positive, but . . . what if he really does sell it? And I never get to set foot in my yard again. And on top of that, since Mom moves to New Mexico with that guy next week, I worry about my dad doing all this alone."

Heath's problems all feel so adult.

A particularly strong breeze passes through, and I shiver. I wonder if Paris has more consistent weather than Ohio. A heat wave on Monday and Tuesday, with temps dropping into the fifties by Friday.

"You okay?" he asks.

"Stop worrying about me! About all of us! We're focusing on you right now." I roll my eyes and toss my backpack into the back of his truck.

"I don't want the focus, though."

He says it in this really low way, and my heart breaks for him. He chews on one of the strings of his Vanderbilt college hoodie. He lowers his tailgate, and the four of us pile onto it.

"Look, it's only one summer," he says. "Next year will be different for me, sure, but we'll all be seniors. I'm excited for that. And I don't know, part of me is even excited to get out of here, for a little bit."

Heath pulls off his hoodie, and I pretend not to see his bare stomach and tufts of light chest hair as his undershirt comes up with it. He hands it to me, and I'd like to protest, but with my five-inch inseam shorts and tank top, I extremely didn't plan for this sudden drop in temperature.

When I bring it over my head, his scent fills my nostrils and his warmth radiates into me. I pull up the hood and look to him. He's smiling, and my chest flutters with so many emotions I might actually explode.

I need to stop tracking what we have (whatever the hell it is) against what Gabriel and Sal have (whatever the hell *that* is). Sure, I wish his arm was around me, but I'm still surrounded by him right now. And it's everything I could want right now.

"Thank you," I say. But I hope he sees the double meaning here, the hidden layer that says what I mean:

I love you.

CHAPTER EIGHTEEN

SAL

IT'S LATE BY THE time Heath drops us off at Gabe's place. Despite my demands that we have only fun during our final Tour-de-Gracemont, everything feels weird.

It's hard to capture the emotion of this moment. We all leave tomorrow, and I think we've all accepted it. I get the nagging thought that something like this shouldn't feel so momentous, but it *is*.

Growing up in the Village of Gracemont is a blessing and a curse. At the end of the day, everyone wants what's best for you, but it's always so clear that no one knows what is "best" at any given time. You watch your classmates grow up saying they want to be doctors and astronauts in elementary school, and by middle school they've been told they can't so many times they start to believe it.

And really, it's true. Mom's always gotten by with strong

benefits and a savings account, but Heath's parents have always been one disaster or one medical bill away from losing their house. We don't have advanced-level classes at Gracemont High, so last year's valedictorian couldn't even get wait-listed at Duke.

Heath has had his heart set on Vanderbilt for years. Reese might apply to an Ivy League school, just to see what they say. Gabriel seems set on a state school. And me? I don't know. I've worked so hard to defy my circumstances, but I'm the most privileged one of the bunch. I have connections; I get to take chances that no one else does. And I still don't know if it's enough.

I want to go into politics, but it seems so unfair that I need to drop a hundred grand and waste away four years of my life to even have a chance.

I lean against my car, and the other boys form a semicircle around me.

"This is it, isn't it?" I say.

Gabe sighs. "This feels like a series finale."

"A season finale," Reese corrects.

"We'll be back," Heath says, a note of finality in his voice.

Gabe and I give hugs to the other boys, and somehow we're all wrapped into a group hug. It's a heavy goodbye, but I feel some hope, and maybe the others do too. There are no tears as we break apart, but I'm still struck with a very clear absence of warmth when Heath and Reese climb into the truck and slowly back out of the driveway.

It's just me and Gabe, and I realize this goodbye is going to be much harder. I wish I could sneak inside and spend the night with him, but we both leave so early tomorrow there's no chance we could get away with it.

I remind myself this is good for us, because I *really* need the reminder right now.

"Take the bus up and see me," Gabe says. "Give me a month, and I promise, I'll be a Boston pro. I'll give you a proper tour of the city, and you can stay with me whenever."

I smile, and nod slightly.

"We're really doing this," I say. I feel a little empowered, and I hope this energy carries me through the next three months.

"I'll save the world, then you can lead it."

"All in a summer's work," I reply. "Seems doable."

He laughs, then closes the distance between us. I place my hand on his hip as he presses himself into me, just lightly, just enough for our bodies to become one.

I kiss him. Slowly, at first, then with deepening intensity. This isn't some messy make-out session; this is targeted. It's clear. It's with such intention that there's a moment when I wonder if I will ever be able to make myself stop.

Gabe pulls his lips away, and mine burn from brushing against his stubble. He leans his head into a particularly tender spot between my neck and shoulder.

"I can't believe I have to say goodbye to you," he says.

"It's only for three months," I say. "We'll be back together before you know it."

He looks into my eyes for one, two, three seconds, then he slightly shakes his head. "Something tells me this won't be the same after we've seen the world. After we've gotten a taste of what's coming after graduation."

I don't respond.

I can't, because I somehow agree.

• Golden Boys •

GABRIEL + HEATH + REESE + SAL

Landed.

I have 185 notifications, so there's no way in hell I'm scrolling up to see what you all said. Flight was so long, and there was a baby crying for about six hours straight, but whatever. I survived, and I'm officially French!

I'm waiting for the bus to pick us up from the airport. It all feels very weird... all the signs are in French and barely anyone in this airport is speaking English, which makes sense but like... I'm def not in Gracemont anymore

R

How's everyone doing? **R**

S Flight was quick and easy. I made it to the apartment earlier today and walked around this afternoon. R-most of those notifications are selfies of me at all the monuments here so you better scroll up.

G Boston is a lot

S I'm all unpacked, and it feels so legit. I'm in an apartment! With a roommate! Who's like five years older than me and also feels weird about our arrangement!

G I'm hiding in my dorm room

S Orientation starts in a couple days. I'm a little nervous, but it's so nice here. Idk I'm excited guys

G Tree nerds everywhere

O...kay. Well, my bus is here. I won't be able to chat until I'm back on WiFi, but it's super late here, so I'll figure it out tomorrow. Miss you guys. **R**

Heath checked in a little bit ago, he still has a little bit left in his drive FYI

Got it.

Miss you guys too

FaceTime soon?

I'll set up a google doc and we can put our schedules into it

Of course you will

lolllll

CHAPTER NINETEEN

HEATH

MY NOTIFICATIONS LIGHT UP as soon as I send the text, with Gabriel and Reese snapping at me for texting while driving. I give their concerned texts a thumbs-up, but otherwise ignore them. They don't seem to understand that the last hour or so of this journey is in fully standstill traffic. But hey, at least they care.

It was a largely uneventful trip, even though I'm fucking *beat.* The road from Gracemont to Daytona is an almost perfectly straight line from the top of the country to the bottom. Ohio was a snoozefest. West Virginia, Virginia, and the Carolinas featured some winding roads and rolling hills, which was a little more interesting.

I've been in Florida for what feels like hours. After Jacksonville, it's a straight shot down the coast to Daytona Beach. I flew down the highway for a while, but then it abruptly turned into this. Standstill traffic with the sun so hot it causes little waves off the pavement and off the hood of my truck. Beachfront shops dot the street, along with some run-down gas stations, auto parts stores, tobacco shops, liquor stores, and fast food. There's even a Cincinnati-style chili place here.

So it's basically a hotter Ohio.

The sun is burning, so much that I scorch my arm whenever I try to rest it outside my window. My truck's done wonders on this drive (the main wonder being that it hasn't completely fallen apart on the side of the road), but I feel it starting to struggle. My gaze keeps darting to the temperature gauge, which has been steadily increasing over the past hour, and the thermometer has officially entered the red territory. Yikes.

This happened before, a few times in Ohio when the humidity and the sun teamed up to kick my truck's ass. Those times, I would usually just divert from the farm-ridden country roads to the more wooded ones, and let the shade do its work. But I haven't seen a tree since Georgia, so I don't have that luxury here.

God, I need a new truck. One that doesn't give me a heart attack every hour.

My stomach starts to sour at the thought of breaking down here, *so close* to my destination. I try not to think about it, but it's nagging at me constantly, especially now that the check-engine light just popped on.

I'm on a two-lane highway with a lot of traffic, but I remind myself: I'm not stuck here. There's always a solution; there's always a way out. I clear my head and look for anyplace to pull over so my truck can cool down. It's just another couple of miles to Aunt

Jeanie's place, but Google Maps says that short drive will take me thirty minutes, and based on the sounds my truck's making, I don't have that time.

I spot a novelty beach shop with parking spots under a weird overhang and breathe a sigh of relief. *It's better than nothing*, I think as I cut across traffic to pull off the road and into the parking spot with the most shade. I turn off the car quickly, my engine temperature fully in the red, and pop the hood, hoping that'll help it cool down faster.

I pick up my phone and drop the boys a quick audio message of me shouting, "I need a new fucking truck!" then follow it up with another message that says, "I'm fine, just venting. Had to pull over because my truck needed to vent too. It's really hot here. Miss you guys."

Stepping out of the car, the full intensity of the salt air pummels my nostrils, and I'm hit with the very real feeling of being on vacation. We've only been to the beach a couple of times—Virginia Beach or Myrtle Beach, never this far south—but Mom loves the beach. Apparently, her sister does too, so much that she stuck it out here. A part of me wonders if they used to come as kids, and that's why Jeanie chose this life over the one they had in Ohio.

I don't know if it's my place to ask, but as my family feels farther and farther away, I hope I get the nerve to someday.

I step into the beach shop and pull out my phone, giving my eyes time to adjust to the lack of sun. The spotty fluorescent lights have nothing on what's happening outside, so I blink hard until I can actually see my home screen. My first urge is to call Reese, but he's on a bus somewhere in France right now, and the other guys seem to be occupied too, so I call Diana.

My cousin picks up on the first ring. "Hey, you already here?"

"Nah, I'm like a mile out, but traffic is nuts and my truck was overheating, so I put it in the shade." I feel momentarily embarrassed about my poor-ass truck, but Diana doesn't seem like the judgmental type, so I don't backtrack. I look around. "Found this tacky beach shop, and I'm kind of obsessed."

She laughs. "Yeah, those are everywhere. You've got to stock up on the essentials."

"Ironically, I did forget to pack sunscreen."

"I was actually referring to airbrushed tank tops and novelty visors, but sure, sunblock is cool too."

I make my way to the rack of airbrushed shirts, and I'm assaulted by the colors, the vibrancy. Long board shorts with palm trees or sharks line one wall, while the tiniest of neon pink bikinis line the opposite wall. The souvenir selection is truly something. They've got the usual: magnets, shot glasses, and postcards, but they've also got a selection of large model boats, some in bottles and some too big for any bottle. The price tags on those have one too many zeroes for me to take them seriously.

I wonder what the guys would think of this, but then I remember they're very far away and my cousin Diana is not, and I'm totally ignoring her on this call.

"They have a good selection?" she asks.

"You've got to see this," I say.

I request a FaceTime, and she quickly switches over. Her face pops up on the screen, bleached-blond hair framing her face as she gives me a wave. A warmth comes over me whenever I remember this girl's my cousin. My *family*.

I have a family, I remind myself, *even if it's not like Reese's. Even if it's small.*

"I need your opinion," I say. "Do you think I should get this tank with the two dolphins humping?"

I hear a gargled laugh come from the phone. "I literally almost spit out my drink. It's perfect."

"Or . . . maybe this one with the palm trees? It's a little classier, I think. For dinner parties, perhaps?"

"Because class is what we're going for, yes."

The guy working the register comes up behind me, and I jump, thinking he's about to scold me for making fun of his collection so loudly. But I see he's clearly not the owner of this store. He's about my age, but my defenses lower even more when I see his grin.

"Need some help?" he asks in a singsongy voice, and I feel my entire body blush, if that's even possible.

"No, just browsing the shirts. It's an impressive collection."

He laughs. "I will say the shirt with the dolphins, uh, doin' it, is one of our bestsellers. But I'm not sure you fit the type. Vacation?"

"No," I say as Diana chimes in with, "Yo! I'm still here!"

"Sorry, sorry," I say, then turn back to the phone. "I'll call when I'm on my way back."

She waves her arms. "Wait, I recognize that dude's voice. Which shop are you at?"

I turn my phone toward the sales guy, who squints to see Diana on the screen.

"It's, uh, Dan's Beach Shop," I say.

"Oh god, you really are close to the house," Diana says. "Hey, Cole, this is my cousin Heath; he's staying with me for the summer. All the way from Ohio." She stretches Ohio to make it sound like a luxurious hot spot, and I almost groan.

"Hey, D. Small world, huh?" Cole says, then he peeks behind the camera to look at me. "Hey, Heath."

"Mom's arcade is, like, two shops down, just off the beach," Diana continues. "I'm going to take my bike down there right now—Cole, keep an eye on him and don't let my darling country cousin make any bad decisions."

I drop my voice to a solemn whisper. "So you're saying I can't buy the humping dolphins tank?"

Diana responds immediately, "That's a no."

I end the call with Diana while Cole takes me to the register to pay for my (not lewd) airbrushed tank. I feel my confidence start to rise as I follow him, because hey, maybe I'm not super close to my cousin, or to this guy, or to this town . . . but with the hint of sunscreen and salt in the air, there is something magical about this place.

That, or I'm suffering from heatstroke.

CHAPTER TWENTY

GABRIEL

I'M NOT SURE WHAT I expected from a dorm room, but this feels slightly more like a jail cell. The concrete walls are painted white; the desks and beds are bare. I guess I should be grateful that they've put us all in singles. I know that's not going to be the case when I finally get to college. I open one of the dresser drawers, and an old musty smell smacks me in the face. The fluorescent light above starts to flicker.

It's only three months, I remind myself.

Three months . . . in this heat.

Boston's Save the Trees was able to partner with a local university to set us up with these dorm rooms, which is cool in theory, but based on all the marketing materials Suffolk County Junior College shoved into my hands as I arrived, I get the feeling this is going to turn into one of those time-share presentations real quick.

But the college is doing it right: they set us up with towels, sheets that fit the extra-long twin bed in our room, and they're even hosting a welcome event in the lobby tonight. My hands start to sweat as I think through the logistics of the evening: writing my name on one of those name tags? Awkwardly meeting new people? I flash back to the time I gave that presentation in the auditorium, when all my friends fell silently, seamlessly into other groups as I stood onstage alone.

I should make friends.

Or I could call Sal.

I connect to the shitty Wi-Fi and send a FaceTime request to Sal, who quickly rejects it. My fists clench, but I don't let myself think too much about why I'm put off by it. I mean, he's got his own life—right now, he's probably climbing the Lincoln Memorial or trying to network his way into the White House, or . . . whatever it is you do in DC.

He sends me a quick text: **On the metro. Call later?**

The fuzziness in my chest eases, so I double tap the message and give it a thumbs-up. He's not doing anything wrong; my anxiety is just making me act selfish. Being away from him is going to be harder than I thought.

Though I still don't know what to do about tonight's welcome event. I mean, it's not required. I pretend this is a conversation with my therapist, where I'm discussing the pros and cons of going. Pros: I could meet new people. It probably wouldn't be awful. Cons: Meeting new people is draining. I'm already tired from my trip here. It might be awful.

105

I wonder, Would my therapist urge me to go, saying that I need to confront my anxiety head-on? Or would she say that it's okay to give yourself a break? I have this habit of convincing myself I'm doing something for self-care reasons, but it's actually me avoiding responsibility. I don't know if this is what I'm doing now, but I can't be sure. Which is why I'd usually go to Sal for a second opinion.

Am I scared? Is it normal to be scared? It's like I don't know my own brain.

I decide that I really can't handle this question myself, so I pick up the phone and FaceTime my sister.

"Gabey!" she shouts in this cutesy way that almost makes me hang up on her. "You're in a dorm room! How does it feel?"

"Honestly? Not great." I sit on the squeaky bed. "It's hot. It's weird."

"Yeah, I get that. I *hated* my dorm room, and not just because I had the world's worst roommate. It's just uncomfortable. You're in this box, and you have to take a key with you to go to the restroom; you wear flip-flops in the shower? Nothing is normal—everything is weird."

I sigh. "Did you get used to it?"

"Sure. I think decorating helped. You took some stuff from your room, right? I feel like you need to get that up right away, so it feels a little more like home. It's looking dreary right now. Put the sheets on your bed. Unpack. You'll feel better, I promise."

I sit on the bed with my back to the wall, to stop her from giving me even more chores to do. "I will, I will," I say. "Also, there's . . . a thing tonight that I really don't want to go to."

"A thing? Like, a *social* thing?" I hear the eagerness in her voice.

"Yeah. In the lobby. It's going to be so cringey."

She gasps. "This is the exact kind of *thing* you have to go to. I swear, events like this got me out of that dark place I was in first semester. Please, promise me you'll go."

"I'm really tired," I say.

"Did you call me for a pep talk, or did you just call to whine?"

I hesitate. "Both?"

"I'm not interested in whiners." she says, and I roll my eyes. "Go to that party."

"It's not a *party*; it's an awkward welcome event put on by the internship and the school."

"We'll call it party-adjacent, then," she says with a laugh. "Seriously, don't get overwhelmed. It's not a big thing, and you are right that it could be awkward and annoying. But you won't know until you get there. I say you set up some rules: stick it out for at least ten minutes, and make sure you talk to at least one person who isn't, like, your boss. You can set a timer, then when it rings, pretend you're getting a call and bail if you're not having fun."

I nod, but I'm not sure what to say. So much of me is resisting this, but I don't think I have a good reason. Getting through a whole party sounds awful.

But I could do ten minutes.

"That makes sense. Anyway, tell Mom and Dad I'm okay. I'm going to unpack," I say. "Thanks for the pep talk, and sorry for whining."

"You can make it up to me by—"

"Going to the *party*," I say, finishing her sentence. "Yeah, I got it."

"You're going to do great," she says. "I'm actually jealous—Mom and Dad are *really* making me remember why I moved away for college right about now."

I offer my condolences, and we end the call. The schedule the college gave me at check-in sits on the corner of my desk, mocking me. Eight p.m., social hour, optional.

Optional.

I mean, I'll see them all tomorrow.

As I unpack my clothes, I look to the bracelet on my wrist, and my sapling stares back at me. The realization hits me so hard I nearly groan:

I think it's time to put that nagging feeling that I don't belong here behind me, and learn how to grow.

CHAPTER TWENTY-ONE

HEATH

I DON'T BELONG HERE. Not like Diana does. She's got this sun-kissed skin and wavy blond hair, a simple tank top and cut-off jean shorts. Her hair's barely long enough to put up in a ponytail, but she must do something with it, because she's got a hair tie or something around her wrist.

The sound of the ocean lapping onto the beach reaches my ears, though I still haven't set foot on sand yet. We're at the pedestrian island on the boardwalk, sitting on a fence, catching up and waiting for Cole to get off his shift so he can join us.

"You sure Aunt Jeanie won't mind that I didn't go right to your place?" I ask.

"Nah, she was napping when I left." She shrugs. "Her nights go pretty late, so she always tries to catch a quick nap before heading to the arcade."

It's a relatively quiet evening, at least from what I was

expecting. There are plenty of people drinking and eating on the patio on the boardwalk, but it doesn't sound like the same thing as Jeanie's arcade.

Diana finishes her slice of pizza and tosses the crust to a flock of seagulls that have started to gather around us.

"This might sound weird," she says, "but it's kind of cool to have a cousin my own age. Some of my friends always bring their siblings or cousins around, and it's wild to think about having family that's in the same stage of life as me."

"Shitty we're only just meeting, though."

She laughs, then reaches for the thin bracelet on her wrist and spins it around a few times. "True. We'll just have to make up for that this summer."

To be fair, we "met" on social media years ago. She found my Instagram and sent me a follow request, and we've had a sur-face-level liking-each-other's-selfies friendship ever since.

"You don't have any other family here?" I ask. "I feel like everyone I know has these huge families with, like, truckloads of cousins, and I have . . ."

I almost say "my parents," but I don't know if I even really have them. I'll have my dad. And I guess I'll visit my mom from time to time. So that's cool.

"I don't have anyone else, really," she says. "Just friends, though nothing like your crew. Oh, hey, Cole's parents just went through a divorce. You might want to talk to him about it. He was really fucked up for a while, but I think he's gotten used to it."

"That's okay." I chuckle. "And you're right—I do have the best friends."

I can't fight the feeling that it's all going to change after this summer. After they get a taste of their futures.

"You miss them? You seem down."

"Yeah, I guess it's that. Or, I don't know." I sigh, and fiddle with my bracelet for a couple of seconds. "They're all doing these stupidly amazing things all over the world, and I'm—"

"—stuck with us?"

Her expression is sly, and she gives a laugh so I know she's joking, or she's okay with the dynamic at least.

"That's one way to put it. I mean, it's awesome being here already. But we're all, like, the top of our class, and they can be super competitive one-upping each other. I just want to get the most out of my summer, and this next year, and hopefully get into Vanderbilt. I don't really have a backup plan."

"I don't know your friends, other than through your Instagram posts, so this may be way off base. But I don't think they're very normal people. This is coming from a straight C student, so keep that in mind, but I don't think you *have* to do all this extra privileged shit to get into college."

"They're not privileged—" I start, but she cuts in with: "Isn't one studying abroad in *France*?"

I let out a bark of laughter. "Okay, fair."

"I'm not saying they didn't earn it or whatever, just not exactly the kind of whim I could find the finances for, you know?"

"I really do."

Cole texts Diana saying he's getting off work and is going to drive home, then walk up and meet us by the arcade, so she hops off the fencing and gestures for me to follow her down the beach.

I strip off my socks and shoes and bury my feet in the *extremely hot* sand. I yelp with pain, which causes Diana to double over with laughter.

"You'll get used to it," she says, "but let's go down to the water and walk that way."

I hop awkwardly toward the water and breathe a huge sigh of relief when I reach the strip of freshly wet sand. Sea foam runs over my feet, cooling them. Eventually, we start our way down the beach, dodging beachgoers as we walk.

"How are you going to afford Vanderbilt?" she asks, and the bluntness of the question takes me by surprise. I *never* talk money, and my friends certainly don't ask these things. But maybe that's because money isn't as big a deal for any of them.

"Scholarships, maybe? Vanderbilt is a good baseball school, and they give out some scholarships for it. I'm one of the best pitchers in the state—at least, that's what my coach says."

"Oh, whoa, that's huge." She pauses. "I'm trying to think of a talent I have to save some face in this conversation, and I'm drawing a blank. Shit."

"There's got to be *something*," I say.

"Nope." She spins her bracelet again. "Perfectly ordinary, I'm afraid."

"Anyway, if I get in, we'll find a way to make it work. Dad says he's got good credit and would cosign on a loan with me. I don't know how I feel about going into debt for this, but I'll worry about that later."

"Ha, you should talk to my mom about loans. She said buying

112

that arcade was the dumbest shit she's ever done, but she's slowly been paying it back. She used to have a ton of savings, but the whole pandemic thing happened, and you know how that goes."

I flinch, thinking about how hard COVID-19 hit Florida. When all your money is in the travel industry, and the travel industry fully collapses, what does that leave you?

"I'm glad y'all made it out of that. A lot of people didn't." I sigh, thinking back. "During the pandemic, they laid off my dad and it was really bad for a while. Gabriel's family struggled a bit too, but the others didn't seem to get just how hard it was for us. Like, I was fourteen when it started, but I still knew we were always one disaster away from losing everything."

"Another privilege," Diana says.

"They all tried to be understanding, at least. Gabriel started all these fundraisers for those in our community who got laid off, and Sal found literally every government relief program my dad was eligible for." I pause. "It was awkward, but it worked out."

The walk down the beach doesn't take long, but I'm already starting to feel like a different person. There's an overwhelming relief that after sitting in a car for fifteen hours, hunched, gripping the steering wheel tightly, just begging the piece of shit I'm driving to make the drive, I step out into this wholly different world. A world where my fears back home seem smaller.

It's nothing like Ohio here, and maybe that's what I did need this summer. The waves crash against the shore, the sun beats down on me, the noise of the beachgoers recharges me. And as we approach the strip of beach outside Jeanie's arcade, I see a now-shirtless Cole laying towels down on the beach. Diana runs to him, and I follow, and he greets us with a smile.

"You brought snacks?" Diana says with a squeal. "I swear, you're always the most prepared person in the world. This is why I love you."

My ears perk up at the phrase, and for the first time I wonder if they're more than just friends. A feeling of disappointment nags at me, followed by a second feeling of disappointment when I realize I shouldn't be thinking of *any* of this right now.

He looks to me as Diana tears into a bag of chips. "She gets hangry really easy. I realized that, early on in our friendship, if I just carried snacks with me twenty-four-seven, she'd be more pleasant."

Friendship, I repeat in my mind. Noted.

"I would argue, but he's not wrong," Diana says through a mouth full of food. "If I'm ever being a bitch, just go get me a corn dog from the boardwalk. Or some doughnuts, specifically maple and strawberry."

"I hope those are two separate doughnuts," I say.

"Yeah, but I would totally eat them together. But really, any food. It's magic."

We settle into our spots and spend the next few minutes covering one another in sunscreen. I watch as Diana slips her hands down his back, and I feel a little envious of her.

Cole is this mix between adorable and hot. *Hotdorable?* No, that sounds awful. But he's got this tan skin, lanky frame, shaggy brown hair, and dark eyes. At first glance, you can't really tell where the brown of his iris begins and his pupil ends, which gives him a sweet but slightly cartoonish look. Add that to his dimples and the light stubble dotting his jawline, and a part of me wants to lose myself in him.

And then I realize I'm staring. So I stop.

He runs a lotioned hand down his arm, then says, "Jeanie says hi, by the way. I dropped Heath's luggage off on my way home."

"Oh, you didn't have to do that," I say.

As I abandoned my truck in the lot, I put my suitcase in his trunk because we realized leaving it out in the truck bed was probably not the smartest decision. But I do feel some relief knowing that everything's waiting for me back at Jeanie's.

"It's nothing," he replies. "I want to make sure you enjoy it here. Daytona gets a bad rap sometimes."

"For good reason," Diana says under her breath.

"But it's *home.*"

Diana doesn't respond, but I see her lightly nodding.

"Well, it's a lot different here. In a good way," I say.

"Tell me about Ohio," Cole says. "I'm fascinated about, like, places that are not here. I've only left the state once, I think?"

"I guess I'm the same way, with Ohio. My family isn't big on traveling, though we did take a few road trips to the more northern beaches when I was younger. Let's see, what's Ohio like . . . ?"

For a moment, I kind of forget what home is like. It feels so normal that it's impossible to describe to someone.

"Corn," I say. Then I realize that's a horrible way to start a description of an entire state, but I've already committed to the corn route, and crap, they're staring, so I shoot out: "I mean, fields, there are a lot of fields of corn and soy. Farms are everywhere in our village. Our farmhouse is actually on one, though the previous owner sold all the farmland around it. It's nothing special, I guess. We have this big weather vane in the yard, and a star on our house."

"A star?" he says.

Diana cuts in. "It's a country thing; I've seen it all through his Instagram stories. All the houses have these big stars on them, and some have flags in their yard. It's *fascinating*."

"Some paint their barns to look like the flag," I admit.

"Sounds, uh, patriotic," he says with a chuckle.

I shake my head. "I'm doing an awful job of describing Gracemont. It's all so small. Our school only has a couple hundred people in it, and everyone's in everyone else's business. It's nice to get away for a bit. But I miss my friends already."

"You'll be back before you know it," Diana says, and maybe I imagined it, but a look of disappointment crosses Cole's face. I tell myself not to read into it.

My voice drops to a whisper. "I don't even know what'll be there when I get back."

CHAPTER TWENTY-TWO

GABRIEL

IT'S FIVE AFTER EIGHT, and I can hear music creeping down the hall. I haven't heard many people leave their rooms, though, so I take a few extra minutes to make sure I'm presentable. There's a tiny sink and a tiny mirror in this microscopic dorm room, but I look pretty good for someone who hasn't slept well in days and is currently fighting off a panic attack. I adjust my T-shirt, which was meant to be a gag gift from the boys last Christmas—a silhouette of a tree on a stark white shirt, with the word "hugger" blended into the leaves. But it's kind of stylish, and I am a tree hugger, so I like it.

And hopefully the others will too. Although I'm not getting my hopes up. I'll fulfill my promises to my sister: I have a ten-minute timer set, and I will speak to one person. Then I'm going to bed.

I hear a door close out in the hall, and I know at least one person has made their way to the event. I give it a second—a weird fear spiking in me that warns me not to be in the hall with another person, lest we be forced into an awkward conversation.

When the coast is clear, I crack open the door. A breeze blows through me as hot air gets pulled in from my open window and into the hall. I take a breath and try to settle my stomach, the heaviness in my chest. It will be okay. I have to do this.

Stepping out into the hall, I triple check that I have my keys, phone, and wallet, and I let the door click behind me. I feel exposed out here, knowing anyone can open their door at any time, but I think I just need to push through.

I follow the sounds of music. I don't recognize the song, but it seems fairly recent, and I'm sure whoever's in charge put on a Spotify playlist to set the mood. Apparently, the mood is supposed to be up-tempo, pop fueled, with a steady beat. Do they think we'll be dancing at this? I almost laugh at the thought.

Stepping into the lobby, I see they've thrown a pretty decent event together in the few hours that passed after I first walked these halls. Amazing what a few well-placed streamers can do. Looking around, I see tables with refreshments, standing bar tables scattered throughout, and even a few servers walking by with passed appetizers.

I pan across the crowd, and a sort of fear strikes me when I see someone who's far more dressed up than I. He looks a little older than me, but maybe that's because he's wearing black slacks and a white button-up. I get the urge to duck out and find nicer clothes, but as my eyes flick to the other attendees, the tension in my shoulders starts to ease. One person's wearing a short skirt with an edgy tee; another guy's wearing a zip-up hoodie and shorts.

I turn on my timer. Ten minutes, one conversation. Totally doable.

I walk in a meandering way—from the outside, it probably looks casual, like I'm getting the lay of the land or smoothly making my way to the refreshments table. But what I'm actually doing is more strategic. I put a round table in between me and the group of two looking up at me from their sodas; I slide casually behind someone whose back is closest to me; I walk in a path where I can evade conversations but still not be rude. It's right where my anxiety is calmest: a place where I can be present but also fade away.

I get to the registration table, where a cute older girl with a Boston Save the Trees shirt is checking off names and handing out our badges. As I arrive, she plucks one out and hands it to me.

"Oh, thanks," I say. "You're the person I interviewed with, right?"

"Yes, I'm Ali! And you're the intern from Ohio, right? Hope your flight went smoothly. I'm really excited to be working with you this summer."

She slides me a name tag and a marker. "Just write your name and pronouns here and go meet some new people. I promise they're all really cool. Twelve summer interns, plus about five of my colleagues are joining me here. Super-small gathering, not much programming, it's all about having fun today!"

I'm unsure about a lot of things, but I obviously know my

name. But when I put my Sharpie to my name tag, I hesitate. It dawns on me that I came here to redefine Gabriel. To be a new person, or at least an enhanced version of myself.

"Careful," she says, noticing my hesitation, "you only get one chance to define yourself here. If you're going for a nickname, you've got to commit. One of my friends decided to go by his middle name, Keith, one summer, and it stuck with him forever. And Keith is such an awful name."

I laugh and thank her for the warning.

It's more than a nickname, though. When I think of who I want to be here, I think of Sal. I think of the person he sees me as. And that's not Gabriel. I'm Gabe to him, and I think that's who I need to be.

I write *Gabe* on the name tag. Then my pronouns, *he/him*.

Then I turn toward the party. Since that chat with Ali doesn't count, I have about eight minutes to make my one conversation before I can officially duck out. So I scan the rest of the crowd.

My heartbeat thuds against my chest, so much that if I looked down, I'm sure I could see it raising and lowering my shirt in a sharp rhythm. I veer around the chatty guy who's too dressed up for the occasion, but he doesn't seem to mind as he's deeply involved in a conversation about hydroponics with a cute guy who looks like he has no idea what that is, based on his blank expression and erratic nodding.

I do my dance, weaving between tables, knowing I could keep this up for the full ten minutes. I shouldn't do that, but I simply don't know how to start the conversation. What if they don't want to meet me? What if I barge into a really good conversation, and it gets awkward after that? What if . . .

My therapist's voice reminds me that shaming myself for feeling so scared right now isn't helpful, and that I need to turn those what-ifs around:

What if it's not the worst thing ever?

What if I have a really good conversation?

What if I even make a new friend?

"Hi!" A short Black girl stops me in my tracks. She's got a subtle, almost shy look about her, which doesn't match up with the fact that she definitely just jumped in front of me. "I'm Tiffany."

"Hi, Gabe." I reply. "*I'm* Gabe, I mean."

My brain already feels fried, and I've barely had any conversations tonight. She gives an awkward chuckle, then waves me over to a table where another intern stands. A napkin sits in the center with about ten toast points with avocado sitting on it.

"I know it looks weird," the other person at the table says in lieu of an introduction. Thankfully, I don't need an introduction because we have name tags, and theirs says *Art, they/them.* "But they only have one vegan appetizer here, which is basically ridiculous because half of us seem to be vegans—I mean, we're all interning to save the damn trees? I swear I'm a good person, but I am not a good hungry person, so please don't judge me for the avocado toast hoarding I'm doing. Would you like one?"

I laugh. "No, they're all yours. I'll grab one of the meat ones next time they're passed, and you can have all the avocado. As long as you don't mind me eating meat in front of you."

"Honestly, you could slaughter the cow in front of me as long as I've got my toast. Live and let live, you know?" They pause. "Okay, that was intense. Maybe not that."

"Wow, great mental image." Tiffany rolls her eyes. "I guess you don't need the introduction, but I *was* going to say, 'Art, this is Gabe; Gabe, this is Art.'"

We shake hands.

"So where are you all from?" I ask. "I'm from Gracemont—I mean, I'm from a little town in Ohio. It's technically a village. In Ohio, you have to have five thousand citizens to call it a town. We have like two thousand. Probably too much info? I am very new to Boston, and I am overwhelmed."

"Oh god, I am too." Tiffany places her hand over mine for a brief second, breathing a sigh of relief. "I'm from a tiny-ass town in Maryland, and this shit is stressful."

"Okay, so you get it. Boston is a *lot*, isn't it?"

She considers my question for a second, then gives a thoughtful nod. "It's pretty cool, though, you've got to admit."

"It's not all bad," Art says. "I'm a local, but I do appreciate you two not being so doe-eyed about it."

"Yeah, I'm not doe-eyed, I'm just scared." Tiffany laughs. "Is that okay to say?"

I feel myself thaw in conversation with them, and I really do breathe more easily knowing that there are nice (albeit toast-hoarding) people here, *and* there's another small-town person here who does not seem comfortable either. Though she did jump in my way to chat, which is way more than I did, so I should be taking notes.

"Have you been here long?" I ask.

"Tiffany and I were the first to get here, actually," Art explains. "We checked in at the same time and got to chat a bit while unpacking in our rooms. Did you just get here?"

"Ah, no. I got here a while ago. I just . . . haven't really left my room."

"I get that," Tiffany says, and I think maybe she really does. "This is all so weird. Like, I have no idea what we're going to be doing. I assume boring stuff—filing papers maybe? Think we'll actually be in the parks at all?"

"If it gets me away from my parents for a whole summer, I would gladly file papers," Art says.

I give them a sympathetic nod, but they jump in with, "Oh god, not like that. They're just really annoying right now. Mostly about college stuff. They're such helicopter parents, I swear."

Another employee, name tag *Laura she/her*, comes by our tables and drops off a few notebooks and folders, letting us know that we don't need to worry about reading any of it yet—just some paperwork and information for our orientation sessions tomorrow.

We continue talking, though the stack of information is clearly taking some of our attention. Art's eyes keep landing on some spot behind me. I want to turn back to see what's going on. They walk away from the table quickly, so Tiffany and I watch as they walk up to the table with the two guys from earlier—the one overdressed, overeager, and *still* talking about hydroponics from the look of it; and the other, who seemed overwhelmed before but is downright flustered now.

123

Art greets both of them, then singles out the scared guy. They gesture behind them with a concerned look on their face. The two guys from the table shake hands as a goodbye before the loud one walks over to another unsuspecting group of people, and the quiet one (who is noticeably less flustered now) finally joins up with us.

"So wait, how do you have my paperwork over here?" he asks, which makes Art laugh.

"I'm so sorry if this is an overstep," Art says, "but I've been watching you drown in that conversation for at least fifteen minutes, and I thought you might need an escape."

The guy—*Matt, he/him*, according to his name tag—fully deflates into the table with relief. He looks up and gives us each a smile. His smile is . . . really nice.

"I tried to get out of that conversation six times," Matt says. "I kept track."

"So did I," Art replies.

"He's a sweet guy, but he's just so freaking passionate about this. I thought I was a tree hugger and all, but wow, I would have fully lit a tree on fire to get out of that conversation."

Tiffany gestures at my Tree Hugger shirt, which makes Matt laugh. "So you understand just how desperate I was. Anyway, hi, I'm Matt, thank you, you're all my new best friends. Art, I owe you."

"Noted," Art says with a smirk.

To repay us, Matt offers to grab us all refreshments. Once he returns, we all get to know one another a bit more over sodas, and the tension about what mysteries are in the welcome packet starts to ease.

"And you, Gabe, with the very stylish and on-brand shirt, I must say—where do you live?"

My phone starts beeping at this point, and for a weird moment I expect it to be Sal calling me, but it's not—it's my ten-minute alarm. I am free to go. I can leave right now, and I'll have completely fulfilled my obligations for the day.

"Sorry about that," I say as I delete the alarm and dedicate my full attention to my new friends. "I'm from Ohio."

• Golden Boys •

GABRIEL + HEATH + REESE + SAL

helllooooooo???

anyone out there?

miss you guys! (H)

(S) Miss you too!

oh hey!

how's DC so far?

pics look great

... hello?

ok good chat (H)

CHAPTER TWENTY-THREE

REESE

AESTHETICALLY? PARIS IS PERFECTION. The stone buildings are all intricately chiseled, and these charming cafés line the network of small angular alleys that make up this part of town. I'm trying to not look so touristy. I'm going to be living here for two full months, and I feel this urge to be immediately comfortable in this new environment. But I find that impossible to do when there's so much to marvel at: a historic cathedral down the street, a storefront with stylish mannequins in the window, or even the cute French guy outside a café who's casually smoking a cigarette, reading the paper, and sipping a tiny espresso.

Logistically, though? Paris is a nightmare. It's not the city's fault, to be clear. But French III did *not* prepare me for how truly *immersive* this immersive experience was going to be. I got a burner phone to make calls, but I haven't been able to add data, which means I can only group chat or FaceTime the boys from my computer or when I use Wi-Fi on the iPhone I brought here. Even more challenging, I don't have a Maps app to tell me where to go.

But on mornings like this, there's something calming about walking the streets without a direction, following the smell of freshly baked bread. There's something freeing about being untethered to my phone, though I'm really starting to miss them all.

Miss *him*, I guess.

It's early in the morning, but the city's starting to warm up, figuratively and literally. I find a corner café that's situated in view of a roundabout, but it's tucked away on a silent, tiny, one-way street. I go up to the bar and order a croissant and espresso in (what I think is) perfect French, but the barista clearly picks up on my American accent and replies in English: "Three five four, please."

I take out an assortment of euros and hand them over, trying not to openly sulk about it.

I take my pastry and espresso to a table outside and watch the passersby as I take off my backpack. I pull out the full schedule and welcome packet I was given yesterday on that massively confusing bus ride to the dorm. I groan, thinking of the state I left it in—I pretty much just dropped my suitcase on the floor and crashed on the unmade bed. I still haven't unpacked, but maybe I'll have time to do some after my first classes today.

I look at my Studio Design schedule, and the class names pop out at me: Typography, Computer Modeling, Fundamentals of Design, Graphic Design Practicum. I wonder if there was ever really a time these classes actually appealed to me. I love illustration and design as an art, but the more I think of it as career, the less I'm sure I want to do it. This is by far the most practical of all the programs, but it's only practical if I want to work in graphic design someday.

I flip through the pamphlets for the other classes and realize a lot of these don't appeal to me either. I'm feeling low on inspiration, which is a laughable thought considering I'm in *Paris*, which is arguably one of the most inspirational places in the world when it comes to art and design.

I watch as a naked mannequin gets dressed and styled with a new look across the street in the boutique dress shop. Outside, a woman's stopped to watch, and I see her tug at her own dress, which is much more conservative in comparison to the flamboyant garment getting put on the mannequin. She waves to the person in the shop, and once she leaves I see the finished product in the window. It's unlike anything I've seen before—a bold look, where a bright red strappy top billows out into a skirt so large it presses against the window. It's impractical, I'd guess, but it makes a statement. Even on a mannequin it gives the feeling of movement, of perpetual motion.

Without thinking much, I pull out my journal and sketch the dress in the corner of this week's plan. In this sketch, it's being worn by a faceless woman, falling downward with her hair flying back, dress wrapping around her, alive with movement.

I look down to my bracelet, and the four dots on the charm stare back at me. An empty box still waiting to be filled in. I realize my hand has rested on a new program, one I hadn't given any thought to when I was browsing the catalog.

The classes in this new program hit me with some unexpected inspiration, the feeling I've been missing: Photography & Fashion Design, Themes in Fashion History, Fashion Design Studio, the Business of Fashion.

I can visualize myself learning how to design dresses or how the fashion world operates, and a nagging feeling enters my brain.

Is there still time to switch? What would my parents think? As they're halfway around the world, they probably wouldn't even have a say in it. Inspiration floods my body for the first time since I crafted these bracelets, and it's so loud I can't ignore it. I shoot back the rest of my espresso and try not to gag at the bitterness. Maybe I'm imagining it, but a rush of energy hits me and I know what I have to do:

I'm transferring to Fashion Design.

• • •

Riley Design is the Paris extension of the famous American design school. When my tutor first brought up this idea, Mom really questioned why I would need to leave the country to learn something I could learn there just as easily. Though I didn't have a great answer for that, Mamma fell in love with the program on my behalf and urged me to apply.

She wanted me to learn something new, to take chances and make this trip memorable . . . and this might be the thing to do it.

The building itself is pretty unassuming, just three floors of a fairly large building in the city center of Paris. When I first got here, I used my student ID to log into the Wi-Fi, then shot off an email to my instructor with my request. All that has led me to this moment, where I'm here, outside Professor Watts's door.

"Come in, Reese." She calls me into her office, and I take a seat on a beautifully designed, yet impractical and slightly painful, chair. "Very nice to meet you in person. We're really excited to have you as part of this program. Did you make it here okay?"

Her accent is fully American, which is a comfort, but it also makes me realize that going to an American school in France kind of negates the immersive experience I was planning. But regardless, it's nice to have a conversation that isn't in my pained French.

"Let's talk through this potential transfer. It's a little last-minute, but I appreciate you coming to me before classes start. We have a lot of students who don't think their classes are a good fit a few weeks in, but by that point the program's almost half over. You'll find that no matter what you study here, this is a very accelerated program, so I want to make sure you're fully ready for what to expect."

"That makes sense," I say, though I'm starting to feel immature for this change, and I wonder if she sees me as just another flighty American who can't make up his mind.

Although, that's totally who I am.

She turns her computer toward me, and on it is the portfolio that went alongside my application. It wasn't much, just a couple of illustrations and promotional flyers I made for student council.

"I will say, these flyers are fantastic—way better than I'd expect any high schooler to do, but I do think you could use some work with typography if you think you'll ever want to work in graphic design. Of course, you're young, you could study it in college, but I think now is a great time to wrap your head around how words fit into your design."

I nod my head, and my cheeks feel warm. I'm used to critique, but it's hard not to take it personally. I mean, I think they look great. But to know that they let me in despite immediately seeing flaws in my work makes me want to run away. But I guess that's why I'm here.

"Spatially, you've got everything down perfectly, which tells me you have a great eye for proportions and an overall aesthetic and point of view, which actually suggests you'd do well in fashion if that's something you're really interested in."

"That makes sense to me," I say.

"These illustrations are also really strong. You're particularly good with landscapes—clouds, capturing all the colors of the sunset, things of that nature. The wheat field here has such a feel-ing of movement, which shows me you don't just draw what you see, but what you feel as well. There aren't a lot of figures in your work, though, so I don't have anything that hints at your interest in fashion. Do you have anything you can show me?"

I slowly take off my copper bracelet, and I realize it's the first time I've taken it off since I handed them all out.

"I made this. Four of them, one for each of my friends, each with a different engraved charm. It's not much, but I really liked the idea of twisting metal to make an understated bracelet that goes with everything."

"Why did you choose copper?" she asks.

I wince. "I liked the color? It was easy to form, and not too expensive to buy. Why? Is it bad?"

"The bracelet's quite nice," she says with a laugh. "Just always curious why artists choose their mediums. It wasn't a test."

"Oh, I also did a sketch this morning of a dress I saw in the window of a boutique. It's *also* not much, just a quick ten-minute pencil sketch." I slide my journal across the table to her. "Ignore all the other stuff."

She flips back to the other illustrations, to the glimpses of my days, my dreams, that accompany my weeks. "This is what I was looking for," she finally says. "Oh, this is sweet—you sketch your friends in this?"

"Sometimes."

"At the risk of sounding condescending, that's really cute. Oh, I love this one with the fire—I love how you played with light and shadows here. This boy's face is positively *glowing*. Again, not much like what we do in fashion, but you're observant, and you have an eye for colors and shadows, silhouettes, and a lot of the basics."

She keeps flipping back, and I feel my cheeks flush with heat. I don't even let my friends see my journal.

"These are great," she finally says. "Every day you use design to tell a story, and that's what you need to do in any of these programs. Back to the first drawing you showed me, though. I don't like that dress—not your fault, I just feel like there's an impracticality here for something that was in a dress shop. Maybe good for the runway, or for editorial, but no woman is going to go down the street and pick this up for everyday wear—regardless, I love how you drew it."

I smile and get the urge to tell Heath about it all immediately, especially the bit about her loving my drawing of him. Silently, I curse the miles between us.

"Anyway, I don't think I can fully transfer you into the fashion program."

"Oh," I say as my heart plummets to my stomach. "Well, um, okay, then."

"I think you'd be better served with a hybrid program. I want you to take typography and fundamentals of graphic design. I don't think you fully know what you want to do, but looking at your work, you'd get a lot out of these classes. The fashion history course would also be good for you, and I know we've got an empty space there. And I want you to get some hands-on experience, so I'll put you in the fashion studio class too. You'll have two classes back-to-back in the morning, then you'll have a six-hour break, followed by your design classes.

"Fashion History, though, starts in about five minutes. It's down one floor and at the end of the hall. Think you can make it?" She finishes scribbling a note on some letterhead and hands it to me. "Just pass this to Professor MacLachlan. I'll email you your new schedule today. And Reese? Welcome to Riley Design."

MONDAY

- O 5-7 PM CLASSES
- O HANG PICS

TUESDAY

- O 3-5 PM CLASSES
- O TAKE A WALK AROUND NEW HOOD
- O POST A FEW SELFIES (FOR MAXIMUM FOMO)

WEDNESDAY

- O 5-7 PM CLASSES
- O CURATE NEW PLAYLIST: "WALKING AROUND PARIS"

THURSDAY

- O 3-5 PM CLASSES

FRIDAY

- O CHECK IN W/ PARENTS
- O FACETIME W/ THE BOYS

WEEKEND

- O TREAT YO' SELF!
  - ↳ PASTRIES? STREAM SOMETHING ON FRENCH NETFLIX?
- O CATCH UP ON SLEEP!

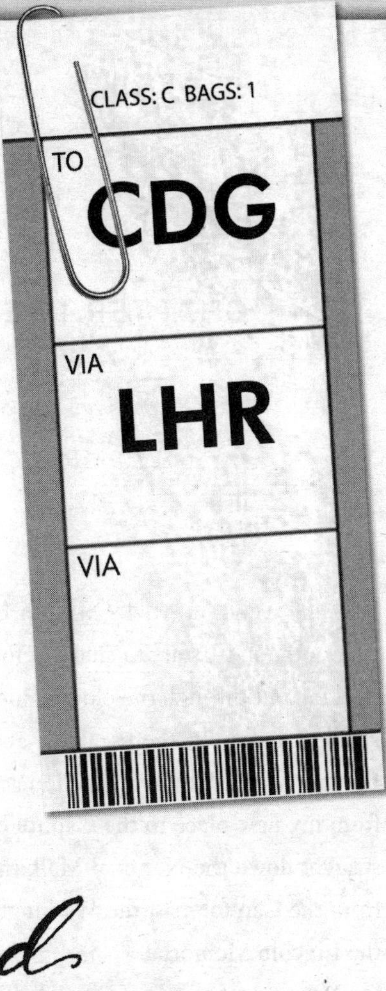

CLASS: C BAGS: 1

TO
CDG

VIA
LHR

VIA

"*find yourself*"

← S MADE ME WRITE THIS

CHAPTER TWENTY-FOUR

SAL

THE ESCALATOR LIFTS ME out of the metro station at Capitol South, and I start to shake before I even step off. The sun is peeking out through the clouds, and it's sweltering, but here I am shaking. I step off the escalator and pull up my phone, though I'm pretty sure I know where I'm going. I did a dry run yesterday from my new place to the Capitol building. From there I walked straight down the National Mall, the strip of parkland that leads from the Capitol, past the Washington Monument, all the way to the Lincoln Memorial.

My new phone background shines back at me. I took hundreds of photos yesterday—not an exaggeration—but my favorite ended up being this one. In between the Washington Monument and the Lincoln Memorial lies the World War II Memorial, which is stunning. It's a large fountain that's surrounded by a walking path, with fifty-six pillars surrounding them, their shadows like spokes on a bike.

Each pillar represents a state or territory that fought in the war, so I walked around until I found the pillar with "Ohio" on it. I took a selfie and made it my phone background. I'm far from home, but I get to keep a piece of it with me through this whole trip. I'm here to help Ohioans, and to work for one of the people who represents them in the Senate.

Maybe that's why I'm shaking. This is such a huge opportunity, and I know I have to do things right.

I check my look in my phone's selfie camera and quickly adjust my bow tie and smooth down my hair—the humidity is not going to be my friend this trip. I walk the short way up to the entrance to the Capitol and wait for my contact at Senator Wright's office to come get me.

This is real. This is happening.

• • •

Thirty minutes later, I'm sitting in a conference room with a large group of interns, and I'm trying to process all the cool stuff that just happened. Meghan—Senator Wright's scheduler—walked me here, and as soon as we left the security area, things started feeling official. Busts of important Americans dotted the halls; flags hid in every corner. Every senator's office was just *right here*, and as I walked by them, I found myself repeatedly starstruck.

Orientation, or whatever this is supposed to be, happens too quickly. The Speaker of the House welcomes us, wishes us all a wonderful summer, and is gone before we have the chance to even process what just happened.

The other interns seem to be a part of a larger program, probably the college one the congresswoman was talking about at dinner. I don't get to know anyone, because there's really never any time, and it all seems a bit chaotic. As we're about to change rooms, Meghan comes in to take me and two others out.

I guess our time is done here.

"What did you think?" Meghan asks. "We wanted to give you a taste of what you can expect here, plus we've been swamped this morning and didn't know where else to put you. I heard the Speaker was going to stop by—did she make it?"

I can barely keep up with her pace, which I admire doubly because she's in heels.

The guy next to me replies first. "She did. It was . . . great!"

"A little rushed," the girl behind us says. She adds quickly: "Oh, but, like, amazing that she could fit that into her schedule at all."

"I would not want to be her scheduler," Meghan says with a deep chuckle. "I'm drowning as it is. We all are—you'll see."

Though I don't want to be ungrateful, it's not the most welcoming environment. But this does feel important, so I work hard to seem unbothered by her blunt tone and the fully disorganized program. I get the feeling we're already a burden to her, and maybe to all of them, so I will not let that happen.

We're brought into Senator Wright's office, where Meghan introduces her arrival by kissing her fingertips and smacking the side of the door frame.

"What was that?" the guy with us says, his voice quiet.

"Probably some secret ritual they're too busy to let us in on," the girl replies.

I laugh but don't add much.

The space is cramped, and I feel a small sense of dread come over the group as they realize they need to fit three more bodies in their office for the summer.

"One day, when Wright's back in town, we'll do bagels and you can get to know everybody more, but for now"—she points to her left and starts gesturing at people, clockwise, around the room—"that's Jenna, staff assistant; Marcus, constituent advocate; Pasquale, chief of staff; press assistant, legislative assistant, and there are a few others back in that room that you'll probably never meet, as they're never in the office."

We're not sure what to do or, like, how to behave, and Meghan takes that pause to usher us into the side room. On one end is (presumably) Meghan's cubicle decked with souvenirs from her university, and on the other end is a round table jammed into a too-tight space. With two chairs, one computer, and two phones.

"Shit, let me grab you another chair. I don't think Cyrus is in today, so . . ." She trails off as she leaves the room, and for one moment I'm absolutely certain Gabriel would lose his mind in an environment like this. He's so easily overwhelmed in normal situations, but something as frantic and high energy as this? I almost laugh at the thought.

She returns with a chair, then says to us in a tone that you'd probably reserve for a group of toddlers, "I'm going to be over here at my desk for the next thirty minutes. I have, like, six meetings to reschedule, and this has thrown my morning off a bit." She pauses. "But get to know each other, since you'll be working together for the next few months. We have coffee in the front room if you want some; there's a water cooler out there too. Lunch is on us today—we're getting sandwiches catered. Anyway, more info soon, I promise."

She turns and puts on her headset, then starts punching numbers into her phone. I turn to the others, a little stunned, and take a seat.

"I think I'll grab us some coffee," the guy says. "Any preferences?"

"I hate coffee," the girl says, "but I think I'm going to need it to keep up with these people."

We bust into snickers—keeping semi-quiet so we don't bother Meghan. I agree, and within minutes we each have a steaming cup of coffee in front of us. It's milky and smells sweet, so the girl and I just go for it.

It's fine.

"I'm Sal," I say. "Though I feel like we're basically old war buddies after the pure chaos we just went through over the past couple of hours."

"Josh. I know they have a lot going on here, but I—I guess I don't know what else I should have expected."

"April. This is fucking bonkers." She smiles. "I kind of love it."

We spend the next few minutes talking about what part of Ohio we're from. April's from Mechanicsburg, a small village far outside Columbus; Josh's from Zanesville, a town known mostly for the fact that it was the capital of Ohio for about two whole years. I'm the only one up north, but I doubt there's much of a difference in our towns. Ohio's a big state, but its towns tend to have a distinct look and feel.

Instantly, though, conversation cuts to colleges. April's going right to George Washington University because she wants to be in DC as soon as possible. Josh is a little hesitant to move, so he has his eyes on a few local universities that have good programs. They turn to me.

"I'm still figuring that out, I guess." I sigh. "Part of me wishes I could just fast-forward to working on the Hill, walking fast, heartbeat absolutely racing twenty-four-seven. But I guess you can't do that without going to college."

I'm met with mostly crickets, so I'm going to assume that what I'm saying doesn't make sense to them. I shrug.

The phone rings, and the three of us all back away from it instinctively. On the third ring, I start to look around, wondering whose job it is to answer this call. I make eye contact with Meghan, who's on a call of her own, and she nods toward the phone and gestures picking it up with her hand.

I look to my co-interns, neither of whom seem interested in answering. So I swallow the fear and do it myself.

"H-hello? Senator Wright's office. This is Sal speaking?"

"Oh great! Meghan got you up to speed. It's Jenna!" She pauses as I cycle through the names I was just introduced to, but I can't remember her role. Something with constituents maybe? She continues, "We're drowning in calls right now because Wright's supposed to be voting on that health care bill tomorrow. Could you help and take a call from a constituent?"

"Oh sure. What do I do?"

"Just let them speak, and you can make a tally of whether they support it or not. Pretty easy. Sending one your way now, thanks so much!"

Before I can hang up, the phone starts ringing again. I see the little red light blinking at me and quickly turn to my shoulder bag and whip out a notebook and Mom's trusty engraved pen.

I take a breath, then tap the line.

"Hello, my name is Lauren Miller and I'm calling from zip code 45345. I'm urging Senator Wright to vote NO on H.R. 19249."

I scribble down the zip code and write *NO* next to it. The lady on the other end is reading from a script that she got online, I'm assuming, because I know the pacing and the structure pretty well. I've been on the other end of them, even, I'm realizing, to this same office. I don't know how to respond—usually I just get rushed off the phone when I'm the caller, but something in me wants to try to connect to this constituent. To give them the experience I rarely get when calling my reps.

"Thank you for letting us know," I say. "I want to make sure you know your thoughts will be passed along to the senator. Is there anything else you'd like me to relay to him?"

A pause, then: "You'll actually pass the message along to the senator?"

"I'll do my best, at least. We're getting a lot of calls about it, but if you want me to say anything specific I will make sure you're heard by someone higher up than me in this office."

"Well, thank you. I guess, I guess I want him to know that this is a really serious issue for my community. I work at a physical rehab facility, and I see patients dropping their programs every day because their insurance won't cover it, and this bill doesn't do enough. It even has the potential to seriously damage the work we've done with these patients." She pauses. "On a personal note, um, breast cancer runs in the family, and my mom overcame it when she was younger. But every time she was out of work, she couldn't get insurance because companies considered it a preexisting condition. Protections aren't in this bill for existing conditions, and I just don't want others to go through the same thing she did before she passed."

"I hear you," I say. "I'll pass the message along, and I'm sorry about your mom."

I hear a laugh on the other end. "Thanks. This is the first time I've called my reps. Would have done it a lot sooner if I knew someone like you'd be answering."

I end the call, and a blush comes over my face.

"What was that all about?" Meghan rolls her chair toward me, and she looks at my notes.

I shrug. "I, uh, have a message for the senator."

CHAPTER TWENTY-FIVE

REESE

WHEN I WALK INTO the fashion studio, I feel incredibly unprepared. I hate this feeling, how it gnaws at me, shames me. There are fabrics on one wall, sewing machines along another, and sketches are taped to a third. I look closely at the board of sketches (mainly so my back can be to the sewing machines, which are currently mocking me for knowing nothing).

"I love this one," one guy says, and it takes me a while to realize he's talking to me. He's got a British accent, and I catch myself blushing immediately at his closeness as we both focus on one piece.

"What do you like about it?" I ask.

I'm petrified of looking like an idiot here, so I figure, when in doubt, ask a question. He studies the pencil sketch, and the model's eyes pierce through me. As my gaze drifts down, I notice just how detailed the sketch is.

"It's asymmetrical, so that's always a plus for me. I love the proportions too; the cinched waist makes it so the rest of the dress falls straight down from the hip. And you can tell the lining at the bottom is a little heavier. It gives it some movement, but, like, defined movement. It's controlled and precise, which fits superbly with the angular makeup."

"Well said," Professor Watts says behind us. "Philip, Reese, I see you two have met. This one was one of my favorites from last summer's program. We were able to get this produced for the summer show, and it worked just as well as you'd expect on the runway."

I raise my eyebrows, as I didn't realize she was the professor for this class as well as the leader of the full program.

"A student did this?" I ask, and I feel overwhelmed again. "This is really good."

"Well, you'll all be able to do something similar once I'm done with you. And if you're lucky, one of you might even get your work shown in our fall fashion show."

I gulp. I'm in over my head, and I don't want to admit to Philip that my only frame of reference for fashion and design is watching *Project Runway* and *RuPaul's Drag Race* over the past few years.

The class takes their seats. I take a seat next to Philip, as he seems nice and smart.

"Nice to meet you, mate," he says. "This is kind of intimidating, innit?"

"I've never used a sewing machine," I admit. "So, yeah, I'm shitting myself, basically."

He laughs. "I doubt many of us know. I mean, I do, but that's just because I used to make quilts with my gran. I don't know how to sew a garment or anything. We must be getting a crash course on everything this summer."

"Well, I'm ready for it," I say, even though that's a full lie.

"Yeah," he replies. "Me too."

Professor Watts walks us through the course, explaining all the projects we'll have to take part in.

"As this is an accelerated program, your first project starts today. You may have seen the sketches on the wall as you came in. Those are examples of the same final project you'll be making, and I want you to know that everyone on that board came in with a fairly limited knowledge of fashion design when they started the program, and they all were able to produce some really smart designs by the end of the summer.

"So, as a sort of base check, so I know where you're all starting from, I want you to design a seventies mod dress that has some connection with your zodiac sign. It does not have to be perfect; it doesn't even have to be *good*. It just needs to exist so we can critique and workshop it at the end of the week. I believe your first week in Fashion History covers this decade, so you won't be totally at a loss, but I suggest you do more research on your own."

She continues teaching, actually showing us some mod prints and seventies fashion. This is my final class for the day, but none of them started with so much of a bang. I'm getting pelted with information. Finally, she takes a breath and tells us to put our pencils down.

"And for the rest of today, we'll be doing some base skills on the sewing machine. We only have enough sewing machines for half of you, so you'll have to share with the person next to you."

Professor Watts passes out templates, some patterned fabric, and fabric scissors as we retrieve our sewing machines. One per table means my new friend Philip and I are on the same machine.

"Looks like we're making a . . ." I pause in confusion. "We're making a fabric lipstick holder?"

"Seems practical," Philip says with a laugh. "And it's a key chain too. What luck!"

"I *do* always lose my lip balm, so I guess I can't mock this too much."

I keep a casual conversation with Philip going as I make the cuts to my beige polka-dot fabric. I line up all the layers, and I take time to do it slowly, methodically, because I do *not* want to be the first one at our sewing machine.

"You want to go first?" Philip asks, and I groan in response.

"I don't know what I'm doing," I say as the embarrassment creeps in.

"It's fine—I can show you."

I line up two pieces of fabric and slide the key chain loop around the middle as the instructions say, and I slide the fabric under the needle.

"Okay, now here's how I like to thread it. You take the spool here and feed it through here. There's a little guide that's supposed to help you thread the needle, but that never works for me."

He sticks the end of the thread in his mouth to wet it, then runs the end through his fingers.

"Perfect," he says, and shows me how he's able to thread the needle a lot easier. "Now just connect this to the machine, and we'll do a little test on this extra fabric. Just twist this slowly and it'll start—move the fabric smoothly so it doesn't get bunched up." He pauses. "Yeah, like that. Hold on, I think the tension is a little too tight for this fabric, and I don't want the thread to snap on you."

I go through the motions, a little flustered by how little I know. But a part of me is friend-crushing hard on his sewing knowledge. As a general rule, I think anyone who has a skill that I don't have is instantly appealing—like how I get chills every time I see Heath strike someone out.

Philip helps me work through the pattern, and I kind of start to get it on my own. Kind of. It's not great, but it's something, and I can't imagine what this would look like if I didn't have help. I see Professor Watts walking around helping others, so it does seem like she's running a whole Sewing 101 lesson today.

As Philip starts sewing his project, I pull out my journal to start sketching the lipstick holder as a memory of what happened today.

"That *dress*," Philip says when he gets a glimpse of the drawing I did this morning. "Did you design that?"

I laugh. "No, it was in a shop. It was on this mannequin, and I kept imagining what it'd look like on someone walking down the street. So I drew it."

"You're skilled," he says. "My drawings are more, like, feelings or impressions. I don't do detail very well."

"Well, if there's any way I can help with your sketches, I'll gladly do it. I feel like I owe you for this crash course on sewing I just got."

He takes his time to finish the last stitches of his project and cuts off the extra thread. He lines his next to mine, and they look nearly identical. Mine's a little uneven, but not bad for a complete amateur.

"Here," he says, taking the key chain I just made and offering me his in return. "It looks like we'll be helping each other a lot this summer."

I take it and feel my cheeks get warmer. I absentmindedly play with the charm on my bracelet. "Yeah, looks like it."

Professor Watts gathers our attention and has us all show our key chains. There's a variety of successes and failures around the room, but the energy is pretty high. Like everyone else, I'm hopeful, at least. I see a potential here.

As we stand to leave, Philip turns to me.

"Hey, want to grab dinner after this? I don't have any mates here, but I hate eating alone, you know? And I'm a little overwhelmed already. If I go back to the dorms I'm just going to start working myself to death on this project, and I'd like to take a breather first."

"Sounds great," I say. "There's a cute café I went to this morning that's open for dinner—it's about halfway between here and the dorms. I could even show you the dress I drew this morning?"

He nods. "You lead, and I'll follow."

CHAPTER TWENTY-SIX

SAL

IT'S LUNCHTIME, AND WE still haven't gotten the training they promised. We helped with calls, though. A *lot* of calls. I have a stack of constituent responses, but it's not totally clear what we're supposed to do with them. The caterer wheeled in a sandwich platter not long ago, but no one's really touched it. No one's even around—Meghan left a couple of hours ago without saying anything, and the others have popped in and out all morning.

"I can't believe that man called me a bitch," April says. "I listened to his full conspiracy theory rant, *all seven minutes of it*, and then when I say I'll pass along the message I just get called a bitch."

Josh sighs. "Sorry, April."

Though it hasn't been long, we've all been hung up on and snapped at by constituents, but no one's been quite that mean to me. There's not much a person can tell about you from your phone voice, but I wonder if April's voice were deeper if the guy wouldn't have snapped so hard. I wonder: If I'd answered the phone, and he'd picked up on the higher pitch of my voice—or how I hold on to my *s*'s just a bit longer than other guys do—what would he have said?

Maybe nothing. But an uncomfortable feeling churns inside me, which sends me back home, picking out an outfit while Mom watches, worried about what I'll say or how I'll say it. A part of me wants to morph, to change, but I steel my nerves. I can't do that.

"I'll take the next call," I say. "In case he calls back."

"Oh, I *hope* he calls back," April replies. "I just thought of a few comebacks to his conspiracy theory comments."

We're brought in to grab sandwiches and are asked to go back into our corner for a few minutes while someone takes care of something. Names and faces are all interchangeable at this point, and I would give anything to just sit down and have a real introduction. But that's apparently not how they do things here.

"Busy day," Meghan remarks to no one in particular as she returns, sandwich in hand, and goes to her computer. A calendar app takes up her screen, and I see her taking notes. She pulls up an email, then spins around with a broad smile on her face.

"Okay, great. The chief of staff talked with the senator about what to do with you all, and I think we finally have a plan. Senator Wright is going to be in Ohio for a few weeks, so you unfortunately won't get to meet him for a little while longer."

"But I thought he had a vote tomorrow," I say.

"Good memory! He's flying in for the vote and for a quick CNN appearance tonight, and he will be back in Ohio by the next day. I just finished booking his flights." She pauses. "You're the intern who's got connections to Congresswoman Caudill, right?"

I nod. "She's my mom's friend."

"Ah, that makes sense." She turns back to her email. "He'll be in her neck of the woods as part of this trip, so he wanted me to make sure you were taken care of."

I tense up, hoping that doesn't sound as entitled as I know it does.

"Anyway, April and Josh, it seems like you're naturals at taking these calls from constituents, so we're going to have you help out more with that."

We all suck equally at dealing with phone calls, so I know her reasoning isn't exactly true. I feel their glares burning into me, but I don't dare turn. Meghan looks to me now.

"And you'll be helping me keep the wheels on the track. Being a scheduler is actually the job of, like, fifty people. I don't complain about it—well, I don't complain about it in earshot of certain people, I should say—but I do need some help, especially those times I literally need to be in two places at once, you know?"

"Got it," I say weakly. "Whatever you need."

I respect Meghan. But I don't want to work with her. *For* her.

A sourness settles in my stomach, knowing I've just been given preference over April and Josh for no reason other than that a member of Congress is a family friend. This job is probably not any better than theirs, but it definitely looks that way. And here, appearance matters.

"On that note," Meghan says while handing me a few papers

slid into a manila folder, "you two can go see Jenna, who's going to do a full rundown of how to handle the phones, check the answering machines in the morning, and all that. And Sal, do you remember how to get back to the entrance?"

"I think so, yeah."

"Great. Two things: First, I need you to go pick up Leona Smith—she's a veteran from Lima—and welcome her to the Capitol. Just bring her here; Jenna will give her a ticket so she can have a seat for tomorrow's vote, and Marcus will have a one-on-one meeting with her on behalf of Senator Wright."

"Got it," I say, though I feel the pressure building up inside me.

"On your way, just drop by Senator Greenwood's office and drop this off with Helena—her name's on the tab there. His office is just down the hall and on the right; you'll walk right past it."

I nod, though I'm not fully sure where I'm even at right now. "I'll find it."

"Great, thanks! I'll have a few other tasks you can help with when you get back. It's going to be so nice having you here this summer."

I turn to go, and my cheeks flush when I think about doing this all summer. I want to help, and maybe this is how I can. A tear falls down my cheek as the emotions battle within me—I've already annoyed April and Josh, Meghan's piling on the tasks with vague instructions, but worst of all, something in me says this "special project" might have been a lie all along.

• FaceTime •

HEATH + REESE

R◀ Hey! I can see you now. The others haven't answered the FaceTime request yet. I guess they're running late. In a shocking turn of events.

H◀ That's okay with me. You and I can catch up a bit. Reese! Ugh, I missed that face. How's the design school?

R◀ It's good so far. Really stressful, don't get me wrong, but it's actually kind of nice. It's like we've all been thrown into the deep end together. Oh, I even made something. Here, look!

H◀ A key chain? Oh, and it holds your ChapStick. Nice. You sewed that?

R◀ I did! Well, actually, this one was Philip's. He showed me how to sew and I'm helping him with some design stuff—trying to teach him how to draw with a digital illustration pen, stuff like that. So he suggested we trade. But mine looks just like this.

H◀ I can't believe you're already making stuff. That's great you're making friends too. So, um, is he the one you've been hanging out with this week?

GABRIEL + SAL

G◀ Sal, we've really got to join the other FaceTime. Reese keeps sending me requests. You know how he is when we're late to stuff.

S◀ This week has fully killed me, Gabe. I think I worked thirty-five hours this week? It's so chaotic, but I don't want to complain to the others.

G◀ You just want to complain to me?

S◀ Actually, yeah.

G◀ That's strangely sweet. But that's a lot of hours. I thought you were only supposed to do, like, twenty hours.

S◀ No one knows what's going on there. It's madness. I haven't felt this stressed in a long time. It's so cool, though, being in the Capitol each day. I think I'm pissing off the other interns, but I've gotten to do a lot of cool things already. I'm so tired.

G◀ You can't kill yourself for this, babe. You have plenty of time to work full-time after this. You need to, I don't know, set some boundaries or something. Before it gets out of control.

S◀ I can't do that. I need this to go well.

G◀ God, I just got another request. Can we talk to the group?

S◀ Fine, let's switch over.

CHAPTER TWENTY-SEVEN

HEATH

DIANA AND I GET to Aunt Jeanie's arcade for my training around noon, and I'm struck by how silent this part of the boardwalk is. Yes, it's a random Monday in the middle of summer, and most of the more rambunctious Daytona Beach partiers are probably sleeping off their hangovers right about now, but it still strikes me as odd.

My first meeting with Jeanie was short but sweet. My second was nearly nonexistent. Diana and Jeanie are ships passing in the night, their only true bonding times seeming to be during the shifts they work together. This family dynamic is light-years apart from the ones I know, but it's still something special.

And I want to be a part of it.

"Your first shift is Friday, so we've got plenty of time to get you up to speed," Diana says as she ducks under the half-open gate that bars entrance from the closed arcade. "You nervous?"

"Should I be?" I ask as I follow her into the dark space. "I'm sure I'll get the hang of it. I've had a few odd jobs—I know how to deal with people."

"*Drunk* people?"

I laugh. "Back when Mom and Dad went to church, I'd have to babysit all the toddlers during service. Toddlers are essentially tiny drunk humans, right?"

She snorts. "Normal drunk and Daytona drunk are very different, you'll see."

My eyes slowly adjust to the light, or lack thereof, in the space. A large bar stands right in front of me. Behind it lies a collection of chips and a deep-fat fryer. Hundreds of giant plastic cups are stacked behind the bar, and it really hits me just how much beer this place must go through every day.

"Jeanie's probably in the back doing inventory. The kegs come in around this time, so I'll give you a quick tour."

She leads me around the space, pointing out some of the most popular attractions.

"Two air hockey tables, which people will wait hours to play. These have been doused in so much beer that it's a miracle they still work. They get stickier and stickier as the night progresses, though, so we have to clean them midshift sometimes."

"Next, we have the shooting games—zombie-shooting ones, deer-hunting ones, alien-blasting ones. All popular with a certain . . . demographic. They usually wear red hats, that's all I'm saying about that. Then we have a row of Skee-Ball in the back, and those basketball-hoop games bring in a ton of money. It's a dollar fifty per round, and you get a lot of bros lining up to prove their sports superiority all night."

I laugh because I definitely know the type. A few guys on my baseball team would have a blast here, me included. I try to think where my friends would gravitate to: Reese would master the art of Skee-Ball, while Gabe and Sal would spend all day duking it out at the air hockey table.

"Heath!" Aunt Jeanie calls from the back and runs over to wrap me up in a hug. She does the same for Diana. "I didn't hear y'all come in. I wanted to give you the grand tour."

She leads us back up front to the cash register and pulls out a stack of coins.

"We don't open until seven on Mondays, so we have some time to kill. Skee-Ball? I'll make us some corn dogs."

I blush. "Oh, I couldn't take that."

"Most of the money comes back to me anyway, so believe me, it's my treat."

"Actually," Diana says, "Jeanie is the Skee-Ball master. Why don't I fry up the corn dogs, and Heath, you can learn from the master."

After a moment of hesitation, Jeanie agrees and leads me toward the back.

"I guess we haven't had any alone time," she says. "As you can probably tell, I work all night and sleep all day, so I haven't been the best host."

"Oh, it's fine," I say, putting in the quarters to start my round of Skee-Ball. "The fact that you're letting me stay here at all is great. Diana's been showing me the beach life."

She rolls her first ball, nailing the corner hundred-point hole. "I'm afraid I'm not sure how to be a good aunt. I . . . you know, I've never gotten the chance. Which is partially my fault."

"Mom's too," I say bluntly. "We always talked about coming down here. Then Mom would ultimately take us to Cedar Point or something and pretend it was the same thing."

"We don't get along much. She always hated how impulsive I was, how I never wanted to settle down. And I thought about coming back a lot, but I was in so much debt because of this arcade. But also, once you've lived on the beach for so long, it's hard to imagine going back to Ohio."

"I bet," I say as I drain a thirty-point shot.

Diana comes by with a platter of corn dogs, then takes a few quarters to start up the third Skee-Ball game.

"I'll teach you how to make those," Jeanie says. "And how to pour the perfect beer. Which, if a health inspector ever asks, you absolutely never do on any occasion."

We laugh, before a loud knock sounds out from the back of the building.

"Ah, that'll be the frozen-food delivery. Got to sign for that."

"Jeanie's trying really hard to be the cool aunt," Diana says. I'm struck then by how unusual this family is, on so many levels. But I feel the love between them, and isn't that all that matters?

"Why do you call your mom Jeanie?" I ask.

She shrugs. "It just fits more than Mom, I guess. She's always let me figure my own shit out. Once I started working here, I always had to call her Jeanie during shifts, and it just kind of stuck."

162

"Think she'll mind if I keep calling her *Aunt* Jeanie?"

Diana smiles. "I think she'd like that."

I do have a family. It's not like Reese's, or Sal's, or Gabriel's, but it's mine. And just as I feel comfortable with that, I get a text from my dad that shatters that thought and makes me realize nothing will ever be the same again.

Good news, bud—we got an offer on the house!

CHAPTER TWENTY-EIGHT

REESE

ALL OF US IN the program have started to fall into these daily routines. I am, fully, a routine person, so I appreciate it. The six-hour break I have is usually spent in one of the lounge areas at school, though I know I could go back to my room, or sit at a café, or even go explore the city. I've seen the Eiffel Tower in passing, but maybe I'll go be a tourist this weekend.

I'm starting to get the hang of sewing—meaning, I no longer break the machine just by touching it. And not surprisingly, I'm doing really well in my graphic design classes. But fashion doesn't come as naturally to me. And a part of me already wants to drop the fashion classes, which feels super immature, but maybe I'm just not cut out for *this* kind of design.

I'm sitting cross-legged in the comfiest chair that the lounge has to offer, studying my design for the first workshop this morning. I think it's okay, though the prompt was bonkers—a seventies mod design that incorporates your zodiac sign? It sounds like a bad *Project Runway* prompt.

What I've come up with is a fairly simple dress. A halter top with thin straps that tie into a bow in the back. The navy-colored dress falls straight down, just brushing the floor, and is lightly cinched with a thin belt. I wasn't sure how to include the zodiac element, so I patterned the dress with the circle-and-horns symbol for Taurus.

I think it's good, but is it enough?

"That your design?" Philip asks, though it's a bit rhetorical. We've been discussing it all week, though I've never felt comfortable *showing* it to him. "That's a great drawing."

"Yep," I say, and I quickly slip the page into a folder and hide my embarrassment.

We file into the classroom, and I get glimpses of other designs. All of them look more polished, more creative, and far more correct than mine. Watts comes in, and we launch right into the presentations.

"Just so it's all fair, names will be picked at random. When it's your turn, present your design and talk us through your design choices, and how you were inspired by the prompts. If you're not presenting, you're critiquing. I've passed out Post-it notes to everyone. Just write some constructive feedback on these; we'll collect them for everyone, then we can have a quick conversation about the highs and lows of each garment. Make sense?"

We all nod, and she goes over to a desk and takes a seat. She clicks a few buttons on her computer. "Okay, first up, Philip!"

His cheeks turn red immediately, and he practices deep breaths as he digs for his presentation.

"Better to go first than last, I guess," he says. "At least this will be over. Wish me luck?"

I smile back at him. "You don't need it—you're going to do great."

And he does. He doesn't have the best art ability, but you can tell he gets style pretty well. The model in his image is wearing a short mod dress in a burnt orange, with a matching handbag.

"Right, so at first look, it's a pretty straightforward mod dress. I chose the color because it fits in a standard retro color palette, but it also reminds me of fire. And Sagittariuses are fire signs. I decided to break it up with color blocking, and you'll see the thick white stripe down her front turns into an arrow, which represents Sagittarius as well."

He continues his presentation, detailing little touches I hadn't noticed before, showing his knowledge of early seventies fashion. It's so hard to be a know-it-all and not sound like you're bragging, but he does it in this humble way that makes me simply envious.

We all applaud when he's finished.

"Well done, Philip," Professor Watts says, then starts listing things she loves about the design.

"I would wear that dress," she says with a laugh, "that is, if you made it in my size."

We all chuckle, and I write my individual feedback on the Post-it. I'm writing all the things I like about it, but I can't find

166

anything negative to say. I write "Loved this!" and draw a little heart in the corner, then start to worry that this is way too familiar for me. But I can't erase this. So as others start passing him their Post-its, I slide mine under the rest.

"You did so well," I say.

He's sweating, but he has a huge smile on his face. I can't help but mirror it.

"Thanks. That was fun. Terrifying, but fun."

A few others get called up and get mixed but mostly positive feedback. Another Taurus drew a smart houndstooth mini-dress with an oversized collar, but he turned the shoulders into full horns to match the prompt, seemingly as an afterthought. A Pisces goes with an even safer route, designing a cute, if not a little boring, retro swimsuit.

"Reese," the professor says, "you're up next!"

I pull out my presentation, and again I feel underprepared. Which is not something I'm used to. Being an A student all my life means I can really only find comfort when I fully understand something. But fashion will take me longer to understand.

"Right." I snap into presentation mode. "I saw that halter tops were pretty popular back in the seventies, so I made this simple halter dress that's patterned diagonally with the Taurus horns. It's a print that I think looks visually appealing from afar, but as you get closer, you can see the horns."

I go on to explain a few smaller details, the movement of the bottom of the dress, and so on. We open to feedback, and I flinch.

167

"Hi, yeah." The Pisces girl looks at her notes, then back to me. "It's a pretty dress, but it doesn't really look mod to me. Maybe you could have done a halter top with high-waisted pants?"

"Oh, that would have been much better," another student chimes in. "And you could have just done the pattern on the top, because right now it's a lot of Taurus looking at me."

"Exactly," Pisces girl says in a knowing voice. "The print is a little obvious, so I would have gone for something more subtle."

"Thank you for your feedback, Noelle," Professor Watts says. "I just want to remind everyone that when we're giving critique, it's always nice to have some other ideas, but I find it a lot easier to highlight potential problem areas but not explain how they could fix it too much. I think we all end up finding ways to incorporate feedback that work for us, but what makes sense to you might not make sense to the original artist."

Meanwhile, I just want to sink into a puddle in the front of the room. That shuts up Noelle, aka Pisces girl, for enough time to let the others start offering critiques. I don't get a lot of positive notes that count—though Philip chimes in to compliment my use of color, which I appreciate.

I keep my head down as the others finish their presentations, and I pull on my shoulder bag as soon as we're dismissed. I turn to leave, but Philip stops me.

"Hey, a few of us are going to go out tonight to celebrate completing our first week here. You in?"

He looks so hopeful, and a part of me wants to just say yes—I mean, we've already eaten dinner together three nights this week, and something about a new friendship with him really appeals to me. But right now, I just feel incompetent around him.

And I don't want to be in a room with Noelle, even if her comments were warranted.

"I think I'm going to turn in early tonight," I finally say, and I see disappointment crash across his face. "Maybe next time?"

"Yeah, of course. I'll walk you back. I have to change anyway."

The walk back is quiet and short. We get to my door, and he puts his arms around me in a quick hug, which is a first for us. When he lets go, I'm reminded of my friends back home. It shows me that I *do* have support here, even if it feels like I'm all on my own.

"Don't worry about what happened back there," he says. "I think when people start to negatively critique something, they fixate on that. Read the Post-its you got; I'm sure you got a ton of great feedback too. At least, I know you did from me."

"Thanks," I say, flashing him a smile. "I will."

When I step into my room, I throw the pile of Post-its in the trash and sit on my bed, begging for the tears not to come. I see the group chat flooded with messages from Heath, mostly selfies of him preparing for his first shift at the arcade. His tan's deepened, and I can tell he's really enjoying his time in Daytona.

He also texted me separately, asking me how the presentation went. But . . . I can't complain to him about this. I want to respond, but I don't even know what to say. I turn on an old season of *Drag Race* and start taking notes on every runway look, every sewing challenge. I consider asking my parents if they can order me a cheap sewing machine somewhere so I can practice while I'm here.

I feel so defeated now, but I can't let this beat me.

CHAPTER TWENTY-NINE

GABRIEL

MY DAYS ARE LIKE this: I get up at five thirty in the morning, dart into the guys' bathroom to shower before anyone else on my floor wakes up, then come back and take a nap until seven or eight. The Save the Trees Foundation's office is about fifteen minutes away, and I usually walk there with Tiffany. Art and Matt usually get up early to grab us all iced coffees, which Tiffany and I appreciate, mostly because we learned early on the office coffee machine is always out of pods.

We technically start working at nine, but it's really hard to consider it work as all we've done so far is learn about the program. A *lot*.

"Welcome to your *final* day of orientation and training!" Ali looks like she's on her third cup of coffee. While everyone else they've had come in for these trainings looks like a human is supposed to at nine a.m.—a groggy urban forester, a half-asleep policy analyst—Ali, grassroots fundraising specialist, is alive with energy.

As Ali gets her slides ready for the last day of training, Tiffany leans over and whispers, "I don't know how much more learning I can do. Isn't it a little weird they still haven't told us what we'll be doing after training is over?"

"I've been trying to pick up bits and pieces from people's presentations. Based on what the urban forester said, it seems like we'll be helping plant trees from time to time?"

"Nah, I don't think so," she says. "He said they do most of their planting in early spring."

We're cut off by three loud claps from the podium, which Ali used to get our attention. Even in this experience that feels so grown up, something like that just reminds me of being in school and being treated like a child. It sours my mood.

"Now we're going to break into partners. You'll be working together in these little teams for the rest of the internship program, so you'll have to get close. We'll just divide you by the tables you're sitting at."

She goes down the rows, eventually assigning Tiffany and me as partners, and Art and Matt become partners too. I don't know what this partnership will entail, and as a rule I hate group projects, but I am glad to be partnered with Tiffany. We get along really well. She seems incredibly normal and not obnoxious, and we can both bond over being super anxious. Art and Matt seem like a good pairing too as they've become fast friends ever since Art saved Matt from the longest, most painful conversation of all time during that first event.

"Okay, now our last speaker of the week is going to walk you through how the first month of this volunteer experience will work, so you'll want to pay close attention as you'll be using all the information you've been getting this week."

My stomach clenches, just slightly, and I feel a bit of excited anticipation for what's to come. We've been learning so much, but not knowing exactly how to apply it. We know how much oxygen the company has brought to Boston through their programs, how they've developed ways to reduce the city's urban heat effect, which is caused by the sun reflecting off concrete and blacktop, causing a sort of greenhouse effect. We know how donations from large donors and small ones alike directly apply to this process. We also know maybe too much detail of how to plant and relocate a tree.

But we don't know what we're doing.

The speaker gets up, and I see him paste on a smile similar to Ali's—large, full of energy, fully unchanged by the time of day.

"Hi, everyone, I'm Casey, and I manage our grassroots volunteer program. While Ali focuses more on the behind-the-scenes aspects of the job, I get to be front and center with the people of Boston, which is really the best place to be." He turns to Ali with a smirk. "No offense."

We chuckle at this, and he settles in to talk a little more about the history of the program and how past volunteers have moved on to work anywhere from local community programs to more-corporate environmental-law roles. I feel a little better knowing this could open doors to me, but still, it's like everyone is on the edge of our seats. *What will we be doing?*

Finally, he explains:

"For this summer, at least for this first month, you'll all be our street advocates. What you'll be doing is so critical to our mission, as it spreads the word about our organization and brings in massive donations in a way that we can never get through other means." He smiles, and it's a genuine smile, but I also get the feeling he's trying a little too hard to be welcoming, as if we're all about to run out the door. "You'll be working in teams to stand on a few busy Boston blocks. You'll be wearing your Boston Save The Trees Foundation shirts, and all you have to do is flag some people down as they walk by, talk to them about the organization, and see if they'd like to donate. It's super simple, but very effective."

"Oh, fuck no," Tiffany says under her breath.

She turns to me, and I feel the color draining from my face as I process this. Not wanting to speak to people in a safe environment at a networking event was one thing, but stopping busy people on the street to ask them for donations? There's literally no way I can do something like this. No way.

Art raises their hand, and once they're called on they say, "I've been trying to ask what we're doing for the whole week now, and everyone's been dodging the question, and I think I'm starting to see why." They roll their eyes. "That's just some feedback for the future—I'm feeling like I was tricked into signing up for something I don't think I would have signed up for."

"I understand that," Ali says, her tone chipper, "but I want to make sure you know we never meant to mislead you. But we do these trainings in this order for a reason. We prepare you with all the information you need, and we'll be passing out a book-let with responses you can practice, tricks to flag someone down who looks like they may not want to talk, and things like that. It's a totally normal, stress-free experience, but we always find it's best to ease our volunteers into the process, you know?"

"So you *did* mean to mislead us," Tiffany says, a little too loud to be a whisper.

"I think we'll all feel a lot better once we get those booklets passed out," Ali says after clapping three times, signaling that this conversation is over.

The next two hours are grueling. My anxiety is spiked so much that I kind of hate myself for being so positive on my therapy call yesterday. My therapist will definitely be getting an earful next week, but by then, I'll already have gone through all this.

The packet is full of information, but it reads like a how-to guide about violating people's personal space. I'm talking about . . . ways to stop someone and trick them into conversations in a way that they can't escape. I now know eight ways to respond to someone who doesn't want to talk to me.

If they say they're too busy, explain that it'll only take a second and launch into the full pitch, hoping they'll stick around.

If they say they don't have their wallet on them, explain how we just need a signature and a pledge and launch into a full pitch, hoping they'll stick around.

If they just say no, appeal to their soft side and remind them that climate change is going to kill us all one day. Then launch into the full pitch and hope they stick around.

"That was a lot, I know, but we do have one last thing before we let you out early on this beautiful summer day. I'll need a few volunteers to start working on our summer outdoor gala in a month or so. We work with a lot of high-profile donors, and we need someone dependable who works well with a team if we're going to pull this off. So do your best, and you might be able to take on a new project later this summer—one that will look great on college applications, I might add."

We break for the rest of the day, and without really even deciding to do it, Tiffany, Art, Matt, and I all walk together to the local coffee shop to decompress.

"Well, this sucks." Tiffany buries her face in her hands. "I hate those people who canvass on the street for donations. They're so annoying, and they won't *stop*. I never thought I'd have to do that."

"I don't really know what they are," I admit, "but it sounds awful."

Art clears their throat, and we all give them our attention.

"Look," they say, "it's not great. I think it's a known fact that everyone hates those kinds of people. But I think I've talked to enough of them to know what works and what doesn't."

"You *talk* to them?" Tiffany asks, which causes Matt to laugh.

"I do, and they're usually normal people, like us, who get treated like shit but need a paycheck. A lot of them really want to help their cause, and some of them just like talking to people, you know the type?"

"Like Allen," Matt says, referring to the guy who cornered him at the first event.

"Exactly," Art says. "That kid will *thrive*, but I think we can too."

"Should we run through some scenarios?" Matt asks, and Tiffany and I groan in response.

"I still haven't processed all this," I say. "I don't know how to do this, and I feel a little sick. I don't think practice will help."

Matt looks to the pastry case. "What if I get each of us a giant cookie?"

"Our tab's already way too high after all those iced coffees," Tiffany replies.

"This one's on me," he says, and walks up to the counter.

• • •

On the walk back to my dorm, I send a text to Sal: **SHIT shit shit shit. You will not believe what I have to do for Save the Trees. Can I call tonight?**

I wait for a response, though I know it always takes him ages to get back to me now. He's been working ten-hour days, which seems illegal to make an intern do, but he doesn't complain. He doesn't talk about it to us. Actually, he doesn't *talk to us* at all anymore.

He writes back: **Busy tonight, sorry. Doing my own shitty stuff for the senator.**

I put the phone away. I'm not sure what I expected from him, but I guess I really am on my own here. I'll try to call Heath tonight, since Reese is equally unreachable. And maybe we can commiserate over how our friends are suddenly too busy for us.

CHAPTER THIRTY

SAL

MEGHAN WALKS *FAST*. I know everyone here does, and maybe it's a city thing, but I can barely keep up with her as she flies down the halls, her heels clacking with each step. We're both dressed up a little more than usual today—her in a short black dress and thick makeup, me in my charcoal gray suit jacket and emerald green bow tie.

My feet hurt. I'm not used to wearing dress shoes for multiple days a week, and my smartwatch says I've walked an average of five miles a day—and that's just up and down the halls of the Capitol. My job feels important: I'm taking constituents on Capitol tours, I'm making sure the chief of staff gets to his meetings on time, and usually as I'm walking, I'm calling airlines to change the senator's flights on a second professional iPhone I have on lease from the Capitol.

It's only been a week, and I already have his birth date and passport number memorized.

But I do have a problem. Well, two: Josh and April.

They *hate* their job. All they do is answer phones and get yelled at all day, and even though they get to leave work right at five, they seem to be spending most of the day in agony. There are times I really do want to swap places with them, to be the one talking to constituents, to try to figure out what's making them tick and find the root of the problem, and maybe that's how they started too. But now it's just a short greeting, a quick tally of whether the caller supports whatever they're calling about, and a rushed goodbye. I'm starting to feel their resentment every time I enter the room, and the worst thing about it is I don't blame them at all.

"A Lyft is waiting for us," Meghan says. "We'll get to the Decatur House a little early, but that should be fine. I always like to get the lay of the land before the senator gets there. Are you excited to meet him?"

"Yeah, definitely," I say. "I wish the others could meet him too."

"The other interns? They will, eventually. You know how it is."

I nod, mostly because it seems like the right thing to do. I don't really know how anything goes here, but from what I can tell, the senator doesn't get much time in the office, and the other interns don't get much time outside the office.

We pull up next to Lafayette Park, beyond which I can see the White House. Tourists and protestors alike stand alongside the fence, but something about this hits differently. I'm walking by the White House not as a tourist, like I did on my first day here. I'm doing it as someone who lives here, even if it's temporary. I'm doing it as someone who *works* here. And I could get used to this.

Meghan and I put on our shades, and she leads me toward

the Decatur House, which is this somewhat unassuming historic brick building at the corner of the park that sits outside the White House. She walks confidently, and I mirror her gait, trying to fit in but also trying on this new DC life. This could be me in a matter of years. Even though it's only week one, I can see that. And I've been so mixed up, I almost forget why I ever hesitated.

But then I remember Gabriel. And the boys. And how I really haven't dipped into the group chat at all this week.

We step inside the building, though, and it wipes my mind clean of all regrets. It's such a beautiful, historic building, and suddenly I know what I'm doing is important and lucky, and my friends will just have to understand.

"This is . . . so cool," I say, wishing I could describe my feelings in a slightly more mature way.

"Never gets old," Meghan replies. "I mean, don't get me wrong, I get extremely burnt out. But every time I get overwhelmed with my job, I try to take in these experiences."

We're some of the first ones to arrive, and Meghan talks with the event manager for a minute, confirming schedules and seats and whether the senator's gluten-free meal is still being provided.

"We're all good," the event manager says, his voice calming and confident. "We'll even be placing a gluten-free roll at his seat."

"You're the best!" Meghan gives him a quick one-arm hug. They start walking down the hall, and she gestures for me to follow them. "Can I see the seating chart?"

"I figured you'd ask that," he says while pulling a folded paper

180

out of his breast pocket. "We shouldn't have any problems—I know Senator Wright's seating preferences by now, but let me know if you have any questions."

"You start to get to know the events people *really* well in this job," Meghan says with a laugh after he leaves. We take a turn past an old grand piano, and she leads me to a door that opens to a shaded, tented outdoor area. "Sorry, next time I'll introduce you. Okay, the boss is at table one. You and I will be in the back with some of the other congressional staff."

"What is this event, again?" I ask with a hint of embarrassment. "I know you told me, but all the events are starting to run together."

"You should have gotten a calendar invite about it, but the luncheon is for the senators on the"—she pauses to think—"Housing, Transportation, and Community Development subcommittee, along with some of the nonprofit political organizations here. It's meant to be some open dialogue between the subcommittee and lobbyists from those groups."

"Got it," I say, though I don't know what any of this means. I'll figure it out.

"This is why the seating is so important—we want the right lobbyists to be at the senator's table. Wright's not the most divisive senator, but there are some bad eggs out there and he's got a bit of a temper. You'll see."

We spend the next half hour running through the program and talking with a few other schedulers who have started to arrive. At the beginning of the week, Meghan's laser-focused, no-nonsense attitude felt a little cold, but I see the warmth in her now, even if the other interns seem to think she's a sort of demon.

Meghan is *busy*. She doesn't have time to be overly welcoming. She didn't ask for three new teenage interns to be dropped in her office space, but she's taking me seriously, which is about all I can ask for. As we walk around, she makes networking into an art. She's got one eye on her work phone, and the other eye out for people she knows, people she wants to know, or people she feels like she needs to introduce me to.

"Let's go get the senator," she says. "You ready?"

I feel a little starstruck already, but I nod and walk through to meet Senator Wright. We walk to the edge of Lafayette Square just as the black car stops. Meghan runs to catch up to him, the sound of her heels clacking across cobblestones as she moves.

The senator and Pasquale, the chief of staff, step out of the car and survey the land. The senator brushes off his suit, though his outfit looks perfectly crisp even after the flight and car ride. Meghan shakes his hand, and the three of them walk toward me.

"And this is our new intern Sal, the young man who's Congresswoman Caudill's family friend."

"Yes, Sal!" Senator Wright reaches out his hand, and I take it in a firm handshake, making sure to look him in the eyes as I do it. I can't believe it—I'm meeting one of my political idols right now. I knew this would happen; I even expected it to happen on day one. But seeing him here, bigger than life, looking more confident than he does even on Sky News, it's overwhelming.

A small voice inside tells me this is who I want to be someday. But that feels impossibly far away.

"Nice to meet you, Senator Wright. Thank you for the opportunity. I really appreciate the chance to work here."

"Is Meg treating you well?" he asks, somewhat jokingly.

She gives me a wide-eyed look, and I realize that as much as I'm trying to prove myself to Meghan, she's trying to prove herself to her boss too.

"She's kept me busy," I say, then quickly add, "and she's introduced me to about everyone in the city at this point."

She seems satisfied with that answer, and so does the senator. Meghan suggests we get a photo of me and the senator to send Betty Caudill. I pose awkwardly next to him, even though he towers over me.

"This is great," she says. When she shows it to me, I can't help but think it looks a little like Take Your Kid to Work Day.

As we walk into the luncheon, the senator says, "If it's okay with Sal, you should have Ari post that to social media and talk about the high school internship program. That would make Betty very happy."

"Ari's the press assistant," Meghan says. "I don't think you've met yet, but you may have seen him around the office."

I nod. "Totally fine with me."

The senator and his chief of staff take their seats at the head table and start conversations with the lobbyists as he unceremoniously breaks into his gluten-free roll. Meghan and I take our seats in the back, and she lets out a big sigh before giving me a tired smile.

• • •

Hours later, still buzzed from the excitement of the luncheon, I float down the halls of the Capitol. I still don't know what future I want, but something about this feels right. Could I work on the Hill someday? Could I be a senator someday? My stride gets more confident as I walk into the office and send a quick wave to Jenna, who smiles and waves back.

I'm starting to fit in here, at least. It's only been a week, but I really feel like this will be something special.

Turning to walk into the office with the interns and Meghan's desk, I hear April and Josh talking animatedly, and for a second I wonder what's got them all worked up. A phone call, probably, as they do have to deal with some of the angriest, loudest people in the state.

"He's such a starfucker!" April is saying as I enter the room.

When Josh sees me, the color drains from his face. April notices me come in, and I see a similar frantic reaction come from her as she quickly turns her phone over. Before it flips, I see she's on Instagram, looking at the photo I just took with the senator.

They're talking about me.

• FaceTime •

GABRIEL + HEATH

G◀ Hey, Heath. How's it going? You… you look so tan already. How is that possible?

H◀ Yeah, Diana and I have been taking advantage of the beach every day. The weather's been great.

G◀ Seems like paradise.

H◀ Ha, I wouldn't go that far. But it's a nice change of pace. It still feels like a vacation so far, but I start work in about thirty minutes. So maybe it'll start to feel more permanent after my shift.

G◀ Makes sense. Boston will never not scare the shit out of me. I mean, nothing about this really feels like home. I'm making friends, and I'm having fun, but it's hard. I mainly just miss you guys.

H Same here. I feel like this is the longest we've all gone without talking to each other.

G Sal only comes into the chat to drop in selfies. Did you see he met the senator?

H Sure did. But at least he lets us know he's alive. Reese is gone, you know? I mean, I get it, I do. It makes sense, he's a whole continent away. But he can't be *that* busy, you know? I just want to make sure he's okay.

G Right. It feels like Sal's a workaholic and Reese is just ghosting us.

H It'll get better.

G You okay? You sound sad.

H Dad said they got an offer on the house.

G Shit. I'm sorry, Heath.

H It's okay, it's okay. I knew it was coming, but I guess

I was holding out hope that maybe it wouldn't sell, and maybe it would work out, or maybe I could save up money and help with the mortgage payments when I got back. I don't know, I was just clinging to false hope.

G At least you have a lot of good memories there.

H Yeah. I do. And I'll make a lot of new memories at the apartment or wherever we end up next. I'm just feeling crappy right now.

G I'll try to set up a time for us all to talk. Having half our group go MIA right now is probably not helping.

H Yeah, that sounds good. I've gotta get changed for my shift. Hope you're settling in over there.

G I... well, some things are good. Some things are not. But I'll let you get changed. We'll talk soon. Love you.

H You've got this! Save those trees. Love you too.

CHAPTER THIRTY-ONE

REESE

FINALLY, *FINALLY*, I GET to see part of Paris. I've been so preoc-cupied with school, I've spent more time holed up in my dorm room working on designs than outside.

Mamma always talks about how the memorable parts of her study abroad in London were the places she traveled, the times she got to eat and drink in pubs across the city, and not so much the learning—but I'm still getting torn apart during every design session.

Yes, my other classes are going fine. Yes, Professor Watts always has kind things to say and suggestions on how to improve. But nothing can cause me to spiral faster than enduring group critique from my classmates.

They say I lack a point of view. They say it looks a little too off-the-rack. I feel totally lacking in inspiration, and something's not clicking.

"Perk up, mate." Philip nudges me in the arm. "This is *the* fashion capital of Paris, which is the fashion capital of the world. Do you know much about the Marais?"

"Not a ton," I admit.

"Well, you're in for a treat. Art, food, fashion, it's got it all."

We probably look like a tour group—all twenty of us Fashion Design students walking single or double file through the stone archways that line the shops. I take my time as we walk along, and a vintage store catches my eye. After our first big project, I'm expecting mod dresses, polished looks from the sixties or seventies, but then it dawns on me that "vintage" could really mean from any decade. In here, it's got it all: ancient leather jackets, denim suspenders, brightly colored tracksuits from the nineties.

It makes me wonder what my classmates would think about any of these designs. Too simple? Too flashy?

"We're getting left behind," Philip says, so we walk quickly to catch up with them.

"Do you think I'm trying to be too 'ready-to-wear' and not couture enough?" I ask him. "Noelle keeps telling me how my looks wouldn't read well on the runway."

"I don't mean to be rude to her, or to any of us, but keep in mind she's seventeen and can barely sew a piece of fabric without spiraling into a breakdown. She gives good critique sometimes, don't get me wrong, but after a certain point, you just have to go with your gut."

"Easy for you to say," I whisper.

"Hey, I heard that!" He laughs. "I get bad critiques too.

Remember when I presented that yellow and brown look and Adam said it looked like a trip to the bathroom? Do you think that's a good observation? Like, in any world, would that be helpful?"

"So why doesn't Professor Watts jump in and shut him up?"

He shrugs. "When we're out there in the real world, we'll get way worse comments than that. Maybe this is all part of the process."

Our professor leads us into a three-story boutique. On the first level, we're greeted with some of the most beautiful woodwork I've ever seen—dining tables and chairs, rustic-looking bookcases loaded with vases and prop books. Strewn throughout the home goods are racks of designer clothes, charming day dresses and thin leather handbags, a selection of discounted jackets and sweaters toward the back.

"I'm actually scared to check how much some of this furniture costs," I say.

"There are no price tags in this store," Noelle chimes in from behind me. "That must mean it's quite a bit higher than any of us can afford."

I chuckle, though hearing her feedback on anything makes me bristle.

"It's brilliant, though," Philip says.

We're led into the back room, and the orderly setup of the store immediately descends into a chaos of scrap wood, clothing patterns, mannequins, and half-finished dresses.

"I'm Talia," the shop owner says. "I want to welcome you all to my store. I understand you're all a part of Riley Design, which is very dear to my heart. I was in your shoes not too long ago, and I decided to come back to the school for their postsecondary program. I partnered with a furniture designer I met there, and ten years later, here we are."

A few of us gasp at the revelation that we're standing in a boutique owned by an alumna of the very program we're in. Yes, she had to continue studying after high school, and this seems impossibly far away. But it's within reach.

I think about all the dresses in the shop. Cute, beautiful, and completely my style, but decidedly *off-the-rack*. Something that wouldn't show well on a runway at all. What would Noelle, or any of my classmates, have said about her designs—or hell, even her finished products?

She takes us on a tour of her facility, and the pieces start to fall into place. I see myself studying at a design school in New York, honing my point of view, then opening my own shop someday.

A spark lights a fire within me, and it's something new—something like . . . inspiration.

CHAPTER THIRTY-TWO

HEATH

FRIDAY NIGHTS USED TO be sacred to the four of us. Sure, sometimes I'd have an away baseball game, or one of us would be sick, but with the exception of one brief group FaceTime, we've barely gotten to keep up the tradition. This Friday is no exception.

Gabriel, or "Gabe" as he goes by now, seems to be fitting in well, but I get the feeling he spends more of his time talking to Sal on the side and less time confiding in all of us, which is such a twist from how things normally go. Reese is five hours ahead, so he's in bed by the time most of us are free to flood the group chat. And Sal has almost evaporated from the chat entirely. He wasn't the chattiest of the bunch, but he used to be around *some* of the time.

I'm not alone here, thankfully, but it does get lonely sometimes not to have that constant group by your side. I think I'm fully settled, or at least as settled as I'll get. After a few training sessions,

I'm really getting the hang of things at the arcade. I know how to fry corn dogs to perfection, I know how to pour beer (though technically I'm not supposed to be serving it, so I have to keep this skill a secret until we're really slammed), and I also know how to clean up messes. And there are so many messes.

I'm also getting much better at Skee-Ball, for what it's worth.

My first real shift is tonight, and I'm actually excited about that. Jeanie's paying me seventy-five dollars for a six-hour shift, all under the table. It's good pay, compared to what I'm used to getting in Ohio, and I'll be able to build up some savings. Maybe even fix my car, so Reese doesn't nearly fly out the window every time we hit a bump.

That is, if he even wants to ride with me anymore after his big Parisian trip.

"You're sulking," Diana says as she throws me a bottle of water. I twist off the cap and consider dumping the whole bottle over me but figure I can throw myself into the ocean if it gets much hotter.

As weird as this trip is going to be, one thing's for sure: when I'm back in Ohio, I will seriously miss sitting on the beach every day.

"Sorry, Di." I shake my head to snap out of it.

"Still missing your friends?" she asks, and there's a hint of sadness in her voice.

I shake my head. "Kinda. I knew they'd be too busy to talk this summer, but I don't know. Guess it's just hard. I'm worried we're drifting apart, or something. It's only been a week, and we can barely have a full conversation—what's it going to be like at the end of the summer? Or during college?"

She shrugs and gives her bracelet a slow twist. "Everyone grows apart eventually. But I doubt you guys will. It'll be all back to normal once you're back, except everyone's going to be hella jealous of your tan."

"Ha, yeah," I say. "Reese doesn't tan, but he sunburns, like, instantly. He came to one of my games once and forgot sunscreen, and he was bright red for weeks."

"Risking skin cancer just so he could see you play," she says, a snarky note in her voice. "That's a really good friend."

"He was *fine*." I roll my eyes. "But for the record, he is a good friend."

I feel a slight tug of jealousy in my gut when I think of his new life, and the boy who gets to show him how to sew and sit next to him every day and eat with him at Parisian cafés. But I shake it off. Reese really needs someone now. I just wish that someone was me.

She pulls out her phone and flips to Instagram. She quickly taps to my profile and scrolls through the photos. "Which one is he?"

The picture she's looking at is one of my all-time faves. It's from early spring.

"The one with the glasses," I say. "I love this pic. We were supposed to go to a party that night, but we started streaming this old season of *RuPaul's Drag Race* and we were so invested that we stayed up until four finishing the entire season."

We all shoved ourselves into the couch in Reese's den. I've never felt so close to them, literally and metaphorically, so I snapped that selfie of us all on the couch.

"Looks like a double date to me," she says. "These two are always touching, aren't they?"

I laugh. "Yes, they are definitely *close*. Which leaves me and Reese together by default. He really gets me. Like, when I'm with him I get that best-friend feeling, like, all the time."

"Welp, I guess I need to step up my game if I want to get the honor of being your best friend," she says with a laugh. "Or do I automatically rank higher because I'm family? Blood over water, and all that?"

"See, this is why I don't pick favorites. Everyone gets jealous."

"You know, I think you're his favorite too. He looks so happy to be next to you, doesn't he?"

She zooms in on the photo so it just shows the two of us, and Reese's arm is casually draped across my neck, his cheek pressed into mine, and he's got this smile that's so sincere and vulnerable. He so rarely shows it to anyone, but god, when he does . . .

A sensation passes through me, a lightness that fills me completely, and reminds me of our last time saying goodbye before we left. How I just wanted him to stay in my truck, how I wanted us to just stay there in that moment forever. And I knew he wanted that too, but who knows what he wants anymore.

"He does look happy," I finally say. "With me."

CHAPTER THIRTY-THREE

GABRIEL

"I HATE THIS," TIFFANY says as the sun beats down on the two of us. "I hate this, I hate this, I hate th—*Hi, sir!* Do you have a second to talk about saving Boston's beautiful parks?"

"Hi there," I say to a woman who's walking down the street toward me. "Boston's parks need your help! Do you have a second to . . . aaaand she's gone."

Tiffany sighs and puts her head on my shoulder. This week has been utter hell, but at least I have a partner through this. I've been doing this for weeks, and most days I'm lucky to get anyone to let me give them half of my spiel.

"This nightmare just won't end," I say.

Tiffany nods. "I have never resented an experience as much as I do this. These people *hate* us."

"I have a feeling Save the Trees is starting to hate us too. We've made a whopping zero dollars so far. Maybe we should watch Matt and Art sometime. They've made so much more money than us."

We take a seat on the bench outside the bank. We've been assigned this corner. It's actually the third location they assigned us—we started outside these hugely trafficked areas, and as the others started to succeed and we started to panic, we got pushed to slightly more obscure areas of the city. There's still a ton of people here, but it's clear this isn't the best spot. We've gotten no donations, but what's worse is we haven't even gotten anyone to sign up for their mailing list.

That's how bad we are at this.

"Let's take our lunch break," she says. We only work about four hours a day, so we're supposed to alternate our breaks so one person is always out there to catch unsuspecting passersby who just can't wait to give us all their credit cards. But she's right, we won't be missing anything.

We decide to grab a salad at one of the chain chopped-salad places, a splurge for us considering our meager stipend. After, I head back toward our bench, our bank, our corner, when Tiffany stops me.

"It's only three blocks to where Matt and Art are." She smiles. "Want to do some spying?"

I laugh. "I would do anything to not have to sit on that sad concrete slab we call a bench."

My tight chest loosens as we leave our cursed street, and I feel my mood lift as we get caught in another conversation about our home lives. Tiffany is fascinated about my close group of friends back home—mainly that we're all in competition for the top of our class yet we're best friends. And she talks to me about her normal summers in the mid-Atlantic, eating crabs with her family at a beach house, and how she'd do just about anything to be there right now.

"This volunteer thing isn't what I expected," I admit. "But if for nothing else, I'm glad I'm finding my own friends here. I love my friends back home; they're my family. But we've only got a year left together, and college is going to change everything."

"It does," she says. "At least that's what my brother says. He's a senior at Howard, and I think he's lost touch with all his high school friends at this point. Except for the occasional like or comment on social media."

"I've been worried about making friends without them," I admit. "But this has been good for me, I think."

"Well, thank god I jumped in front of you at that first party."

We make our way to Quincy Market, this giant food hall with shops that sits in the city center of Boston. Eventually, I find Matt talking animatedly with a tourist about the foundation. They're laughing and smiling, and I feel my cheeks lift up along with his.

"How is he the most charming human in the world?" I ask, which makes Tiffany snort laugh. "What? He *is*."

"Yeah, he's fine. I see that look, though—don't be crushing on him like that. You're just jealous he's able to hold a conversation with a stranger."

"Can't it be both?"

"Not when we only have a couple of months left here."

Her words settle in within me, and I nod. It is silly, but it feels special that I am crushing on someone who isn't Sal. Even if it's just secret envy of his conversational skills, it's a first for me.

Matt keeps talking while the man takes the tablet, fills out his information, and swipes his credit card. They talk a bit more, and there is something captivating about the way he talks, the light and kind way he approaches the conversation. He's so happy. I envy that joy, and I know part of the reason I'm not like that is my anxiety, but there's got to be a way I can do this, even if the thought of going back to the bank corner makes me actively want to die.

Before I know it, he's spotted us. "Hey, guys, what's up? Better luck today?"

Tiffany scoffs before saying, "Love your optimism, but no. Not even close. We're going for our eighth zero-dollar day in a row."

"I'm sorry," he says to us both. "It's really hard. I can't believe we have to do this all summer. But, um, I got you two something. It's silly. But it might help."

He crouches down and pulls off his backpack. He wipes his brow with the back of his arm.

"I picked it up at the dorm's front office this morning, but you were already gone, so I was going to drop by on my lunch break and give it to you. Ah, here we go," he says as he pulls two shirts out of the bag.

He passes one to me, and another to Tiffany. I shake mine out, and I see it's a pretty simple shirt: a light gray tee with I AM SORRY in giant, bright pink letters on the front.

"What the fuck is this?" Tiffany asks with a laugh.

"I know you two are having a rough time getting people to talk to you, so I was trying to think of something funny and, I don't know, maybe you could turn it into some silly talking point that works. You both are really good at self-deprecating humor."

"We did say we should just start opening our conversations by apologizing for how bad we were at this," I say.

"Exactly," he says. "I hope you don't mind. It just sounded like a good idea. I asked Ali your shirt sizes, since I knew she had to get those Save the Trees shirts for us all."

"Thoughtful," Tiffany says in a sincere tone, but as my gaze meets hers, she throws me a smirk.

Art comes up and joins us, and they laugh when they see us holding our shirts.

"I know we're supposed to wear the official Save the Trees shirts and all that, but I hope you'll give those a shot," they say. "It's all about throwing them off guard, then surprising them with all the tree-adjacent information they never knew they needed to care about."

Matt puts an arm around Art. "You should hear their one-liners. You could say Art makes this into an art."

Art rolls their eyes, and I do too.

"Thanks for the shirt," I say. "Tiffany and I were actually going to spy on you for a bit and try to pick up tips."

"Stay as long as you want," Matt says, then smiles at me, and I feel an intense blush coming on, so I look down at the ground.

I don't fully know the feeling that's brewing inside me, but I know one thing. It's not just envy.

CHAPTER THIRTY-FOUR

SAL

WALKING INTO THE CAPITOL building never gets old.

It's six forty-five in the morning. I sip my coffee after another smooth trip through the metal detectors that line the entrance. Work doesn't technically start until nine, but Meghan gets in at eight, and she has a tendency to flood my work inbox as soon as she arrives.

Though I wake up early, like *super* early, I always try to do something that gives me that trademark DC rush to start the day. Some days, I'll sip my iced coffee while taking a walk on the National Mall. Other times, like today, I'll wander the halls of the Capitol. Each corridor has a new bust or a new painting I've never discovered. A plaque or an ornate decorative detail I've never noticed before.

Of course, I want to be back here someday, but I want to take in every moment I'm experiencing now.

"Hi, Pasquale," I say as I walk into the office.

He gives me a quick smirk. "Early day?"

I shrug. "I'm pretty sure I intern for the busiest senator on the Hill."

He laughs. "Well, I appreciate it. When the other two come in, can you walk them through this briefing sheet? Wright's announcing a new stance on a student-loan-debt-forgiveness bill, and we want anyone answering the phones to be ready to address it."

"Got it," I say, taking the instructions to Meghan's corridor of the office.

I log into Meghan's computer using my new email address—and I still beam with pride every time I type my shiny new "dot gov" email address—and sort through the messages Meghan sent after I left last night. She usually works late, but I have emails as late as eleven at night this time, which is unusual.

I click the first email.

Sal—
A family emergency just came up. Can you cover for me today? It's a pretty slow day, two quick tours with a few lobbyists before they meet with Pasquale. I'll forward you anything else that comes up. Thank god you're here to help!!!
All best,
Meghan

I sit up straight and get to work. Twenty emails later, I have a list of running questions for Meghan ready and I'm starting to get hungry for breakfast. As I leave the office, I run into April in the doorway.

It's awkward.

"Oh, hey," I say. "I left some scripts on the table in there. Wright's got a new stance on student-loan forgiveness, and they want you to be prepped for any pushback."

"Hmm," she replies, "is he for or against it?"

"Against, I think."

She brushes past me. "Figures. College cost like fifteen dollars back when he got *his* degree. Why should he care about anyone else?"

I follow her into Meghan's office and sit at the desk. I'm still a little peeved at April for what she said about me, but I do want to be on good terms with my colleagues here.

"College feels like a scam, sometimes," I admit.

She eyes me over the script she's holding. "It's definitely a scam. But it's a necessary one. I mean, look at Meghan's desk, it's just covered in University of Dayton gear."

"My friend's dad is the same way. You'd think he just graduated from OSU last year with how much he talks about it."

She laughs but doesn't offer much more to the conversation. I stand again to go grab some breakfast, then give her a rundown of the senator's schedule and let her know that Meghan's out for the next few days.

She still doesn't make eye contact, but she nods.

"Sure thing, boss."

• • •

The day seems to last forever. I'm running on my fourth cup of coffee, and it's starting to make me a little jittery. But I've gotten so much done.

"Hey, Sal, I think we're going to head out," Josh says. "Are you . . . coming? It's past five."

"Yeah, even Pasquale left," April adds. "And he gets paid a lot more than us."

"He's still working," I say after clicking to my calendar app and into Pasquale's schedule. "He's got a meeting with Senator Halwell's chief of staff at Showtime Lounge."

Josh laughs, then puts a palm on my shoulder. "That's a dive bar, Sal. He may call it a meeting, but it's happy hour. And you could use one."

"We found this Mexican restaurant in Adams Morgan that doesn't ID, so we're going to try to get some margaritas. Do you want to come?"

I know networking is a really important part of working on the Hill, but something about leaving all this work undone makes me hesitate.

"I can't. I'm still on hold trying to upgrade Wright's flight tomorrow, and Megan just forwarded me like six more emails." I sigh. "Next time, I promise."

April and Josh make eye contact, and I hate feeling like I'll be the topic of their happy-hour conversation, but they don't understand what it's like. They don't understand how I *have* to make this work. Meghan needs me. The senator needs me.

And I need this.

CHAPTER THIRTY-FIVE

HEATH

"AND HERE'S YOUR ROOM."

Dad finishes his virtual tour of our new apartment by opening the door to a decently sized, surprisingly bright room. I look at the blank space—just white walls and beige carpet—and try to really imagine myself here. Where will my bed go? Where will my desk go? Will I keep the baseball trophies on my dresser, or should I change things up?

I guess Dad gets to decide that, and I can change things once I'm back.

"It's nice," I say. This whole time we've both been trying to keep our spirits up, but I really just want to say how much this sucks. I don't want to move.

"Good," he says. "I was hoping you'd like it. This room seems to get a lot of light, which is nice."

"It looks bigger than yours," I say.

He pauses. "I mean, it is. A little. I thought you'd like this one better. I don't need much room, and you'll be hanging out with your friends, so it makes more sense for you to have the big room."

I try really hard not to think about the fact that he might one day need more space, because then I'd have to come to terms with the fact that he might one day be dating again. But as tempting as it is, it's not fair for me to take the room.

"I don't want the big room, Dad. I don't need the space, or the light, or whatever. I'll be fine wherever, you know that."

"I know," he says. "But I feel bad. First we make you sit by as we sort out our whole divorce, then we make you move away for the summer. It only seems right to give you the best room."

"I want the smaller room. Please? I would feel bad taking it. I've got eight billion extracurriculars, so I'm never home as it is. Not to mention—"

"I'll be an empty nester soon enough?"

I laugh. "I wasn't going to put it in those words, but yeah. Seriously, take the big room."

He agrees, after some hesitation, and I feel a little bit of relief when we finish the call. Diana, who sits next to me, nudges me with her elbow.

"That was very big of you," she says. "I know we've got a three-bedroom, but whew, the things I'd do for a bigger room. Not that any of us are ever home anyway."

"He was just being nice," I say with a shrug. "It's really the first time either of them have admitted they're putting me through something shitty, so I kind of have to give him credit for that. But once I get back, I only have a year or less left."

"Until you're at Vanderbilt?"

"That's the idea."

"I don't know, maybe I'm not as pure and kind as you, or whatever, but whenever Jeanie feels bad for working too much or making me pick up extra shifts, I milk that guilt for all it's worth. It's gotten me so many doughnuts over the years," she says. "Anyway, beach time. I'm going to run by the arcade to harass Jeanie a bit before her shift, but you can go straight to our spot. Cole should be there."

Before Diana and I part ways, I give a wave at Jeanie, and I feel oddly grateful for what I've got. Maybe I won't ever have a huge family. Maybe I won't ever be able to go into the house where I grew up again. But I like what I do have. And I hope I can hold on to that.

I make my way down the beach and spot Cole immediately. Things are good, I think. Things are weird with Reese, and Sal might as well be in another universe, but I'm getting a little closer to Gabriel, and I'm getting to know Cole better too.

"Hey, Heath," he says. "Diana bail on us?"

I laugh. "Nah, she's talking with Jeanie."

"Gotcha. Thought we'd finally get some alone time."

I blush as I lay out my beach towel. I strip off my tank, and for a moment, I think I see Cole's eyes sweep over my body. But then he stops, and I'm left to wonder about exactly what passed during that gaze.

He puts his shades back on and goes digging through his tote, and I lie back and close my eyes for a bit. A part of me feels awkward, and I can't fully put my finger on why. I guess people never really look at me like that. At least, guys don't.

There's something captivating about Cole, and I've been good at ignoring it. That is, until now. He grabs a semifrozen bottle of water out of his bag and takes a sip. The condensation drips onto his chest, and I find myself watching it slide down his stomach. He pulls the bottle from his mouth, and my gaze snaps to his lips. And . . . now I feel like a creep.

I've never even kissed anyone, but yet . . . there's this attraction here.

"I come bearing gifts," Diana says as she returns. She takes her seat between us, and I breathe a sigh of relief as she throws a Gatorade at me and sets out a paper tray with three corn dogs.

"After this trip, I'm never going to be able to eat one of these again." I dunk the tip in mustard and take a bite. "Okay, that was a lie. These are so good, oh my god."

Not even two minutes later, we've devoured our food. It seems wild that this is my life right now.

"This is the life," I say. "I miss Ohio, and I miss my other friends, but this? This is perfect."

"You haven't even been to one of our beach parties yet," Cole says. "Now, those are perfect."

"He's right," Diana adds. "We have a friend who has a little private beach that we'll go to at night, set a fire, and get a few drinks. You'd love it. It's like one of those, um, farm fires that you do sometimes."

"What?" I ask as she tries and fails to remember the word.

"Barn fires?" She flicks my bracelet and points to the charm. "I don't know, this thing."

"Oh, right. *Bon*fires." I look at the charm, and a hollowness grows within me, thinking about how long it's been since I've spoken to Reese. The best I get nowadays is the brief moment when I'm getting off work at two in the morning, he's just waking up, and we're able to text. About the projects he's working on. About how he's learning to sew. About how these accelerated classes are really getting to him.

We've got a little tradition going, though, sneaking texts between time zones, and I like that.

I look to Cole and think about how easy it would be to be with him this summer. About how there are moments of obvious attraction. How if I asked if I could kiss him, I somehow know his answer would be yes.

What I have with Reese is less obvious. So much less obvious that I can't even be sure it exists. But it feels real, and safe, and it's what I want.

But then again, Reese isn't here. And Cole is.

CHAPTER THIRTY-SIX

SAL

MY BODY IS NOT cut out for ten-hour workdays.

I'm shaky all the time, either from the caffeine or lack of sleep, my feet are always sore, and my mind's so frazzled I keep making small mistakes. Though the small mistakes are getting bigger: first, a typo in an email, then forgetting to double check the senator's gluten-free meals at his last event, and earlier today I had a ten-minute conversation with a constituent about how Wright supported the Green New Deal when, officially, he doesn't.

April's and Josh's comments have become more pointed lately, and April sarcastically calling me "boss" still stings.

I want to pull them into a long talk and explain everything, but I haven't had the energy to address it, because I'm so strung out, I can barely find time to eat unless I'm at an event and Meghan forces me to take a break. At least she appreciates me. She's started to bring me iced coffee to start every day. I know I'm making a great impression, at least.

I can do this. Even if it doesn't feel like it right now, I *know* I can do this.

I only have nine weeks left, and I want to know that I've made a mark when I walk these halls for the last time.

Some days I walk into the Capitol with such pride, such confidence. Other days? I can barely convince myself to get out of bed.

I'm fully lost in one of those stare-at-the-wall reveries when April puts her hand on mine, just lightly. I snap my attention to her and pull my hand away.

"Wow, sorry. I've been zoning out a lot lately."

She smirks. "Well, it's Friday at four thirty. I think that's expected."

"What's up?" I ask, desperate to switch the conversation away from my current spiral.

"Josh and I were going to check out this new bistro on Fourteenth Street after work," she says while giving a somewhat awkward glance to Josh. "Did you want to join us? Or . . . do you need to stay late again."

"I don't have to stay late, actually." I feel bad for how things have been lately, and I regret opting out of their last invite, so I can't really say no. "Sure, that sounds nice. Thanks for the invite."

"Sure," Josh says, a bit cautiously.

After work, the three of us pile into a busy metro car and transfer to the Yellow Line to end up a few blocks away from the restaurant. This area of DC is new to me, and it's instantly so much more uplifting in a way. It's a bustling neighborhood, half small-town feel, half big-city life. The crowd gives me a second wind, and I feel the fog lifting.

"Thanks for getting me out of there," I say. "I can, like, feel my heartbeat slowing."

April laughs. "Yeah, it's a little less intense in our world. Kind of how it should be, you know?"

Josh nudges her with his elbow, and it's like they're speaking in some language I don't know. In that language of friendship, where you don't have to say the words, just a gentle nudge and a certain look with your eyes can get your message across fully. For a split second, I feel sad. Sad that I haven't spoken to the boys in so long. Sad that I missed my chance to make friends with these two.

But I guess that'll change tonight, even if just for a little bit.

We take our seats on the patio, in perfect view of the pass-ersby. As soon as I open the menu, I almost fall off my chair at the prices, but it's not like I've spent my stipend on anything so far—I've been too busy—so I can afford it. But still, wow. These are *adult prices*.

"Where are you staying, Sal?" Josh asks.

"A place in Foggy Bottom," I say. "My mom's college friend's daughter, who is way older than me, had a summer sublet fall through, so they set me up with her. It's a small two-bedroom, but it gets the job done. Kind of weird to share an apartment with someone who's even older than Meghan, but we just kind of keep to ourselves."

"That's an ideal roommate," April says with a laugh. "Quiet, mature, stays out of your business."

We keep the conversation casual as we get our drinks and put in our order. Once the server turns, April sets her fists on the table with a thud.

"Okay, we've got to talk," she says. Her tone startles me—it isn't angry, but it's urgent. And I feel some of the stress I've been feeling for the past few weeks suck right back into me.

"April and I have been talking lately," Josh starts, "and we're a little worried about you."

"I'll admit, I was insanely jealous when you started working with Meghan. Like, furious, seeing red, ready to call the senator's office with a complaint—"

"If you did, I'd have been the one answering the phones, and you know I love to hang up on constituents." Josh jokes.

"Shut up," April says, rolling her eyes.

"We were both pretty angry with you," Josh admits, "and with Meghan, and with this whole office. We did not expect glamorous jobs as teen interns, obviously, but you kept getting to do all the cool stuff, while we were just getting shouted at by strangers, endlessly."

"I would be lying if I said I didn't know all that," I say. "I'm sorry, I feel so entitled. My mom helped Betty Caudill with her run for office, and she knew I wanted to go into politics, and that's why she put me up for this. I wasn't trying to get a better gig out of it."

"Well, that's the thing: you didn't get a better gig," April says.

"And that's what finally calmed us down enough to think through it. We've watched you fully deteriorate over the past few weeks, and it's so damn hard to be mad at someone who's struggling so much, you know?"

Embarrassment tugs at my gut. "I thought I was holding it together better than that."

"Meghan thinks you are," Josh says. "Everyone does. Really. You're doing way better than I would. It's just, I know how tired I am every night, and I only work six hours a day. You're there before I get in. You're there after I leave. When you finally get a chance to sit at the table, you just kind of zone out. Until Meghan comes back and you snap to attention."

"What they're doing isn't legal, Sal." April shifts uncomfortably in her seat. "There was this huge thing about interns in DC years ago. They told us a time commitment of twenty hours a week when we got the offer. They all signed that offer, and you've been working, what, forty hours a week?"

"Fifty," I say quietly. "Well, I got to come in a little late today. So forty-eight."

"We have to go to them about it," Josh says, and April nods.

"I need this experience, though." I cling to my water glass. "It's *good* experience. I might never get another chance like this."

"You'll have plenty of chances," April says. "Besides, we're not staging a walkout, we're just reminding them there are laws they need to follow."

I'm still clinging to the idea that maybe, *maybe* I can come back here, in some way, directly after high school. That I don't have to waste four full years to get to where I want to be. Maybe it's impossible, but I've got to try.

I've done everything by my mom's playbook: how I dress, how I speak, how I act. But Mom not standing up for me during the last week of school? That put everything into focus for me: I don't want academic success; I don't want more school—I want to make a difference.

"You can go to them, but I won't." I say it firmly, but my insides are a little more Jell-O–like about it. "I don't want to mess this up, guys."

They look conflicted about my answer, but before they can try to argue, my pocket vibrates. A chill sweeps through me. I pull it out to see a text from Meghan.

"Crap," I shout, and scare myself a little for the outburst. "It's Meghan. Wright missed his first flight, so she and Pasquale are stuck at the airport waiting for him, and she needs someone to receive the catering to the office before the vote tonight."

"Don't respond," April pleads.

"You're off the clock," Josh says. "You've worked forty-eight hours this week. You don't owe them anything else, Sal."

They're right. I know they're right. But . . .

I type a response to Meghan, and I find myself dripping with guilt as I hit send. I look to the two sets of pleading eyes and shake my head.

"They're sending a car for me," I say. "I've got to go."

CHAPTER THIRTY-SEVEN

GABRIEL

TODAY IS THE DAY.

Today is the day I get my first donation.

I've tried every technique in the guidebook. Some made me cringe so hard, like when I stopped a lady to ask her to "Name a state that starts with *T*!" (Apparently, asking people an easy, unexpected question throws them off enough to stop, and answer. When they answer, they feel more of an obligation to keep participating in the conversation.)

This lady, however, replied with "Tenne*see you later*!" and just kept walking. Which, in retrospect, was such a power move.

I'm tired of feeling useless. I'm tired of feeling anxious. But mostly, I'm tired of feeling like a failure. Today, I'm wearing the shirt Matt got for me, with I AM SORRY written in a large font across the front. I've decided not to go by the guidebook anymore. Making people feel awkward and uncomfortable makes *me* feel awkward, which is why I can't get any of my prepared talking points out.

Here, standing in the middle of our busy sidewalk during lunch hour, I keep an eye out for my target. But before I can even make eye contact, people are veering around me. The iPad I hold gives me away as someone who's about to ask for money. I don't blame them, but also, I'm about to explode.

My therapist says it'll get easier. Sal says not to worry about what others think. But no advice has made this any easier.

I throw my head back and take a deep breath.

"Does *ANYONE* want to talk to me about Boston's parks?"

I shout this, and immediately feel embarrassment flood my exhausted, sunburnt body. And then, I hear a faint, "Sure."

A businessperson stands before me. She's in a light gray pantsuit, and she is someone I'd never have marked as a target—the more dressed up they are, the more of a hurry they're usually in. They also tend to be rude, but to be fair they have to deal with people like me every day for god knows how long, so I don't blame them.

"Wait, really?" I ask.

She laughs. "I've got a minute. I love Boston's parks. Give me your pitch."

"Wow, okay. I'm with Boston's Save the Trees Foundation, and we're raising funds to help make our parks safer, more accessible, more sustainable places." I veer off script. "In full transparency, I'm not from here, but that's actually made me love the parks more. Could you imagine what the city would be like if there weren't community parks every few blocks?"

"I truly couldn't," she replies. "I take my lunch break in the park two blocks down every day I can. It's the only thing that keeps me sane."

"I never knew just how much it took to keep these parks running. These spaces didn't just . . . show up, you know? I think sometimes we take it for granted, but taxpayer dollars only go so far. Our programs pay for the planting of new trees in parks just like the one you visit every day."

I wait for her to stop me, to say an abrupt thank-you and walk away, but she doesn't. I go back on script, letting her know the different donation tiers and what our goals are for this summer program.

"If you're up for it, I could . . . get you all set up to donate right here and now. I know it's a little weird, but it's totally safe and takes about thirty seconds. You just put in your email and swipe your credit card."

I wince, because even on the rare occasion someone lets me get this far, *this* is when I get let down easy. It takes a *lot* of convincing to get someone to give you their credit card.

But instead, she pulls a wallet out of her purse.

"The highest tier—you said I'd be sponsoring ten trees and I'd get access to some of your webinar programs?"

I nod. "And you get a laptop sticker with our logo on it."

"Well, in that case, I'm sold," she says with a laugh.

She hands over her credit card to me, and I quickly swipe it, then let her put in her information.

"I can only imagine how hard it is to be out here in this heat, but you've got a good cause. I know not everyone gets it, but a few people do. I'll try to send a few of my more philanthropic colleagues this way."

"Wow, thank you so much."

I croak out the words because I'm damn near speechless.

As she walks away, I look at the confirmation screen on the iPad. One hundred dollars has just gone straight to the organization, and for one moment, this all seems worth it. A tear falls down my cheek, and I feel so goofy for being this emotional about a hundred bucks, but I did this volunteer experience so I could make a difference.

I really did it.

CHAPTER THIRTY-EIGHT

REESE

AFTER CLASSES, AND AFTER dinner, I go right into sewing mode. I don't need to be an expert at this class, but every time Professor Watts works with us on a project, I feel the class separate into two groups—adept sewers like Philip, and absolute messes.

I am many things, but I am *not* a mess.

"Did you thread a denim needle?" Philip asks. He's been such a huge help every time I have one of these catastrophes that he's basically started coming right to my room after classes. This project is simple: I'm turning a pair of jeans I brought into shorts. But the thread keeps getting caught.

"I think it's the tension," I say, but Philip shakes his head.

"You always think it's the tension. You need a stronger needle for denim, and stronger thread. I think this thread is okay, but let me go grab a better needle from my kit."

Compared to this, I'm flying through my other classes. Fashion

History is fascinating, but mostly consists of memorizing designers, looks, trends. If there's one thing I can do, it's memorize. Flash cards are my love language.

My graphic design classes are pretty straightforward too. Our main project in typesetting is to make a graphics collection for a company that advertises a special sale. I'm learning how to work with text more, and I'm picking up on things I should have done differently with my school projects.

But this . . . it doesn't come naturally to me. I hate not being good at something.

I think of Mamma, who constantly mended clothes when I was growing up. I remind myself that she had years and years of practice. I'll get there someday.

Philip returns with a needle. An uncomfortable smile crosses his lips, and I notice he's holding a folder too. He sighs.

"Could you, maybe, take a look at what I've got for my project?" he asks. "You've got a better eye for design than me. I like what I have so far, but it's missing something."

"Yeah, I owe you that much," I say with a laugh to ease the tension. He's an adept seamster, but I guess we all feel vulnerable about some things.

When he opens the design, the first thing I notice is that it's another gown drawn fully out of pencil, but as I look, I do see small details that pop out. It's a tight pencil dress with a thick mock mink collar. The body seems to be made out of a thick, unmoving fabric. He's cinched the waist with a thin belt, and he's styled the model's hair in a tight bun.

"This is fancy," I say. "What color?"

"I'm thinking black, or charcoal gray."

"It's dark," I say. "Your other drawings have been lighter. What's your inspiration?"

"I know we've hopped all over the place in fashion history, but I got caught up with 1950s Balenciaga. I think this will be really smart, flattering, a touch retro." He scrunches his eyebrows. "I don't know if it's enough."

"It's nice, though. If you like it, you should go for it. I mean, it's not like the grades we get in this will, like, stay with us throughout school."

"I could say the same to you," he says with a laugh as I finish changing out the needle. "I'm fine not getting high marks, but I want this to be a real contender for the showcase this fall, you know?"

"I get that," I say. "I don't know why you're coming to me for advice. The class seems to *hate* my looks."

"Your looks are good. People just love to hear themselves talk, you know? Remember when Nico called that green dress I did frog-leg couture?"

I think seriously about it, then say, "He wasn't wrong."

"Hey!" Philip snaps, and I laugh.

"You're right," I finally say. "I've been trying to keep my chin up after our last chat about our classmates' 'creative critique.' It's just hard to pick out what's worth keeping in my mind, and what's not. It's so much feedback, and I never know if I disagree because I'm being defensive or if it actually doesn't match my vision.

Anyway, I don't know how to judge my own drawings, but at least I *do* know how to judge my sewing. In that it's consistently bad."

I finish sewing one leg of my shorts, so I cut the thread and shake them out, looking at the hem.

"That right there is *not* bad. You did well, love." Philip beams.

"Thanks for your help. I guess I can't always blame the tension when things go wrong."

"These machines are temperamental. I wouldn't feel too badly about it. My gran and I made this denim apron for my dad when I was younger, and I remember having the same problem. Even she didn't know what do to, but we read this old, huge, dusty manual until we figured it out." He chuckles to himself. "She'd wondered why she had all these different needles, but it turns out she'd never changed the one that came with her machine."

"Are you still close with her?" I ask, sensing a hint of sadness in his voice.

"In a way," he says. "I think of her every day."

I hear what he doesn't say and reflexively put my palm on his back. He looks up at me and smiles.

"She's my inspiration for this design," he finally says. "She was *not* a fashionista by any means, at least not when I knew her. But when we cleaned out her house, we found all these old dresses from the sixties, back when she was a teen, and it was a side of her I'd never seen. I wanted to draw something that she would have worn, I guess."

"That's sweet," I say. "I get why you'd want to see it walk the runway too. I think the design is good, though. You might want to

223

add some accessories, maybe a white glove and a brooch on the collar? That feels very 1950s couture."

"I thought that might be too much," he says. "But it does feel right."

"Then go for it! If you think it's *too* retro, you can play with the fabric or the colors and say it's a nod to the era."

"I could swap the colors—a dark glove with a light dress."

"Winter Queen realness."

"Exactly. Well, let me think on this. Thanks, Reese." He slides his drawing into his folder and sits back as I finish the other leg of my shorts.

"So what's your inspiration?" he finally says.

I think of Heath immediately, and I feel a bit of shame for how much I've left him in the dark this trip. I miss talking with him, I miss riding in his truck, I miss spending so much time next to him that it sometimes felt like we were two sides of the same coin.

"It's nothing as sentimental as what you're doing for your grandma," I say. "My inspiration is my best friend back home. He's actually, well, he's more than that. Kind of. Or at least, I want him to be." I sigh. "Like, I want to be able to show him this design and have him miraculously know I'm in love with him. But . . . I don't know how to capture his essence and put it into a design."

He sighs. "Yeah, I get that."

I look at the charm on my bracelet, and his comes to mind. Bright yellow, alive with flames. It's the only thing that works, the only thing that blends his warmth with my fiery passion for him.

I've decided: my inspiration for this final project is fire.

• iMessage •

REESE + SAL

Hey Reesey. Can I talk to you about something?

You're up early.
Sure, what's up?

Yeah, I'm on the way to the airport to pick up the senator and traffic is awful.

Okay, so this is hard for me to talk about, but this internship is going so well I'm having second thoughts about college. In that, I don't want to go. I've been essentially doing the job of four humans in this office for the past month, and I don't know how

college could possibly make
me more qualified.

I'm going to talk to my boss
about it at some point, just
to see what she says. She's
a little college obsessed
but I think she'll get it.

Oh whoa. But you've always
wanted to go to college?

My *mom* has always wanted
that. My list of schools, my
major, the campus tours I've
already taken? I just woke up
one day and realized I had
no say in any of this. These
were Mom's words. Mom's
suggestions that I always take
without question.

That's true. You two do talk
from the exact same talking
points. I just thought you
really bought in.

I did, for a while.

Until I didn't.

I'm not going to judge you,
and I have a feeling you
wouldn't care if I did. I think

226

you'll crush it wherever you go and whatever you do. And after what your mom pulled on the last day of school? *chef's kiss*

I really just want to be in the room when you tell her you don't want to go to college.

Ha! I really think this could work out. Not sure I can get by with some of these education requirements in the job postings I've seen so far, though. Maybe starting out in local government makes more sense?

I'm sure the mayor of Gracemont could always use some help.

Oof. Not that moron.

Side note, how weird is it to have a full text conversation without Heath's manic key smashes or Gabriel's average of two words per text?

It's unsettling, to be honest………

227

R sksksksksks

S 😄 😄 😄

R There, that's better.

S Ok we're at Dulles now. Thanks for talking this out with me. Miss you!

R 😄

CHAPTER THIRTY-NINE

GABRIEL

What do you think about this? I text a picture of my outfit to Heath, who replies quickly with a **Cute!**

He's also said this to my last three options. I appreciate the positivity here, but I need *help*. Of course, this isn't his fault—I'd normally go to Sal or Reese way before him, but right now only one of my besties is responding to any texts I send, and well, I have to make peace with that.

Heath's wardrobe ranges from T-shirts to long-sleeved T-shirts, and he'll still somehow be voted Most Fashionable for our senior superlatives just because he has big arms. Meanwhile, I'm trying on my fifth patterned button-down because I really want to look good tonight.

I pick up the phone and call him. "Heath, I love you, but I'm spiraling, and I need you to have a preference here."

"They're all good!"

"They can't all be equally good! Which one is better?"

He sighs. "Gabriel, my love, chill. Why are you spiraling about a shirt?"

"It's not the shirt; it's who will be *seeing* the shirt." I clench my teeth as I finish buttoning up my latest look, which isn't anything special. "I want to look casual, but a little better than normal. I'm having dinner with my new friends, but two of them can't make it. So this one is kind of . . ."

" . . . a date? Oh my god you should have led with that!"

I blush. "It's not really a date. But I would be okay if it felt like one, for a little bit. Matt's really cute. He's the one who bought me and Tiffany those shirts."

"Those shirts were cute too," he says. "But anyway, if you're trying to look chill but interesting, go with the pattern with the little trees on it. You said he liked your tree-hugger shirt? This is, like, an elevated version of that."

"Elevated?"

"Excuse me, I know *fashion* words," he says with a laugh. "And if you must know, it brings out your eyes."

I blush, then pause to consider this. "You don't even know what color my eyes are, do you?"

"Greenish brown-blue. Something like that." He pauses. "Well, look at that, my shift's about to start. Good luck, wear the trees, let me know if he's a good kisser byeeeeeeee!"

Heath hangs up. I want to be annoyed at him, but he did help me out. I worried the trees would be, like, too much, considering we're all a little sick of our tree-vangelism right now. But Heath is right.

If there's one good thing to come from all this, it's really nice to get closer to Heath. He's always been a calming force, and someone I love hanging out with, but between Sal taking my attention and Reese claiming his, we never used to talk one-on-one.

Not talking to Reese is shit, though. Not talking to Sal is torture.

"But I'm not thinking about that right now," I say to the guy in the mirror, who's looking pretty cute if I might say so myself.

I meet Matt in the lobby, and I find myself lost in his smile. There's a sort of smile that he saves only for me, it seems, where his eyes get a little wider, and one cheek turns up a little higher than the other in this casual smirk. He could so easily be a jerk and get away with it because he's so freaking hot, but he's not.

"Always with the cute shirts," he says. "I really need to increase my number of tree outfits, you know? I felt like I knew so much about you from that shirt you were wearing when we first met, and now I feel like I'm getting it again."

"You look nice too," I say, and he shrugs.

"I tried to pick out a nice shirt, but truthfully I'm a little behind on my laundry and this is what you're stuck with." He cringes. "Didn't need to tell you about my dirty laundry, I guess. Ready to eat?"

The four of us go to the same restaurant a few times a week. It's close, it's cheap, and it has such good food. So it follows that we'd go there even if it's just the two of us. But when we get to the restaurant, he hesitates.

"Question. You'll be getting the chicken parm again, like every other time, right?"

I laugh. "Sorry, I'm a creature of habit. Why? Did you want to split something else?"

"Whew. No, no. I just. Hold on one second, I have a surprise."

He ducks inside the restaurant, and I stand kind of awkwardly outside. Should I follow him inside? Will this be long? I find a bench near the entrance and sit there, letting my mind wander. It's an odd request, and I generally don't like surprises, but ... I'm intrigued, to say the least.

A couple of minutes later, he returns, holding a tray with two large plastic drink cups and a bag filled with plastic containers.

"We're getting this to go?" I ask.

"Okay, so. I should have asked first, but I called in our order ahead of time for pickup." He gestures across the street. "I walk through that park every day to go to Quincy Market, and there are so many great spots for a picnic, and this is hands down the coolest day we've gotten all summer. I thought maybe you'd enjoy it?"

I feel a blush take over my whole body, and for some dumb reason, Sal comes to mind. How comfortable I feel with him, but how he'd never do something like this. (And how I'd never think to do it for him, for that matter.)

"Silence is never good," he says, almost to himself. "Crap, sorry. Maybe if we go in they can just let us eat this at a table?"

"Oh, no," I say quickly. "This silence is good. I promise. That's just ... super thoughtful. Here, let me carry something."

"Whew, good." He sighs. "And no, I'm carrying the things tonight."

He carries all the things—his backpack, the drinks, the food—across the street and into the park, and I follow behind him with my arms folded, wishing I could be more useful. It's a kind of weird chivalry that I'm not used to.

We pick out a spot that is semi-shaded in the setting sun. The shadows of trees fan out over our spot, and I take the blanket out of his backpack and spread it across the grass. He sets down the food and passes me tiny plastic silverware.

"I got us the zucchini fries to split as an appetizer, in Art's honor. Though I guess this was our one chance to get a nonvegan appetizer."

"But it's tradition," I say before popping one into my mouth. "And it comes with ranch dressing, which I find comforting."

"Midwesterners are so predictable," he replies.

"Says the guy from New Jersey!" I laugh. "What do you know about the Midwest?"

"Hey, I say this out of respect. I don't think I ever told you, but most of my dad's family is from out that way. They're in northern Indiana, so not exactly close by. But we visit a lot. I have, like, sixty cousins."

"Oh, no way. It's weird, before this trip I'd have said that was impossibly far away, but now that we're all the way in Boston I count all the Midwest as next door."

We start eating our main courses, which is a little hilarious because I'm trying to saw through a chicken breast with a tiny plastic knife while Matt can't find a level place to set his Diet Coke, so it keeps falling over.

"Tell me about your friends," Matt says. "We don't have many people who are out at my school, so it's hard for me to imagine having all my best friends be queer. What do you like about them? What do you secretly hate about them? Who's dating? Who's hooking up with whom? That kind of thing."

I blush. "Well, um, right now no one's hooking up with anyone."

"Right," he says pointedly. "Seriously."

"None of us have ever dated, but it's complicated, I guess." I stuff some pasta in my mouth and look away, giving myself time to decide that honesty is probably the best answer. "I've hooked up with Sal before, my friend who's in DC. But that's over now. It was strictly a friends' thing. But I don't think the other guys have done anything. If they have, they've been super secretive about it."

"I'm being invasive," he says. "Sorry, just fascinated."

"I mean, I get it. But I don't want you to think we're in this liberal haven or anything. We're basically the only out teens at our high school, and we just kind of found each other early on. Thankfully. It'd be a whole lot harder going through anything without them."

"No, no, I didn't think that. I just have a hard time making queer friends. And then I see people like you and Art talk about your ride-or-dies, and I want that, you know?"

He's avoiding eye contact with me now and instead turns his attention to his dinner.

"I also should have thought more about this before impulsively ordering the steak special when I called in the order." He's

234

sawing furiously at the steak, which barely gives in to the plastic knife. He sighs and resorts to picking the steak up by hand.

"I know Art's a pretty tolerant vegan, but they would lose it right now," I say as Matt takes a bite from the steak he's holding. He shrugs.

"Anyway," I say, a more serious note to my tone, "I know having these boys be so close to me is so special, and I wouldn't change what I have with them for anything, but I think it ends up holding me back sometimes. I don't know how to make friends on my own. I don't know how to pick out a shirt without running four options by them. They haven't been as accessible lately, and it's been pretty lonely."

"Well, I think you're great, and I'm glad we're friends now. I know I don't compare to them, and I don't expect to—especially when I'm sitting here eating a steak like corn on the cob—but if you're ever lonely, you can talk to me. Text me to approve all your outfits. Hang out in my room. Whatever you want."

I smile. "Thanks, Matt."

We finish up our meals as the sun's nearly set over the trees. The park closes at sundown, and we should be going soon, but I feel the urge to stay. I like Matt—not as a replacement for my friends, or even a remedy for missing them. But I genuinely like him. And the rest of our little volunteer crew.

"Park closes at sunset. I hate to say it, but we should get back," he says, and we start to pack up our trash. I fold up his blanket and pack it away in his backpack. I feel a smile lightly tug at my cheeks as I think about just how special this evening was.

We walk back, and I get the feeling he's walking slower on purpose. Like we're trying to get every extra moment we can squeeze from this maybe date. Along the way he's talking about this new reality competition he's been streaming lately. He's talking faster, and there's a hint of nervousness in his tone, and I wonder ... am *I* making him nervous? Sal was always so sure, so confident around me, that seeing this sort of vulnerability makes my heart ache in the best way.

It's like every time our eyes meet, he blushes and looks away.

"I started watching it because they billed it as this florist competition, and flowers are cool, but when the florists get there they realize it is more about designing these huge floral installations, like, almost architecture stuff, and it's like none of them knew what they were signing up for. I put it on for background noise the other day, but it's strangely addictive. I only have a couple of episodes left."

"That sounds interesting," I finally say.

I feel bold. And scared. And this feels right, so I add, "It's still kind of early. Would you want to watch a couple of episodes together?"

"Back in my room?" he asks, and I see a smile come over his face. "Yeah, yeah, of course! I've been trying to get the nerve to invite you over this whole time. Yeah! If that's okay with you?"

I laugh. "I'm the one who suggested it. So yep, very okay with me."

When we get back, we sit next to each other on his bed as he excitedly explains all the posters and illustrations that line his walls. He turns on the show, and we're just barely touching. I reach out, slowly, for his hand . . . and lightly link his fingers through mine.

A calmness comes through me, and I can't even hide my smile. We just sit there, holding sweaty hands in his hot dorm room and watching this terrible reality show. And for once, I really feel like this is enough.

More than enough.

CHAPTER FORTY

HEATH

AUNT JEANIE IS LIGHTNING quick, and it's pretty clear that she is the master of this whole arcade. I've worked a few odd jobs, and I know the type. The manager at the local diner who knows that table nine needs exactly two sugar packets under one leg to balance it out, plus which chairs to sit guests at and which ones squeak. The grocery store cashier who knows every single produce code by heart and can spot the difference between yellow onions, white onions, and Vidalia ones from three aisles down.

Jeanie knows everything. How to fix the ticket jams in the basketball machine, how to pour the perfect beer, how to spot a fake ID from just about any state. These things come to you after years of doing the same thing. Kind of like how I practiced my slider about ten thousand times with Dad before perfecting it. It's that kind of knowledge I can really appreciate.

But it's not something I can keep up with.

I don't burn the corn dogs anymore. And I can carry in the kegs from the back. But when things are busy, like this, I feel useless.

"Behind you," Diana says, carrying two giant cups full of Bud Light. She exchanges beer for cash in a flash, and almost immediately, she's got the next order down.

I dump another round of corn dogs in the draining tray, and I start loading in another batch.

"Behind you," Jeanie says now. She's got five full beers in her arms, which she carries to the counter without a tray, never spilling a drop. *How are these people even human?*

The music is loud, like always. The crowds are rowdy, as always. And I'm kind of over it today. I don't mind helping out, but so often I feel like I'm in the way, like Jeanie and Diana have to spend more time correcting my mistakes or teaching me how to do something than if they just did it themselves.

"How are we doing, Heath?" Aunt Jeanie asks.

"Okay," I say, putting on a good face. "I only burned one batch today, so that's progress."

"You're doing great. It's even starting to die down a bit. Hey, why don't you go back early? You've been working later than we agreed the past few days, and I feel bad. I know I'm not paying you much. Diana loves the company, but she and I can probably take care of things till closing."

"Are you sure? I really don't mind. And you're paying me too much as it is. I should be paying you rent—"

"We've gone over this," she says in mock disappointment. "You're family; you've always got a place to stay for free."

I laugh, but I feel a blush come over my cheeks at the mention of family.

"Sure there's nothing else I can do? Any kegs need to be changed?"

"Lug one more of those Bud Lights up here and that's it for your shift."

"Not fair!" Diana shouts as she comes across with two more beers. "I'm suing! Child labor laws are strict here in Florida."

"No laws are strict here in Florida," Jeanie snaps back.

I try to hide the smirk on my face as I grab the keg and drag it over to the taps. I give them a wave as I leave the place, and head right to the beach. It's not the fastest way to get back, but it's a little more peaceful. Except for that time Di and I caught a couple, um, having some *cake by the ocean*.

I pull out my phone and see that it's coming up on two in the morning. A whole hour before closing time. I put in my earphones and give Reese a call, hoping that it doesn't go to voice mail like my last few tries.

A groggy voice reaches the phone. "Heath?"

"Yeah! Hey, Reese. Did I wake you?"

"It's seven, so yeah. I missed your last few calls, but I kept my ringer on this time so it'd wake me up. You off work?"

I smile, knowing that there's someone out there who's willing to get up at seven a.m. for me.

"Yeah," I say. "Jeanie let me go home early, so I'm walking back now. I miss you."

A rush of embarrassment floods my body as I realize exactly

240

what I just blurted out. Of course, it's true, but I didn't need to tell him that.

"I miss you too. It's been a while. I guess I'm not in the group chat much anymore either."

"You're *never* in the group chat. But you at least have the Wi-Fi excuse. Not sure what Sal's is. You know, Gabriel had to ask *me* for fashion advice? I know I'm his dead-last choice, but I was honored to be asked either way." I pause. "Sorry, I feel like I'm talking too much. How are you? Have your projects been going any better?"

He groans in response. "Yeah, they have. I think I'm getting used to this whole group-critique thing. I'm working on my final project now. The only prompt is to take something that inspires you and turn it into a garment."

"What inspires you?" I ask, and I'm met with silence.

"I'm not sure yet. I have some ideas, but I don't know. When it's right, it's right. But Philip has been giving me sewing lessons, which is really saving my ass."

"Oh, that's great. Is sewing a big part of the class?"

"About as much as the design stuff we do," he says. "Oh, and it's really been helpful to know how the fabrics kind of sew together, which stitch works with which fabric, so I know what the different stitches, threads, and all that will look and feel like on the final product."

An unusual part of me comes alive as he talks, when he mentions Philip. I know nothing's going on there, and even if there was, that's . . . great for them. I mean, I can't compete with anyone when I'm frying corn dogs and he's studying abroad in France. But I feel this jealousy building up inside me, and I want to tell him about hanging out with Cole, just to see what he'd say.

But it's not like anything is actually happening here. And it's unfair to hold this over him.

"When do you have to get up?" I ask, because I don't want this conversation to end.

"I'm up now," he says with a laugh. "But I should probably jump in the shower in an hour or so. I've been trying to get espresso and a croissant at this café nearby every day to really drive home this whole French thing."

"Sounds wonderfully cliché." I laugh. "I'm glad you have a routine, though. Do you want to go back to sleep until then? I just got back to the house. I can let you go if you want."

"No," he says. "I've missed talking with you and hanging out with you. I know I've been flighty lately, but I'm just drowning over here. I'm getting super homesick, though. Wait for this—I even miss your truck."

"That seems impossible, but I will let her know you've been thinking about her. I think I finally saved up enough to get the shocks fixed for you. Once you're back it won't be quite as bad."

"It wasn't bad," he lies. I appreciate the gesture. "So we can keep talking? Unless you want to go to bed?"

"Never," I say. "You're worth the lack of sleep, Reesey."

CHAPTER FORTY-ONE

SAL

IF YOU ASKED ME where I'd be six weeks into my internship, I'm not sure even I could clock the fact that I'd be helping manage a black-tie event at the W Hotel. I'm fully suited up with my black silk bow tie on, and I feel good.

After this event, Senator Wright leaves DC for the next week. It's the week leading up to Independence Day, and the senate is officially out of session. Which means, as soon as I get through this last fifteen-hour workday, I can finally sleep.

I'm no less stressed right now, though. Because this is a *solo* event. Meghan is back at the Decatur House for a VIP cocktail reception between a few senior senators, the vice president, and other high-profile Democrats. Wright should be leaving that event any minute now to head here, and I have to make sure every-thing's ready for him.

"Excuse me," I say, flagging down a catering staff person with a clipboard. "Can you confirm the gluten-free meal for Senator Wright, table two?"

He flips through a couple of pages on the clipboard. "I don't see any gluten-free meals here."

"Can one be added?" I ask, panic creeping into my voice. I've already been dinged once for screwing this up, and I can't let that happen again.

He hesitates. "I don't know. You'll need to talk to the event manager, Brittany. We're not supposed to make any changes unless they come from her."

"Do you know where she's at?"

"I'm sure she's in the back somewhere." He takes a step away from me. "Sorry, we've got to finish getting the place settings ready before doors open."

He walks away, and I pace the room, looking for Brittany—who I've only met once. She has a habit of disappearing during events, I remember Meghan saying. I shoot off a quick text to her.

Brittany disappeared, help! I type, adding four siren emojis to get the point across.

She responds immediately: **Kitchen. Loading dock. Smoker.**

I dash back into the kitchen, even if I'm not fully sure I'm allowed to, and head back through the steel door. Brittany sits on a bench smoking with some of the catering staff, seemingly unaware that their event opens in two minutes.

"Brittany!" I say. "Hi—I'm with Senator Wright. Need a gluten-free meal. I called to confirm yesterday, but the caterers don't have any record of that. Can you help?"

"Oh, right! Is Meghan coming? I haven't seen her in a while."

"Yeah, later," I say, trying not to be too short with her. But I can't screw this up again. "Can you get a gluten-free meal ready for the senator? He should be here in fifteen."

She looks at her watch. "Oh wow, doors should be opening soon. Yeah, I'll get him a meal, sorry about that."

"Totally fine, thanks," I say, then turn to head back into the event when she calls out to me.

"We had to tweak the seating chart, by the way. Wright's at table three now."

"Oh, okay," I say. "I should confirm with Meghan. Let me give her a call."

While Brittany and I walk through the kitchen and back into the event, I text Meghan and call her twice, but the calls go straight to voice mail. Brittany hands the seating chart to me, and the names of the lobbyists all blur in my mind.

"It's mostly the same group as what Meghan approved last week, I wouldn't worry about it."

I sigh. "Okay, fine. As long as you can get the gluten-free meal there?"

Guests start to arrive as I walk back into the event, and I get caught up in the wonder of it all. Elegant dresses with pearl necklaces, sleek tuxes and gold watches. Light piano music pours into the welcome hall as guests grab crystal glasses of bubbly.

Since the senator's going to be late anyway, I take my time touring the space. DC architecture feels so ancient and stately, and I can't imagine there's anything like it in the world. I feel so at home here—not only at events like this but when I'm walking the diagonal streets, passing embassies and government buildings, riding the metro, walking the halls of Capitol Hill.

Out of the corner of my eye I see Meghan and Pasquale rush into the building. I sprint toward them.

"Meghan!" I say, "I had a question about—"

"Phone died," she says, cutting me off. "Need to find a place to charge. Take Pasquale and Wright to their table."

Meghan leaves me in the presence of the senator and his chief of staff. Heat creeps up on my cheeks, and I feel a little unprepared.

"Right, okay. This way." I pull back my shoulders and walk them into the space. "How was your other event?"

"Oh, it was fine. Necessary," the senator says. "Let's just say I'm ready to clock out and go see my family. It's been a long month."

"I hear that," I say, mostly to myself. We weave around the various round tables in the space. I point to one in the distance. "Table three is over there. Your gluten-free meal is in the works, so we shouldn't have any problems there."

A surprised look hits Pasquale's face as Wright takes a few steps over to his table. He shakes hands with a lobbyist there, and they fall into a quick, noticeably tense conversation. Wright turns and waves us away with a wide-eyed look at Pasquale.

"Fuck. Who approved that change?" Pasquale demands as he leads me toward the back of the room. "This is not where he's meant to be."

"The events person said they needed to shift some people from table two to three. Is there a problem?"

"That lobbyist Senator Wright is talking with is the problem. The last time they were in a room together, it ended with Wright storming out midevent. Did you not read all about it in *The Hill*? God, this is bad."

"Meghan!" Pasquale snaps. She turns in surprise with a look of fear. "Your intern put Wright with Cal Hewitt—fix this."

He storms back to the table to presumably help facilitate the conversation.

"Oh no," Meghan says. "This is bad. There's so much press here. We need Brittany."

She leads me toward the loading dock, where Brittany enjoys yet another smoke break.

"Brit," Meghan says, "you know we can't have Wright and Hewitt at the same table."

"The kid said it was okay," she replies, pointing to me. "It's too late—everyone's already in their seats."

Brittany walks past us, and I feel Meghan's rage boiling over next to me.

"Can I do anything?" I ask.

"You can start praying that we don't lose our jobs. I knew I shouldn't have trusted you with this one." I pull back, and she gestures at me to leave her alone. "Never mind. I'll fix this."

• • •

I fucked something up for the senator, I text Gabe.

I don't know who else to go to. After wandering around the parking lot, I finally find the courage to return to the event. In the very back, there's a bar with a few college-age interns at it.

Programming—speeches, award presentations, the works—has started in the main event hall.

I sip my water, and I feel the exhaustion creeping up on me. A tear slips down my cheek, then another, and I'm barely able to stop the rest.

"Two rum and Diet Cokes, please," Meghan says, taking the stool next to me. Once they're poured, she passes one to me. "Well, that was a mess."

"I'm sorry," I say.

She sighs. "Pasquale is furious."

"What about the senator?" I ask.

"Wright's probably pissed too, but he can't show it. He's actually been great with Hewitt. Not sure if Hewitt's being less of a dick this time, or if Wright's just too tired to put up a fight." She shrugs. "Whatever, these things happen, right?"

"Do they?" I take a sip of the drink. "Do they always feel this bad? You should have seen the look in the senator's eyes. And the tone in Pasquale's voice. Heck, even you looked like you wanted to kill me. All I wanted to do was make a good impression here, but I feel like I've messed it all up."

"We all mess up," she replies. "I shouldn't have let you take this event, and I guess I didn't brief you enough on this drama. Brittany is also fully useless and makes these kinds of changes all the time."

We sip our drinks in silence for a bit, and I wait for any sort of relief to wash over me. But I still feel like a failure.

She shakes her head. "You've made a good impression here,

Sal. Even if Pasquale's a little scary sometimes, he'll be the first person to write you a recommendation for college, I promise."

"Can I be honest with you?" I say, my exhaustion finally taking over. "I've been debating whether I even want to go to college."

She laughs, but her expression drops when she sees that I'm serious.

"Oh, really? Then why are you doing this internship? Don't you want to work on the Hill one day for real?"

"Well, I was hoping that maybe I could skip all that?"

"Sal, *no* office here would hire you without a college degree. Plus, college is so much fun. Honestly, I get why some people say it's the best time of your life."

"It seems like a waste of time, though. I've learned so much about your job in just over a month, and I learned by *doing* it. Sitting in poli-sci classes for four years isn't going to make me any more prepared for it, you know?"

"I don't disagree—it is a bit of an apprenticeship here. Or at least, you learn by doing it. But that's just not how the system works." She sighs. "Look, if you play your cards right you'll have a recommendation from Betty Caudill *and* Senator Wright under your belt. But that can only get you so far."

A part of me wonders if I should just give in and go to college because it's what I'm supposed to do. But I'm sixteen—that's a quarter of my entire life that I could put to better use.

"I could work for local government, probably. Right?"

"Sure, but it's not the same there as it is here. I did an internship with Wright's home office during his first term, and it almost scared me out of politics forever. Though I guess I was just answering phones and dealing with constituents."

"Like April and Josh are doing?" I ask, and she gives me a glare.

"Firstly, they're getting paid and I was not. Secondly, they get to do it in DC, in the Capitol. His home office isn't quite as glamorous." She looks up, like she's thinking really hard about how to say something. "I guess the thing is this: you seem to thrive in this environment. Not a lot of people do, and I think that's special."

She gives me a kind, slightly condescending smile, and I feel the heaviness of the past few weeks snap inside me. I deflate so hard I almost collapse on the bar.

"I'm not thriving," I say. "I hate this, actually. But I just keep my head down and push through it, because it's such a good experience for my résumé. I'm doing it for the recommendation letter; I'm doing it because I thought if I did a good enough job I could just, I don't know, skip the whole college thing. But if you're telling me there's no chance, then you're right: What am I doing here? Why am I working fifty hours a week?"

"You're not working fifty hours a week," she says in this slightly unstable way, like she can't quite be sure if what she's saying is true.

"I've tracked it. It started out as a pride thing—I worked thirty-five hours in my first week, and I was, like, 'Wow, this is basically a full-time job. I could definitely come back and do the same thing for real.' Then that increased each week. I worked fifty-two hours that week you got stuck at the airport.

"Josh and April have been working up to thirty hours, and

they're starting to notice that Jenna is taking longer lunch breaks while they take over the phones every day. I have a signed offer letter that says my commitment is twenty hours a week. Josh and April wanted us all to talk to you guys, to tell you it wasn't okay, but I wouldn't join them. That was yet another mistake of mine."

Meghan just stares at me, like she honestly doesn't believe it's possible.

"Uh . . . ," she starts. "Holy shit. I'm so sorry. Pasquale never told me about the twenty-hour limit. I just assumed you were all just along for the ride. I don't know why I didn't ask. And believe me, I didn't mean to keep you that late. You're just so put together all the time. I didn't realize the sort of stress I was putting on you."

"I fell asleep on the train and ended up at Franconia-Springfield last night," I say. "And it's all for nothing. Do you think this experience will even be relevant when I get out of college in, like, five-plus years?"

"Maybe . . . maybe you should take the rest of the week off. And we can play next week by ear, maybe longer. God, if Betty Caudill knew about this, she'd freak. I'm going to email the others and cut their work hours now. We'll figure this out."

And just like that, it feels like my internship is over. Fifty hours a week, I put my all into this, and in one moment, it's gone. Even if I come back, it'll never be the same. But who cares if it is?

I've lost so much precious time this summer, and for what?

As I leave, I pick up the phone and call Gabe. He'll know what to do.

251

CHAPTER FORTY-TWO

REESE

TODAY, LIKE EVERY OTHER day for the past week, started with a call from Heath. It feels good to be close to him again, and I'm starting to rely on his early morning pep talks to keep me going throughout the day. Especially on critique days.

As we come up on four weeks left in the program, we've started weekly one-on-one consultations with Professor Watts about developing our design.

"It feels very Hunger Games right now," she says. "Ever see that movie, the second one?"

I nod. "Without the magic fire?"

"Ha, right. But that's a little of what I'm seeing here. The movement, the gradient from black to fire red. I like it, but it's lacking a bit of practicality. What fabric are you thinking? How would it be dyed?"

I pause, considering it. "Linen, maybe? It wouldn't have the movement, but it would be easy to dye."

"Cotton batiste, maybe? It would be sheer, so you'd need something with a bit more heft for the body, and these could be decoration. But then it looks a little—"

"Flamboyant?"

She laughs. "It does look like what the gals wear at my local drag show back home. Not that that's bad. There's a market for that—we've just never had a drag queen on our runways."

"I wasn't really going for drag, but I guess a lot of what I know about fashion is from drag queens I follow on Instagram."

"I think, whatever you're going for, just commit to it. Think about the fabric. Next week, I'd really like you to come in with a couple of samples of fabrics for this look. It's coming together, though. You've improved a lot so far, but again, for *this* assignment, think equally about practicality, cost, production. Things like that."

"Got it," I say.

"I only have the budget to get one of these designs produced for the show. And there are times I've given better grades to projects that didn't end up winning because they weren't feasible for the runway. Stick to the assignment." She lowers her voice. "And don't give this up."

That makes me smile, so I just repeat, "Got it."

I leave her office, thinking briefly about how much more confident I feel now than I did the last time I was in there. I came into this program with no direction and no clue what I was doing.

But I've figured it out along the way. Thanks in part to Philip, who's waiting for me as I walk by the lounge.

"So? How did it go?"

"It went well. I mean, she said it looks like it was made for a drag queen and I have no practical way to make it, but it's a start."

He laughs. "That's a compliment."

"Oh, absolutely. But I don't think this school is ready for their first drag runway." I pack my drawings away, and he stands to join me. "Café?"

"Actually, I was thinking. It's pretty early, and you haven't been a proper tourist. Want to change that?"

I pull back, a hesitation gripping me. "I mean, I was going to do the Louvre and stuff when my moms visit. And I've been so busy."

"But you're not busy now."

I pause, then slowly nod. "I guess that's true."

"So let's go. Save the Louvre for your mums, but there are plenty more museums to see. We can just go to the Eiffel Tower if you want. Please?"

"Sure." I smile. "I need some new selfies for Instagram any-way—I haven't made enough friends jealous, to be honest. My friend who's in DC keeps sending us pictures of, like, him with the senator he's working for, or him at every monument. It's gross. I really need to get him back."

Philip laughs at that. "Then it's a deal. We'll make all your friends jealous."

As we walk the angled streets through the city, Paris comes alive around me. This area isn't like our neighborhood, which is quiet and full of small shops and restaurants. This neighborhood is loud, bustling, cosmopolitan.

For once, I recognize that I'm in a big city. I feel like Gabriel must, with his long threads in the group chat early on panicking about Boston. It's overwhelming. It's too much. And I kind of love it.

"How lucky are we?" Philip asks, somewhat rhetorically. "Studying fashion in Paris. I might come back here for undergrad."

"That would be amazing. I think we'll be back for a week next year for French IV, just a class trip, though. But I have my eye on a few graphic design schools back in the US. I don't think I could be away from my family for that long, you know?"

As we walk down the Champs-Élysées, we instinctively slow to window-shop at the obscenely expensive shops. I think of the people in class who want to design looks like this. Powerful business looks, expensive fabrics, and I almost laugh when I picture my dumb little fire dress in here.

"This is not my vibe," Philip says. "But I appreciate these looks. If that makes sense."

"Definitely. It's, like, when I go to modern art museums—I don't always get it, but it still makes me feel something. But really, I'm more of an impressionist guy."

"Wait, you are? Have you been to Musée d'Orsay? It's, like, *the* impressionist museum. Largest collection in the world. Want to go there after this?"

I nod, and we launch farther into the city. Our first stop is the Eiffel Tower. The sun is hot overhead as we join the other tourists meandering around and through the legs of this masterpiece.

"Want me to snap a few pics for you?" he asks, and I shake my head.

"They've got to be selfies, since I'm trying to properly mock what Sal's been sending our chat."

I pull out my phone and focus on the tower in the background. I take a few photos, some with portrait mode on—which really just blurs the tower, but it makes my skin really smooth.

"We should get one together," I say. "We're sewing-table buddies, and that means we're bonded for life."

He chuckles at that and comes around. He puts an arm around me and leans in close, and I snap a picture. When I pull it up, I look at how happy we are, and I feel instantly grateful that I made at least one friend here.

"This is going to sound incredibly corny, but do you mind if I sketch this a bit?" I pull out my journal. "Just a quick one."

"Of course. Let's find a spot to camp out, and you can tell me more about your friends."

This week's journal page is full of sketches of accessories, since that was the focus of our most recent Fashion History lecture. Belts, bracelets, and earrings line the page, but I find enough room to pencil in a quick sketch of the tower.

As we continue the walk, I'm able to connect to a Wi-Fi hot spot, so I drop the picture in a text to the group chat and send it off. He ushers me away, and we start the long walk toward the impressionist museum, pausing at times to take in gorgeous, sunny views of the Seine.

"So does 'the chat' know about me? Or do your friends just think you magically got good at sewing."

He gets my elbow in his side for that. "Heath knows about you, but I haven't really talked to the others much about it. I did show them the jean shorts I made, though."

"Heath is . . . the fire guy? You've told him we're just friends, right? I don't want to accidentally put out that fire. This whole thing has my girlfriend pretty concerned, if we're being honest."

"Heath isn't like that," I say. "And sorry about that. Do you want me to explain to her just how bad I am at sewing? Would that help?"

"It's not that. She's just *very* straight and was raised a little closed-minded." He throws his head back. "She was always fine dating a guy who was pansexual, but, I don't know, I think this whole fashion-school thing is making her paranoid. She doesn't fully get it, I think."

"That's rough. I guess it's hard for some people. I feel like we've been pretty lucky back where I grew up, but there was an incident near the end of the school year. Hopefully she's just a little insecure, and she'll get it eventually."

"What kind of incident?" he asks.

"Oh, you know the kind. Name-calling, threats, critique of my fashion choices. Things like that."

He tilts his head. "Is that why you take everyone's feedback so personally?"

"What? No, I don't." I pause, thinking of my instinctive flinch every time Noelle or Adam makes a cutting remark on my work. They're not bullies, but he's got a point: my brain still interprets critique as an attack. "Hmm. I never thought about that."

"Can't let people like that win, you know?"

I nod. "Absolutely. And I don't think he has won. Thanks in part to the constant pep talks you and Heath give me, I've been more clearheaded about my critiques lately."

He stops walking, and I turn to him.

"You're a good mate," he says. "It's nice to *finally* have a gay friend. I know it makes Emily a little uncomfortable, but she tries, and she's a good person. But she also needs to know that I need friends like this. Friends who get what it's like."

"She'll get it, eventually."

As we walk the streets of Paris, I really start to appreciate this new friendship I've made. It's always felt so one-sided—me depending on him to fix my sewing machine every time the thread breaks—but I had no idea all of this was lying under our friendship. And I hope we can keep it once I'm back home.

MONDAY

- O 5 - 7 PM CLASSES
- O SEWING W/ PHILIP?

TUESDAY

- O 3 - 5 PM CLASSES
- O CALL HEATH?

WEDNESDAY

- O 5 - 7 PM CLASSES
- O CALL HEATH?

THURSDAY

- O 3 - 5 PM CLASSES

FRIDAY

- O ACTUALLY CALL HEATH! *
     (STOP PUTTING IT OFF)

SAT / SUN

- O FAMILY ZOOM

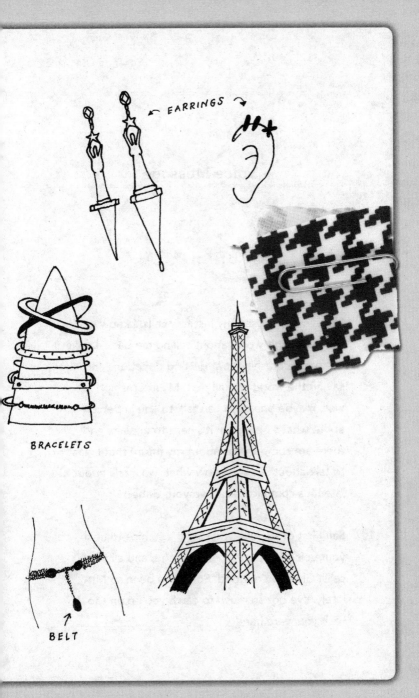

EARRINGS

BRACELETS

BELT

• Voice Message •

GABRIEL + SAL

[S])) Hey, you've missed my last few calls. I know you're busy, so don't worry about calling me back. Looks like you're crushing it at getting donations and saving the world and all that. My internship . . . well, maybe one day I can talk to you in person about what's going on. It's hard to explain, and there are some things about my future that I want to talk about . . . You know what, we'll talk about it later. It's complicated. Love you, Gabe.

[G])) Sal! First of all, love you too. It's so nice to hear your voice. Just got your message, and all your calls. Glad you're good. Sorry I've been so MIA lately. I've got so much to catch you up on too. I wish you were here!

CHAPTER FORTY-THREE

SAL

THE FIREWORKS HAVE STARTED. I feel them, more than I see them, but every time the bus turns just the right direction, I can see the small pops and fizzles from my window seat. Happy Independence Day, DC.

And, goodbye.

I still feel bad about being the one to confront her about it, since April and Josh wanted to do this whole structured intervention. I might never know why they lied for me, or why they continued working thirty-hour weeks for me, but I owe them so much for letting me get to the obvious realization—that I was being overworked for no damn reason—on my own terms.

I don't blame Meghan. I don't blame the senator. They're so busy and scattered that I really don't think they realized how much they were overworking us, and Meghan's face turned fully white when I told her our offer was for twenty hours a week. I wonder if all the offices have that kind of full communication breakdown, but then I remember the frantic energy on the Hill. It must be that way.

But I can say goodbye to that now. I've been told to take the rest of the week off, along with April and Josh, while they re-collect. I don't know if I'm coming back. Who knows if they even want me to, but if they do, I'm not sure I *want* to go back.

Which is why I'm all packed up and sitting on a bus right now.

GABRIEL

"I wouldn't have bought you those shirts if I knew you'd catch up to us," Matt jokes.

Tiffany, Art, Matt, and I are spread out on a blanket in the park, waiting for the fireworks to start. Fourth of July is a huge thing back home, and I feel this nostalgic warmth about sitting with friends, making a picnic, as fireflies dot the dimming sky.

The four of us, unexpectedly, received the most donations for Boston Save the Trees during the month of June. Tiffany and I slightly edged out Matt and Art, but we decided to call it a tie, because Tiffany's family came up to Boston for a surprise visit last week and dropped a spontaneous donation that pushed us just above them.

But cheating aside, we've done really well.

"You should see our dearest Gabe now," Tiffany says. "He will literally jump in front of tourists to talk to them about trees, and

I think he's so awkward people just let him talk, then he somehow cons donations out of them."

"Yeah, yeah, good for Gabe." Art rolls their eyes as they grab a scoop of hummus. "When are the fireworks going to start?"

Smaller fireworks have been popping up all evening, and it reminds me a little bit of being home. Where you can turn in any direction and see someone's (possibly illegal) fireworks show popping up over the trees. If I were on a roof right now, I bet I could see dozens and dozens of them, all over the city.

Matt snuggles up to me a little bit. We haven't told the group much about whatever we have going on, which has so far consisted mainly of watching Netflix in his dorm room and holding hands, resting slightly against each other—and if we're feeling really bold, he leans his head on my shoulder, and we just stay like that for hours.

Now that we're in the dark, his hand finds mine, and I grip it tightly.

What we've had has been slow and sweet, and it sits in a completely different world from what I had with Sal. There was nothing slow about my relationship with Sal, but we weren't ever caught up by these real feelings. Everything is different with Matt, and I've let him set the pace, partially because he's never dated anyone before, but also because I'm scared to mess this up by treating him like Sal. By going too far and taking it for granted.

The first few fireworks fly, and the park gasps with awe. I turn to Matt and see the flashes of light bounce off his face. He leans into me, keeping his eyes on mine the whole time. I close the distance, and our lips meet as the crowds cheer and the rockets explode . . . just for us.

SAL

Gabriel hasn't been responding to my texts all night, but at least I got to talk with him through a couple of disjointed voice messages this week. Though I was calling to tell him about my utter meltdown. I couldn't do it. I couldn't utter words that showed how much of a failure I am.

I know now that I'm not a failure. But I was in a dark place. I went from working fifty hours a week, all leading up to this imaginary moment where I didn't have to spend four years and a hundred grand in college . . . to nothing. No work, no one to talk to, and nothing to do but sit with the mistakes I made this summer. And in that dark place, I bought this ticket, so I could flee DC. Part of me already regrets it.

Maybe I'll end up going to college; I don't know. While Heath was busy working and Gabriel was busy doing whatever it is he does, I was able to talk to Reese about it more. College is a scam, but it's a necessary one sometimes.

This morning, Reese actually threw out the idea of me running for office after high school, which of course has me thinking. I would love to show our joke of a mayor the door. And with our tiny town, could it be much more than running for student council president?

Is that just a pipe dream?

At least it's nice to dream again, I think as I settle into my seat on this empty bus. I use an old Cornell sweatshirt as a pillow, and I drift off to sleep, calm for the first time since I showed up in DC.

GABRIEL

Matt is a good kisser. Not that I have a ton of experience, but I at least know he's not a *bad* kisser, and that's key. Though with his slightly tousled hair and his eager expression, he could have bit my face off and I'd probably still have enjoyed it.

"I'm not sure if you two saw, but the fireworks show already happened," Art says, which makes Tiffany giggle.

She stands and starts to pack a bag. "Were you trying to watch it, like, through the reflection of each other's eyes like some sort of eclipse situation? I don't know, we couldn't really tell."

"Something you want to tell us?" Art asks pointedly.

My cheeks burn red, and I don't dare look at Matt, who's fallen into a fit of nervous giggles.

Tiffany shakes her head in a mocking way. "I just can't believe you're sleeping with our competition. We were supposed to be a team!"

"We'll take your silence as an apology for having to witness your big ol' public display of affection," they chime in.

"I get it, guys, oh my god." Matt can't stop laughing.

We start on our way back, but it's clear neither of them will let this go *ever*. They've both made it clear they approve of us, if only by the fact that they won't shut up about this. Matt takes my hand, and when I look into his eyes, we smile. And it's so sweet to be in a friend group where we don't have to hide, or lie, or wonder if people are secretly judging us.

"I knew I should have been partnered with that hunk from Houston," Tiffany says. "If anyone deserves a make-out session, it's me."

"I can't believe we're going to be third wheeling it for the rest of this summer," Art replies. "I guess fourth wheel? But that'd just make us a car."

"Maybe they're flat tires in this analogy?"

"Yeah, we'll go with that."

Their banter continues, and at a certain point we stop even pretending to be annoyed with it. Six weeks in, I'm walking through the city, holding hands with a cute boy, surrounded by obnoxious friends. I'm not sure why I ever worried about this experience, but it's everything I've ever wanted.

SAL

Eight hours on a bus with only one stop is not my ideal way to travel. But it was cheap, and I could book it impulsively, so it'll do. I feel a sense of home, of familiarity as I step off the bus. I grab my suitcase and roll it down the sidewalk. It's dark but not silent

268

here. Apparently a few fireworks shows or celebrations must have happened recently, because it's impossibly busy tonight.

I pull up my phone and flinch when I think about who I'm letting down by leaving DC. How I'm going to have to admit that I wasn't cut out for it. But now that I'm away I feel a sort of ease reach my chest, and I know I've made the right decision. I don't have a ticket back yet, but once I clear my head, maybe I can try this whole internship thing out again. Or maybe I'll just stay here.

GABRIEL

We say goodbye to Art and Tiffany at the front of the dorm. They've finally dropped the topic of me and Matt, and Tiffany gives me a tight hug before she leaves, and I get the feeling that she approves.

Matt and I talk into the night, watching drunken strangers stagger around and hearing residual booms from fireworks off in the distance. July nights used to remind me of summers with my friends, drive-in movies, and bonfires, but I know that now they'll only remind me of Matt. Of our hands sticking together in the humidity, of his lips on mine.

He rests his head on my shoulder, and we watch the people go by. And I think I spot a familiar face. It's happened before, me seeing his face in crowds of people, and each time it tugs at my heart in an awful way. But this time, as he gets closer, the recognition doesn't fade.

It's Sal. He's *here*, in Boston.

The past crashes down on me all at once.

CHAPTER FORTY-FOUR

HEATH

TONIGHT'S SHIFT WAS BRUTAL. We knew to expect it—people in Daytona are wild as it is; add in a national holiday and people are likely to go far out of control. Jeanie's a force to be reckoned with, though, which she showed by throwing three people out of the arcade before we even got to midnight.

The only thing that got me through it was my midshift texts with Reese. It was such a weird dynamic: he was up early getting ready to start his day of sewing, and I was lugging kegs around this never-ending rager. We largely communicated in emojis and short texts, because I didn't have time to do much else, but it was something.

I've never seen people so drunk, but before this, I guess I wasn't around it too often, if ever. The guys and I have gone to parties, and we've been able to sneak a couple of six packs out to a bonfire before, but I've never been like *that*.

Maybe that'll change tonight. Diana and I show up to the Fourth of July beach party after everyone else, but we didn't have much of a choice—it was all-hands-on-deck at the arcade, and even Diana knew not to try to get out of it.

I go to knock on the door, and Diana laughs.

"They're all on the beach out back. No one's going to hear you knock." She confidently opens the door to this bizarro mansion beach house, and with the exception of a couple making out on the sofa, she's right that it's basically empty here.

"You nervous?" she says coolly.

"A little, yeah. I'm not usually nervous meeting new people, but something tells me we're going to have to drink fast to catch up."

A case of beer cans are lined up on a table next to a cooler, like someone started to fill it up but promptly got distracted and walked away.

"Nice and warm, just like I like it," Diana jokes as she palms a can.

She throws it to me and gets out her keys. "Let's step back and shotgun this, then we can fill up the cooler and bring it out to them. You'll be a hero."

We step out back, and I scan the beach. About twenty teens are spread around in every direction, with the largest cluster around a tiny beach fire. It's no bonfire, that's for sure, but it's something. Just looking at it brings me back home for a second. Even if nothing else is the same.

I've never shotgunned a beer, but Diana shows me the ropes—I poke a key into the side, bring the hole to my lips, crack the beer, and chug. I spill a little bit down my shirt, but otherwise I'm able to finish it pretty quickly. My stomach feels warm and gross all at the same time, and I wait for the buzz to kick in.

"All right, now that that's done, let's go take over for whoever was supposed to fill up the cooler."

When we come back in, I see that sand's been tracked all over the kitchen, and I realize just how late we are to this party. Diana says they last well into the morning, but after that shift, I'm not even sure I want to stay up.

"Thought I saw you guys," Cole says as he enters the kitchen. His eyes are a little glassy, but compared to the couple who just rolled off the couch mid–make out, he seems a little more in control.

The buzz starts to hit me, and it churns up a different warm feeling. Cole gives me a sidearm hug and plants a quick kiss on my cheek, and I almost light on fire.

"Good party?" I ask before looking in the freezer for any more ice for the cooler. I find none, but I guess the others are too far gone to really care.

"Better now that you're here. I was talking with Ashlee most of the night, but then, well, she found Bryce while he was restocking the beers and, well"—he gestures at the couple making out on the shag carpet—"you get it."

Diana reaches into the fridge and grabs a box of Franzia, this cheap boxed wine she's apparently so happy is here, and we head out back. We claim a towel near the fire and don't bother mixing in with the other groups of people, who barely know we're here.

I send the group chat a selfie I took of me and Diana shotgunning, and receive an immediate thumbs-up from Reese.

REESE

There's such a vast difference between three a.m. and eight a.m., especially when it's a holiday in the US and life moves on as normal over here. I'm feeling a little under the weather today, though I think it's this weird combo of homesickness and fatigue, and I scratch my plans to sit at the café.

It's raining anyway, and though Paris is pretty in any weather, I'm feeling intensely homesick. My parents threw this family party for the holiday, like always, and just about every one of my cousins sent me photos and said they miss me. Ariana just got her braces off, and she looks like an entirely new person. In the selfie Isabella sent me, I swear Lucia's grown since my goodbye party.

And that was just about six weeks ago.

Though Philip's idea of doing undergrad in France was tempting, it's just unrealistic. There's nothing like a big, life-altering trip to realize you're a homebody. I want country fried steak at Melody's Diner. I want to give Heath a huge hug after he pitches another perfect game.

I want to *be* with Heath.

He sends a selfie to the group, and in it he's shotgunning a beer with his cousin, which makes me laugh. Whenever we drink, which isn't that often, he's always the babysitter. Making sure everyone has water, that we pace ourselves. If I got sick from drinking too much, I know he'd be the kind of guy who just sits in the bathroom with you, rubbing your back, distracting you with jokes or stories.

I should have told him how I felt before I left, I know that. But what we have right now is special. We've cobbled together a friendship with late-night texts and early morning phone calls. I'll send a travel selfie while he's at work; he'll respond with a voice message for me to wake up to in the morning.

It's not perfect, but it's ours.

HEATH

"Okay, I'm feeling it now," I say after my third cup of boxed wine.

Diana twists her bracelet a few times, and I realize I've never asked her why she does that. Is it a nervous tic? Is it just out of boredom?

"What's that bracelet about?" I say. "Is it like the one Reese made me?"

"This is literally a bunch of thread that's tied around my wrist. Yours is this copper-wire hand-crafted masterpiece." She laughs. "So, no, it's not like that."

"But you play with it a lot, usually whenever you're anxious. It almost rubs your wrist raw when we have busy shifts."

"It's a reminder, I guess. I used to be"—she drops her voice to a dramatic whisper—"a bad kid."

I laugh at the drama of it, and she elaborates.

"Okay, fine, it's not that deep. I used to smoke cigarettes, though. I'd steal them from Jeanie back before she quit, and I'd find ways to get my own. I was up to a pack a day at one point—it was pretty bad. I guess I was just acting out, but I found myself actually needing a cigarette every time I was stressed or anxious. After I quit, I found this string lying around, so I made this. Every time I have a craving, I just twist it, or spin it around, and focus on that until the craving passes. It's worked for about six months so far." She sighs. "Much harder when I drink, though."

"It's been six months, and you still get cravings?"

"Oh, constantly. It's awful, I could pick it back up today, this very minute. But Jeanie . . . Mom, she was able to quit. And she got so mad when she caught me smoking. I don't know, we don't fight much, but that was a bad one. So it's a reminder. Something to focus on that isn't a nicotine addiction."

"Good for you," I say. "I didn't realize you were dealing with all that."

"I got off on being a 'bad kid' for a while, but that felt a little too cliché for me. Really, I just want to graduate. Get a good job. Maybe take over the arcade one day."

I laugh, and she shoots a glare at me.

"No, sorry," I say. "I'm just drunk. I pictured you owning the arcade, but in the mental image I got you had renamed it DIANA'S ARCADE, like, in all caps. And that seemed silly. I don't know. You'd do a great job, though."

She laughs. "Thanks. We'll see."

Diana and I have talked over the past hour, with Cole popping in and out to pile more driftwood on the fire. The sun is still hours from coming up, and the temperature's dropping to this perfect humid cool.

I send Reese a couple of texts, because I miss him and I want to tell him that. But after a little back and forth, I force myself to stop before I trap him in a drunken FaceTime with me. Even I can tell when I'm being annoying.

I spot Cole standing alone, even closer to the fire. I notice a slight chill in the air, so I leave my phone in my chair and go join him.

"Hey, Cole," I say. "You in charge of the fire?"

"More or less. Everyone freaks out when the fire goes out, but none of them care enough to grab a piece of driftwood." He shrugs. "I like to be useful."

"That's thoughtful," I say.

"I can't wait for the sunrise," he says. It's a non sequitur, but I let the conversation drift. "It's always so beautiful, and I always try to pace myself so I'm this perfect amount of drunk to appreciate it."

I laugh. "I should probably slow down, then. We've been try-ing to catch up to everyone, but it's all catching up to me. Every time I turn to look at you, it takes a second for the world to catch up. Does that make sense?"

"Franzia will most definitely catch you up, and fast. That's why I only stick to beer." He hiccups. "Though that has its drawbacks."

We stare at the fire together, and I'm a little mesmerized at how it flickers. Cole shifts, almost imperceptibly, but I feel our bare arms touch lightly, and I savor our closeness. I turn my face to him, and he just smirks at the fire.

There's a fire in me, a pot that's been close to boiling over for so long now. Seeing Reese's pictures with Philip awakened something weak and petty in me, and I hate that feeling.

"There's something about beach fires that always feel romantic, you know?" Cole says. "It's nice to be around someone who appreciates that." He turns to me, and I know the warmth in my cheeks has nothing to do with the fire blazing in front of me. "Can I just lay all the cards on the table here? You're, like, this incredible hunk, you're impossibly sweet, and I really want to kiss you right now."

My gaze drops to his lips, and I slowly lace my fingers through his. His directness shocks me, brings me fully into the present, and the jealousy inside me feels muted now. A cool breeze cuts through us as I close the very short distance between us.

I'm always too cautious. I never go for what I want.

But this time? I think I can.

REESE

It's nice to see Heath let loose, though it's hard to fully understand his drunken ramblings when that idiot turned off autocorrect again. *If there was ever a time for autocorrect, this is it*, I think.

His last text, though, struck me as odd: **i hppe u and philip are happy**

I started typing out a quick response to dismiss it, explaining that Philip is very much taken, and it's not what he thinks, but there's this undertone to the text that I can't ignore. It's almost like he's jealous. But Heath *doesn't* get jealous. Not when someone does better than him on a test, not when I told him I was moving to France for the summer and he replied telling me how his parents were moving him to Daytona. Not ever.

And if he's jealous, I wonder if that means . . . he has feelings for me.

It's a long shot, I think. Or maybe it's not. But before I can talk myself out of it, I send a FaceTime request his way, hoping that I can gain something from a real chat with him.

He answers, but Diana's face floods the screen.

"Reese!" she shouts, a little drunkenly. "How are you? I can't believe I'm finally meeting you—Heath hasn't shut the fuck up about you and your friends all summer."

I laugh nervously and talk with her a bit about my summer in Paris, and what they've been up to tonight. I keep waiting for Heath to pop his head in, and she must notice my distraction, because she finally says, "Oh god, you're looking for Heath. Let me go find him. He's going to be so happy to see you."

She flips to the front-facing camera and pans the party crowd. It seems like one hell of a party: loud music, plenty of booze, and a beach fire. She walks around calling his name, and for the briefest moment, I find his silhouette next to the fire. *Of course* he's by the fire.

"Heath, you got a phone call!" Diana slurs, but he doesn't turn.

She walks closer, and the phone shakes with every footstep, but as he comes into view, I see that he's not alone. He's with another boy, and their mouths are pressed tightly against each other.

And I get to see my worst nightmare play out in front of my eyes.

CHAPTER FORTY-FIVE

GABRIEL

THERE'S A SPECIAL KIND of hell you fall into when someone you're just starting to date meets someone you've hooked up with. When I got Sal settled in my room, Matt just kind of lingered outside. I didn't get much information from Sal, other than that he was going through a rough time, but I couldn't fully focus because the whole time I was just thinking *Matt knows Sal has seen me naked* on repeat. Funny how our brains work. And by funny I mean fucking awful.

Now, after the most awkward fifteen minutes of my life, Matt gives me a long hug outside his dorm room. There's a silent desperation in how he clings to me, and I want to promise him that what Sal and I had is in the past, but I feel the past clinging to me like condensation on a glass of water. He's everywhere around me; he's my relief and my protection.

"Is he going to be okay?" Matt asks. "He seemed really stressed."

I nod. "His internship wasn't going very well. I think he just needed a break. I let him know he could visit whenever, and I guess he's cashing in on that. But please, don't worry."

His eyes are uncertain, but I feel his tension lighten when I give him one last hug.

I leave without giving him the chance to kiss me good night, and I wonder if he'll read into that. I wonder if *I* should read into that. When I open my door, Sal's sitting on my bed, curled up against the wall, and he's looking embarrassed.

"Okay, I'm sorry, I should have told you I was coming." He shakes his head. "I should have known something was going on, after how you talked about that guy early on and how you haven't answered any of my calls lately. I'm sorry. For coming here like this."

He does this thing, sometimes, where he gets overly apologetic in an attempt to shield himself from any critique. And I get why he's doing it now—he's not used to feeling so insecure—but I will *not* let him flip this on me.

"Let me stop you," I say, and take a seat next to him on the bed. I kick off my shoes and pull myself up against the perpendicular wall. We're both looking just past each other. "*You* ignored my calls for weeks. I know you're busy, but you and Reese have been fully MIA from the chat lately. At least Reese has the time-zone excuse."

"I've been working fifty hours a week. Apparently everyone there sucks at communication, and I was doing a whole bunch of stuff I wasn't supposed to do, and it all felt wrong, but I kept saying yes to things, thinking it would get me ahead or something."

My gaze drifts to him, and my expression must be some mix of disbelief and shock. "Fifty hours? Really?"

"I tried not to complain. I mean, we've all had fifty-hour weeks if you count all the extra crap we do for school. This was decidedly harder. I think I had a breakdown."

He says that last part quietly, like he's ashamed to admit it. Like he's not saying this to the actual King of Breakdowns right now. I almost laugh.

"You could've talked to us, you know? I get that it's hard, but you can be, like, a *fraction* vulnerable with us, your best friends. I know you better than anyone else does, I think, but even I don't get this. Let me in, *tell me*, because otherwise you kind of just look like a tool."

He pauses, and buries his cold toes under my thigh. "Fine. Can I tell you something?"

SAL

"I don't want to go to college," I say.

Gabe considers me with this subtle squint before confusion takes over his whole face.

"O . . . kay? When did you come to that conclusion? Is it just because of this internship?"

"No, it's not that," I say with a sigh. "I've been thinking about it a lot lately. Even before I left for DC. I think I even word-vomited

283

about it to Katie that last day before I met you on the baseball field. Until earlier this week, she's really the only person I told."

"The only person you told about not wanting to go to college was my sister? Even though you've been, like, researching where you wanted to go to school and which schools have the best poli-sci programs, and talking to me about this on a near-daily basis since preschool. What changed, then? I don't get it."

"Don't judge me," I say as I come around to his side and rest my head on his shoulder. He flinches, so I pull back, but then he wraps an arm around me and pulls me back into him. "Lately I've just felt like college is this big scam that delays your dreams for four years. I mean, even Katie is liking college *not* because she's being prepared for a career but because she's made friends. Your dad just talks about how much fun college was. His major has nothing to do with his job."

"But I still think his job required a degree," Gabe says softly. "I don't disagree, though. I wouldn't mind a few more years to figure out exactly what to do, and I think I need environments like that to make friends. But Dad would kill me if I didn't go. I think I could go to Michigan and he'd feel less betrayed."

"Ha, your dad?" I scoff. "My mom started sneaking me in to meet with the guidance counselor for college prep conversations back in seventh grade."

"Ew, she totally did," Gabe says with a laugh. "She will flip out. But it's not a big deal, really. Not everyone has to go to college."

"She's been prepping me for this for so long, and it just took me so long to realize that my thoughts *weren't my thoughts*. My need to go to a good school, maybe even my career path, it's all her. I've got all these competing voices in my head, and I've been trying to figure out which voices are mine—the ones that keep pushing me into a career in politics, basically, and which are hers—going to a 'good school' and getting perfect grades and getting put on this pedestal."

"This isn't some elaborate plan to get back at her for what she did—or, well, didn't do—when that guy harassed you at school, right?"

I shrug. "That helped me realize some things about my dreams and my plans, but no, I'm not punishing her for that by trying to abandon our college plans."

"Right," Gabe says thoughtfully. "So wait, does this mean you're giving up on being our valedictorian next year?"

I elbow him lightly in the gut. "Don't count me out just yet."

My mind is swimming, and I feel the sharp spike of anxiety hit my chest whenever my mind drifts back to DC. I had to run away—physically leave the city—just to clear my mind. It was the only way I could force myself not to go back to work. There are so many untied ends back there, but for once, I let myself sink into this moment, and eventually, these thoughts take the back burner.

"But really, I am sorry for ruining your evening," I finally say. I pull out of his embrace and look in his eyes. "It's so nice to see you, Gabe. And wait, why did Matt call you Gabe earlier? Do people call you that here?"

He laughs and looks away. "I wanted to reinvent myself, like you said. I was at the table on the first day, making my name tag, and I thought about who I wanted to be. And that person was . . . the person *you* see me as."

"Is that Matt guy your boyfriend?" I ask tentatively. I don't want to mess up anything he has, but his closeness, his scent, brings me so much comfort that I can't not ask.

Gabe swallows hard, then shakes his head. "He's . . . not."

My hand climbs up his back, lightly gracing his neck, until the back of his head fits in my palm. I hear his breath, I feel my heartbeat. I lean into him, and I push him back onto the bed. Our lips lock, and it's just like before.

And for one moment—with his tongue on mine, and my body pressed into him—everything is back to normal again.

DIANA + REESE

Fuck that was bad I'm sorry

This is Diana

Nothing is going on with Heath and Cole ok? I don't know what that was, but it's not... it's not anything real

I've seen your pictures and I hear how Heath talks about you

You're so special to him

I just need you to know that

I'm sorry

CHAPTER FORTY-SIX

HEATH

IT'S ABOUT NINE THIRTY, and Diana and Jeanie are still asleep, so I take a walk. I think about going down to the beach, since the beach is never so peaceful as it is before ten. But we certainly got enough of it last night, watching the sunrise while the last of the fireworks were shot off down the coast.

I'm extremely tired, but not hungover. When we got back, Diana was militant about us taking ibuprofen, vitamin B3 (a hangover life hack, according to her, and probably not science), and chugging a Gatorade each before we got into bed.

The only problem was that I stopped drinking once Cole and I started making out, and Diana did *not*. I was drunk, but she was in rare form. For some reason, she just kept drunkenly apologizing to me all night. There's no amount of B3 that is going to prevent *that* hangover.

I can still taste Cole's lips, and when I think about it, it's like a blush takes over my entire body. I have no frame of reference, but that felt so good. I've never felt free enough to pull someone into my arms like that. I'm almost giddy, but I can't say the feelings I have for him changed much overnight. Turns out he's a great kisser, but I'm not looking for anything more with him.

There's this regret I feel, though. And I wonder if things will be weird between us now. The feeling seizes my chest every time I think back to last night, though so much of it is fuzzy, and it feels like how Gabriel describes his panic attacks. Sudden, gripping pain, then this sheer embarrassment like I can feel the color dripping from my face.

But then I think about the smile on Cole's face, and feel the smile on my own, and think that whatever happened last night couldn't have been that bad.

REESE

I can't stop thinking about that guy. To Diana's credit, making me see it was a complete accident, and she seemed to know that Heath and I had something special going on. Even if she didn't name what it was, and even if I couldn't name it, she made it known. She turned off the FaceTime as soon as she could (too late), then I suddenly got iMessages from a number I didn't recognize, all saying more or less the same thing: that wasn't real.

But god, did it seem real.

I've been a zombie all day, just going through the motions in class. I can't even tell you what we learned in any of them, and even Philip seemed to get the hint that I wasn't up for it today. After the third time he asked me if I was okay, I snapped at him to leave me alone, which was unfair.

Which is why I'm outside his door right now. Hesitating before knocking, because I don't know if he'll want to see me. But I have to try.

"Hey, Reese," he says. "Two visitors in one day. What are the chances?"

He opens the door and gives me a cautious smile as I enter. A girl's sitting on his bed. She looks disheveled in a slightly purposeful way and is wearing an oversized T-shirt and torn jean shorts, with her flats resting on a suitcase just to the side of the bed.

"Oh wow, hi!" I say, suddenly caught off guard by seeing anyone else in his room. "You must be Emily. I've heard so much about you!"

I don't say that the things I've heard about her aren't exactly the best—her insecurities about Philip's pansexuality, her hesitations about him studying in school here. But I feel like what Philip needs most is for me to act like everything is normal. So I do that.

"I didn't realize you were here. Why don't I come back later?"

"Is everything okay?" he asks, and I hesitate slightly before nodding. "You've been weird all day. I was excited to tell you Emily was arriving today, but you seemed a little out of it. Not to mention, you were late to just about every class."

My facade breaks, slightly. "I just had a bad morning. But I really don't want to bother you guys. It looks like she just got here."

"Oh, no, I got in this morning." Emily laughs. "I took a quick tour of the city while you were in class, and I've been avoiding unpacking ever since."

Philip hops onto the bed with Emily, and I take his desk chair. We talk a bit about Emily's flight, the cooking classes she's been taking over the summer, and the conversation flips to our designs.

"It's amazing how much Philip's designs have improved since he got here." She shakes her head. "And you letting him borrow your illustration tablet was key—have you seen his final project?"

He hesitates. "I actually haven't shown him yet. I will, but it has to be perfect first. No offense to Emily, but Reese's designs are professional level, at this point. And I'm still learning how to use the illustration pen."

"Mine are *not* professional level," I say with a laugh. "Ask literally anyone in class. I can't wait to see yours, though. I loved where you were going with it before."

"So how *is* your project?" Philip asks, and I see that he's trying to dig into my issues.

I've told him about Heath. About fire. So I answer in a language only he and I will understand:

"I think . . . I've lost my inspiration."

HEATH

Diana's a mess, as expected. Jeanie thankfully left to oversee the deep clean of the arcade—something she has to deal with after every holiday, apparently—which leaves Diana, alone, moaning dramatically in her room.

I open the door, and the smell of sweet, stale alcohol hits my nose.

"Oh my god, you smell like a box of Franzia," I say. "Here."

There was a Dunkin' on the path back, and by now I know Diana's preferred hangover food: one maple doughnut, one strawberry doughnut, and an iced coffee roughly the size of her body.

"One, how are you able to function?" She takes a bite of her maple doughnut. "Two, how the hell did you remember my Dunkin' order? You are literally the best cousin who has ever existed."

I sit on the bed as she devours the doughnuts and sucks down her drink.

"You didn't get any?" she asks.

"Oh, I ordered your hangover special too, but there was no way my two doughnuts were going to make the six-minute walk back untouched. You're lucky I didn't break into yours."

After the doughnuts are gone and the rush of caffeine and sugar starts to hit, she sits up in bed. There's a lot weighing her down right now, and I feel like it's not just the hangover. Like, the silly side of Diana has left the building.

"We need to talk about you and Cole last night," she says, and my mind starts racing, wondering if I crossed some sort of line.

"I'm sorry," I say. "I don't know why that happened."

"Don't apologize?" she says like it's a question. "You two were horny and drunk and that's what happens at parties. Hell, *I've* made out with Cole at parties. And Ashlee. At the same time."

I blush, but I feel a little grateful that what I did wasn't exactly out of line.

"Have you talked to Reese today?" she asks, and his name sends a dagger through my heart. "He FaceTimed you yesterday, after you left your phone on the chair and started talking to Cole. I answered, and we talked, and I went looking for you."

She stops, and my heart aches, because there's only one way this story ends.

"I turned the camera toward the fire, because I knew you were around there, and I thought it'd be cute if you looked at the phone from afar and got all excited about seeing his face on there. But . . . *your* face was occupied."

I pat myself down for my phone, and I realize I've left it in my room. I stand slowly, and turn, and I can't really think of the words to say.

"I really fucked this up. *Fuck*." I pull at my hair. "This is, like, the one time I just did something because I wanted to. The one time I didn't overthink it. And there was a fucking camera on me."

"It's going to be okay," Diana says.

"You don't know Reese," I say, and walk out of the room.

REESE

"It's all over," I say when I get to our usual café table, two espressos in hand. I hand one to Philip. "It took years to get to where we were at before this summer fucked it all up. Before *I* fucked it up.

He was always right there for me. He's kind and thoughtful and perfect to everyone, but it was like overdrive for us. The way he would come give me a huge, dirty, sweaty hug after his baseball games, even in front of the whole team. How he'd always take side roads when he was driving me home, just so we could spend a few more minutes in his truck together. And I was just waiting for the 'right' time to say something."

"I know how it looks, but let's remember that it was three in the morning and he was drunk. It's not like this new guy's going to be coming to his baseball games next year. I'm not up-to-date on your country's geography, but when I went to Disney World I'm pretty sure that wasn't anywhere near Ohio."

I look past him. "But how did they get there so quickly? We've been so close for a decade, but they have six weeks together and that's enough for a drunken make out? I thought Heath was just timid, but apparently not."

He pauses to let me panic, taking small sips of his espresso, then says plainly:

"It doesn't sound like a real relationship, Reese. It's just convenient; it's just easy. In my experience, it's much harder to go from friends to lovers than it is to go from strangers to lovers. If that makes sense."

"Was Emily your friend first?" I ask, and he nods.

"Going from friends to more felt impossible. Because I really didn't want to mess up what we had as friends. And I guess I really could have messed it up. But at a certain point, my friendship with her was solely rooted in how much I wanted a relationship with her, and that didn't seem particularly healthy either."

"That makes sense. But I still feel like shit. And I don't know how to even be friends with him after this, and I feel like such a dick for saying that."

"It's okay to be hurt," he says plainly. "But your being hurt by something doesn't mean Heath did anything wrong. Try to keep that separated, and I think you'll eventually find your way through this."

"Emily should be all unpacked now," I say. "So we better get back. I'm glad she suggested you come chat with me. I feel like that's not something you do if you're, I don't know, *worried*."

"She's come around and apologized," he says. "I think being apart was hard on her, so it unleashed all these weird insecurities she didn't know she had."

I chuckle, because if there's one thing I fully get, it's that.

HEATH

My shift started thirty minutes ago, and I've already burned two batches of corn dogs. I haven't really spoken to Diana since she broke the news. I just want to go home—*home* home—but I can't even do that, because Dad's moving out of the house this week.

When I got here, I was so worried about my family—or lack

thereof—and my friendship with Reese and the others. I try not to bury myself in negative thoughts too often, but all my fears really came true. My home is gone, my family is broken, and I've fucked things up with my best friend.

I drop another basket of corn dogs, then zone out a bit, staring at the people starting to fill the arcade. The smell of beer hits my nose, which makes me cringe after last night.

"I hate to say this, but maybe you should go home," Jeanie says with a quiet voice. "I love having your help here, but something's off today. Even Diana's on her game, and she's *obviously* hungover."

I look up to Jeanie, and she just laughs. "I can tell these things, especially when y'all come rolling in at six in the morning. But you don't seem as bad, so I'm trying to figure out what's wrong."

"Just a hangover." I flinch with the lie, but it's a whole lot easier to explain than what's really going on. "I thought I was better about hiding it, I guess. I'm really sorry."

She reaches past me and pulls up a basket of overfried corn dogs and gives a hefty sigh. "Heath, I love you, but you're killing me tonight." She gives a defeated laugh. "Go home, okay?"

I walk straight home and turn on the box AC unit to high so I can curl under the covers. I type a message to Reese and delete it again and again, because I can't find the right words to say. The only words I want to say are the words he'll never want to hear.

I love you.

CHAPTER FORTY-SEVEN

GABRIEL

SAL WAS MY PAST, but now he's my present. I slip so easily back into what we had before that I almost forget about Matt. But he's there, in the back of my mind. Every time Sal and I kiss, every time we touch, Matt's there, and I know this is wrong, but Sal needs me.

And I need him.

"Did you want to grab takeout again?" Sal asks, even though our trash can is full of three days' worth of takeout. *My trash can,* I correct myself. He's taken over the space so fully it's hard to remember what's mine anymore.

I don't get tired of having him in my bed, though. I hold him against me, and I remember how special our relationship is. It heals this homesickness I never even knew I had.

"Maybe I could introduce you to my Boston friends?" I suggest. "They're doing dinner at the restaurant we usually go to.

They have a good chicken parm, though I know Italian's not your favorite."

He shrugs. "I don't really feel like meeting new people."

I hesitate, thinking about how to respond. Truthfully? I don't want to sit around while Sal sulks, but god knows he's had to deal with my sulking for years, so isn't it fair if I stick around until he's feeling better?

But then I realize that no matter what, I still need some boundaries. Even back in Ohio, we'd hang out a lot. But never seventy-two hours in a row. That's a lot.

"Then, do you mind if I go?" I ask. "Without you? We could use an hour apart anyway, and they're all kind of wondering why I've been shut in here."

He looks up with these sad eyes, and I feel myself start to crumble. He has this power over me, and he has no idea how much it affects me. I start to rescind my suggestion, but I don't want to back down, so I take a second to collect my thoughts.

"I'm going to the restroom," I say, and I duck out the door. I breathe easier as I step into the hall. When I reach for the door-knob to the restroom, it suddenly opens, and Matt's surprised eyes bore right into mine.

"Matt," I say.

"Gabe." He looks so uncomfortable, and I know it's because I haven't really been responding to him. "How are you? How's your friend? He still here?"

I read eighteen other questions in between those, and each one is a dagger to my heart. He runs a hand through his coarse hair and puts on a smile, and I feel like melting into the floor.

Pursuing Matt was nice, but I remind myself that it's not smart. This can't go anywhere, right? He lives too far away. We could never make something real work between us.

But a louder, more confident part of me tells me what we had was real. *Is* real.

"He's still here," I say. "Look, we should talk about this. I feel really bad about—"

"It's okay, really. We both knew there was an expiration date on this, right? You've known him since you were, what, four? I can't compete with that."

My voice is quiet as I say, "I guess so."

"Look, I need to change before dinner," he says. "I assume you two will be busy?"

I hesitate as I look back to the room, and Matt releases a soft sigh.

"Thought so. Just . . . be careful." He turns to go, and I watch. He starts walking backward, and even though he's facing me, he still can't look right in my eyes. "Miss you, Gabe."

When he's gone, I shut myself into the restroom to think. But really, what do I have to think about? I need to be there for Sal, but I need to learn how to be there for him as a friend. I've grown more confident this summer. And I know how to advocate for what I need.

As I walk into my room, Sal looks up to me, and I give him a confident smile.

"Okay," I start, "so here's what we're going to do."

"I've been dating Matt," he says. "I'm sorry for lying about it, but I really wanted to be there for you, and it's so hard to resist what we have, you know? But this thing with Matt, it's real. It's new, and I know it probably can't go anywhere, but he's sweet and nice and we were taking it slow and I really liked it."

I wince. "I thought there was more to you two than you let on. I'm sorry, Gabe."

"But you're my best friend. I mean that." He sighs. "And as a best friend, you absolutely take priority. So if you need another day of sulking and Thai takeout, we can do that, but I'm only giving you one more day."

"No," I say. "I don't need takeout; I need to remember how to exist as a human again. This internship *broke* me. I've never worked that hard on anything, and everything I dealt with seemed so intense and so important that I just crumbled. But I think you're right—meeting new people would help. And we can do it as friends, no benefits."

"It just can't be awkward," Gabe says, and I laugh.

"It's going to be awkward, but I think we can get through it." I smile. "Together?"

"Okay." He starts pulling clothes out of his dresser. "Then you've got to help me pick out an outfit, and get it through your head right now that when we go to bed tonight, you're keeping your hands to yourself."

"Friends cuddle," I say plainly.

"Yeah, well, *we* don't." He laughs. "You'll understand when you get to know Matt."

He reaches out to me, and I take his hand.

"I'm new at this confidence thing, but hear me out." Gabe clears his throat. "I think you really have a chance to go back and get this right. To figure out your place in politics, to make this internship work for you *and* the senator, to leave your mark on the Capitol."

I nod, so he continues, "There's no non-corny way to say this, but you can do anything, Sal. I know you. *You* know you. I'm not kicking you out, but if you don't go back, you're going to regret it. And if you do go back, don't fall off the grid again, please."

As Gabe jumps into the shower, I pull out my laptop. With a heavy sigh, I look up bus tickets back. I know what I'm doing here isn't only unhealthy for me; it's screwing him up. I look to my bracelet, and the bow tie stares back to me. I need to be bold, polished, and I need to make my statement in DC.

I can't do that here.

Gabe and I arrive late to the restaurant, but his friends welcome us immediately. Tiffany is shy at first, then launches into these bonkers stories of the random people she's met on the street. Art acts slightly above it all, but based on some of their experiences living in the city, they absolutely seem like the coolest person in the world.

Matt is quiet. And I know that what he and Gabe had needs to be resolved on their own, most likely *far* away from me. But he's still so kind. He reminds me of Heath, but he's got an edge to him, chiming in from time to time with the perfect joke or pun.

I launch into a few stories of working with the senator, and within minutes, they're all pretty much scarred on my behalf. It helps remind me that what I went through was not at all normal, and I was right to put a stop to it . . . even if I did it during a poorly timed, frantic breakdown over rum and Cokes.

I love all of this, but nothing compares to seeing Gabe in his element. This is his group. In six weeks, he really did it all: crushed his internship, made great friends, found a boy. All I have to commemorate my first six weeks is a few great selfies and probably an ulcer. But I have time to salvage some of this.

When we get back, I start packing up my suitcase, and finally come clean.

"I bought a bus ticket to DC for tomorrow morning. I'll wake you before I go, but I need to go back and figure my life out."

He hesitates, then pulls me into a hug. "What are you going to do about your internship?"

"No idea, but I can't figure that out here. I have seven or eight hours on a bus—that'll give me some clarity. Heck, I might even stop in New York and be a tourist for a bit. Send the group chat a selfie with the Statue of Liberty. That'll really throw them off."

He laughs. "You texting the group chat *at all* would throw them off."

"I'll be better about that. If I go back, it'll be twenty-hour weeks, max."

He helps me pack up, then we turn off the lights and slide into bed. He puts his arm around me, but I don't push it further. I just enjoy his closeness, and I wonder if we'll ever fully be able to pull off a normal friendship.

Or maybe this is our normal, and this is okay.

"Before I go, I want you to know this." I turn to him and smile. "You were *always* amazing. And I'm sorry if I ever fed into your insecurities or anxieties or made you feel like you needed to change. You never needed reinventing, you know that now, I hope. The person you were tonight, the person you've been all summer? He's perfect."

It's dim, but I see his eyes start to tear up.

"The only time I felt confident was when I was in your arms," he says. "I loved what you brought out in me. Not just the sex stuff, though that was fun. I liked myself more when I was with you. And I think I needed to be away from you to figure out how to like myself all those other times."

"But that was you, that wasn't me. I need you to remember that, and maybe we won't fall back into this so easily next time."

I bring my forehead to his, and I feel his breath on my lips. But for once, we don't give in. We don't lean into each other. After that, we don't have much else to say, so we fall asleep like this— forehead to forehead, pinky in pinky—for the very last time.

CHAPTER FORTY-EIGHT

GABRIEL

THOUGH I'VE GOTTEN THE hang of canvassing on the street for donations, one thing is for sure: I still absolutely hate it. A hugely high percentage of people treat you like the scum of the earth when you try to get their attention, and though I don't take each rejection as a personal attack anymore, I still find it impossible not to let it wear on me after a while. Thank god for therapy.

That's why this Monday, on our seventh week of this internship, I am thrilled to be back in the office for some sort of meeting with our quasi manager, Ali. We're back in the training room where we had orientation, though that feels like ages ago. Just like those early days, Matt surprised us all with iced coffees as we arrived.

"You are a godsend," Tiffany says as she lunges for the drink.

Art grabs their drink as well. "So, anyone know why we're here?"

Matt takes a seat next to me, and our closeness gives me that same rush it always does. I feel it every time he's around, whether we're at dinner, passing by each other in the hall outside our dorm rooms, or walking to our designated canvassing areas.

But things aren't the same with us, which infuses this purely amazing feeling with this frustration. At myself. At Sal. At everything that led to things being awkward for us. I still try to show him I care, but Matt says he needs time, and I've respected that. Even if it's eating up the last weeks we have together, I'm willing to wait.

It's obscene how quickly Sal and I fell into our routines, and how quickly I gave up the promise of something new for the familiar comfort of what we had. But that's firmly behind me, for now at least.

"Art and Tiffany can't do dinner tonight," I say. I let the fires of embarrassment run over my face as I form my next sentence. "Would you want to do something instead?"

He considers this, and there's a hint of sadness in his expression that makes me wonder if his mind went right to the picnic he planned with me, because that's definitely where mine went.

"Sure," he says. "We haven't done a one-on-one thing in a while. Maybe no picnic this time, since it's a hundred degrees?"

"I may have something planned," I say with a cringe, "and we may just have to sweat it out."

"Wait, really? You're planning something?"

I shrug. "Guess you'll have to wait and see."

"Well, it won't be hard to beat me breaking multiple plastic forks and having to resort to eating a steak with my hands."

"I promise that whatever happens, you'll have appropriate silverware."

A smile comes over his face, even as his gaze falls. He looks like he wants to say more, but Ali comes in and welcomes everyone back into the training room.

"Hi, everyone!" She's impossibly perky again, but this time I think we're all a little more awake than before. I guess getting up early to get yelled at by strangers has recharged us. That or we've had so much coffee it's built up a caffeine reserve in our bodies.

"I wanted to thank you all for your help. In the past six weeks that you've been out on the street, together you've raised more than twenty thousand dollars for Boston's Save the Trees Foundation. So give yourselves a round of applause."

We do, and for a second I feel super energized that I was a part of that. That Tiffany and I were a part of that.

"As you might know, our Summer Gala is coming up in a month, which will coincide nicely with the end of your experience here. We wanted to let you know that each one of you will get a ticket, as our way to thank you for all your help. We'll even bring you onstage and talk about the program, but I swear we won't embarrass you too much.

"But that leads me to my next announcement. We need a few extra hands in the office to help our fundraising coordinator in advance of the gala—it's a fundraising gala, after all, and we have a lot of big guests on our contact list, and that means a lot of work. We'll be bringing in a few of you to help in the office over the next month based on who was able to get the most donations so far this summer. And for those of you who don't get picked, we're giving you the rest of the day and all tomorrow off as an extra special thank-you."

She pulls out a binder and flips open to the first page. "I'm so pleased to announce that the team with the most donations is Art and Matt!"

We all applaud for them, and I start to enjoy the idea of the rest of the week off, though I worry I'll have even less time with Matt if he's in the office all the time. But then Ali says, "And the second-place team, who will also be joining us in the office for the rest of the internship experience, is Tiffany and Gabe!"

• • •

When Matt opens his door, he looks so cute that there's a very real part of me that wants to lean in for a kiss. Once we got back from the office, or what Ali dubbed double orientation, Tiffany and Art both left straight to their other plans, and we barely had time to change before meeting up.

"You look nice," I say. "I feel like I've seen you in that shirt before."

"I only packed, like, ten shirts, so you've seen it a few times. But it's my favorite. I wore it the first night we met, just like that bad boy." He flicks the center of my tree-hugger shirt and laughs.

"This is our seven-week friendiversary," I say, "so we're obviously just feeling nostalgic."

We walk next to each other, down the street past our usual restaurant, so far that we find ourselves in another neighborhood.

"Do you know where we're going?"

"Just a bit farther. Sorry, we should have grabbed a cab."

"No, no. It's a nice day."

"Matt, it's literally ninety-five degrees and humid. It's not a nice day."

He laughs. "And I'm willing to lie about my comfort levels to you. That has to mean something right?"

I snicker, but think, *Yeah, that actually does have to mean something.* I bat at his hand playfully and lead him up the stairs to a Chipotle.

"Not to offend, but I think we passed four of these on our walk here." He hesitates dramatically. "Is this Chipotle special?"

"Shut up," I say. "You told me you loved Chipotle earlier this week. This isn't the *date* part of the date. That comes after."

We order our food and eat at one of the two-person tables by the window, watching the after-work crowd flood the streets. We don't have much of a conversation, but we talk a little about the new tasks we'll be doing at the internship. We don't know what to expect, but we're both pretty much thrilled that we don't have to be outside anymore this summer.

We head out, and I lead him into a park. This time I've got a packed bag, and just as we start to take the stairs down into a second section of the park, it clicks for him.

"A movie in the park!" he shouts, not unlike a child would. "I've always wanted to do one of these. What are we watching?"

"Okay, don't laugh, but I don't exactly pick the schedule. It's *Jurassic Park*, the original, and it might be awful."

"Oh, a classic. Dad watches it all the time, still. Have you never seen it?"

I shrug. "I haven't, but I'm glad it gets the stamp of approval from your dad."

We set the blanket down, and I pull out a bag of popcorn I

popped just before we left, a couple of cans of Diet Coke, and a few bags of candy.

"I wanted to show you a little bit of what my life is like back in Ohio. There's this drive-in theater we go to a lot, it doesn't matter what's playing, and we all sit in the back of my friend Heath's truck and just hang out. It's one of the things I miss most about being away from Ohio in the summer, but then I saw this and thought it might be fun."

"I'm glad you're letting me in on this tradition, then." He smiles at me, and as the sun goes down, he moves closer to me.

I place my hand on his, just briefly.

"Is this okay?" I ask. "I'm so sorry. There's so much I want to say, but I—"

He places his finger over my lips, and I hush.

"Just tell me this: Are you serious about this? Whatever this even is. I need to know that you're not just messing around. Or if you are, I guess that's fine, but I would still like to adjust my expectations."

"I don't know what this is either, but I can't believe I screwed it up. With Sal, there's a history and it's complicated, and we can talk about all this later. I promise, I'll be honest with you. Just know that, right now, I'm serious about *this*. You're really special, Matt. Whatever this is, I'm all in, and I don't want to waste another minute of this summer."

He leans in and gives me a light kiss. "Then let's just enjoy the movie, and we'll take it one step at time."

CHAPTER FORTY-NINE

SAL

IT'S A DIM, WINDY day in DC, and though the humidity is high, I feel like I can breathe for the first time in weeks. It could be that it's not ninety degrees and sunny for once, and I'm not running from an event venue to the Capitol in a bow tie or something. But it also feels like something's been lifted from me, and that's good.

But things aren't resolved, at all.

April, Josh, and I are returning to the office at ten this morning. I have no idea what to expect when I get back, though I know it won't be the same. When Meghan called me to check in, on my bus ride back from Boston, her tone was delicate, and I knew that whatever I'd done had struck a chord.

Since the weather broke unusually for a July day, I'm just walking the Mall, which is pretty quiet compared to my first time here. Tourists wind around the World War II memorial, and I just walk the loop, my eyes drifting to each pillar. I pass

District of Columbia, Massachusetts, and Ohio, and suddenly feel very homesick.

"Hey, son," Mom says as she answers the phone. "It's been a while. How are you? How was DC for Independence Day?"

I'm glad this isn't a FaceTime, because my face freezes in a seriously awkward position. There is *no way* mom would be cool about my spontaneous trip to Boston. I'll have to come clean to her eventually, but now is just not the time.

"The fireworks were fine," I say, hoping she doesn't press me for details. "I just went back home after."

"How's the senator? You haven't sent me any more pictures to get framed lately!" I hesitate again, but she continues on her own. "Oh, of course, the senate's not in session. He was probably right out the door after the Fourth."

"Yep, he was at his lake house in Michigan with the kids all week," I say, then feel super weird about knowing so much about this guy's personal life. "No clue when he's getting back, though. I actually have to tell you something about the internship, but I need you to listen, and not get mad."

"Oh no. What did you—"

"Mom, you need to listen. And maybe dissect why your first response was to assume *I* did something wrong." Before she says anything else, I launch into the story of how I fell into this bonkers full-time job on the Hill with little to no training, and how major miscommunications led to me being overworked and all three of us being underappreciated.

By the time I finish, I'm about halfway between the Washington

Monument and the Capitol. Each step heightens my anxiety some, but I need to go through with it. I need to walk through those doors and finish this experience the right way.

"I'm calling Betty. This is not okay. You should have told someone right away—"

"I was just trying to keep my head above water and do a good job. But I did tell Meghan, eventually. It just took some convincing from April and Josh. And, Mom, Betty *knows*. The senator knows. Meghan made it very clear when she called me back in that everyone knows they messed up, and they're trying to fix it."

"I'm still going to call her. I don't want Betty thinking I knew about this."

I release a dry laugh and stop in my place. I'm staring at the Capitol steps, and a part of me can't believe Mom's worried about how *she* might look.

"Really?" My voice squeaks. "That's why you're worried? Because it might make you look bad? Typical."

"I raised you better than that," she says with a scoff. "You know I'm very upset about what happened to you."

"I've heard that before!" I shout. "The last day of school, you tried to reassure me that you were upset about me, but what exactly did you do to fix it? Remind me. Did that asshole not call me and Reese faggots—"

"Don't say that word—"

I raise my voice as I say, "—and threaten to hit me *to my face* before graduating *with honors* that very weekend? Was there really nothing you could do?"

"Oh, Sal, that was an entirely different issue. There was nothing I *could* do. He wasn't a student anymore."

"Did you even try, though? Did you have to smile when you shook his hand at graduation? Did you really, honestly have to brush it under the rug that quickly?"

For once, she's silent, and I have the answer I already knew.

"What you don't get is that fifty people who watched that happen now know they can do the same thing and get away with it. You don't know how *fucking* dangerous that is." She starts to speak, but I talk over her. "Call Betty so you can clear your name. I have work to do."

My cheeks are on fire, and as I hang up I see April and Josh sitting outside the entrance by Capitol South. I pause to tie my bow tie in the reflection of a car window and join them.

"How was Boston?" Josh asks.

"You missed one hell of a fireworks show," April says. "Meghan got us tickets so we could sit in the stands. Each office only gets a couple, so she basically called every other senator to ask if they had anyone going on vacation. It was an adequate peace offering."

"Boston was . . . necessary. But now I'm jealous, so thanks for that," I say with a light laugh. I'm still a little shaky from snapping at my mom, but trying to start something new, something better with April and Josh for this last month, is worth the work.

"It looks like we're going to be split up," Josh says. "April basically grilled Meghan on the plan, and she's going above and beyond to make us happy, so she told her everything."

"God, that woman means well." April shakes her head. "She's

only five years older than me—my eighteenth birthday was last week, while you fled the district, by the way. She seemed so old and mature when we started, but, yeah. She may be a killer scheduler, but she has no idea what she's doing when it comes to managing interns."

"She's really hard to hate," I add. "Like, she would make me stay until eight at night and not realize that I was about to collapse from exhaustion, but then she'd really make me feel appreciated. Like I single-handedly saved the campaign every time. But anyway, they're splitting us up?"

"I know, and we were all *so* close," Josh jokes, which earns him an elbow in the ribs from April.

"Betty Caudill is *pissed*. She and two other members of Congress got together and created a new monthlong high school internship program from scratch. We'll actually have mentorship, we'll learn about *all* the roles in the office, and we won't just get yelled at by strangers and watch you and Meghan dash off to meetings anymore."

"I think you're with Betty," Josh says. "But we'll find out soon. I'm just so glad this is going to be a real thing. You know I never got to actually meet Senator Wright? I was in the bathroom the one time he came to the office and had time to say hi."

"And I was on the phone," April says. "So. I got the world's fastest handshake, and that was it."

"Sorry I didn't come forward earlier," I say. "You were obviously right, but I was just clinging to this experience like it was going to define my future or something."

April shrugs. "It's fine. It's hard to be angry with someone who's such a mess."

"What she means is," Josh says before sending a glare her way, "*you* weren't the one who screwed us over."

"I'll take that," I say as we make our way toward the entrance.

We stand at the doors, and I know everything will change as I step through them. And I'm so *fucking* ready for it.

GOLDEN BOYS

Good news, I said the f-word on the phone with my mother earlier today. **S**

G … which f word?

Oh god.

Both, actually. **S**

H You know you're allowed to say fuck in the group chat right?

R Come to think of it, I don't think *I've* even heard you say those words out loud.

G What happened babe?

I told her about me being overworked and everything that went down, and she said she had to tell Betty that she didn't know. I literally saw red, it was just like what happened the last day of school.

Did you flip a table this time?

I wanted to. But I did tell her how her not even trying to punish that jackass sets an awful precedent and that she basically failed as a mother and as a vice principal. That felt good

YES EXACTLY

Good for you!

Thanks, Sal.

CHAPTER FIFTY

HEATH

IT TAKES ALL MY energy to stay normal in the group chat. When real-life me is spending most of his days in bed sulking. I kind of hate the person I've become over the past couple of weeks. I don't shame myself for kissing Cole—I mean, he's cute and sweet, and in that moment, I knew I wanted him to be my first kiss.

And I doubt that was just the wine talking.

Reese is complicated and delicate and beautiful, but Cole is simple. It's like how Gabriel described his semirelationship with Sal: easy, fun, but ultimately, not real. I wanted something that wasn't real, something distracting. But I don't want to be distracted anymore.

As I'm zoning out, Diana barges into the room, which makes me jump.

"Didn't walk in on anything, did I?" she says bluntly. "Assumed you'd be too sad to be doing anything *unsavory*."

She sits at the foot of the bed and hands over the crumpled Dunkin' bag in her hand and an iced coffee.

"Here," she says, and the sincerity in her voice wavers. It's always felt tricky to have a deep, serious friendship with her. She turns anything sincere into a quick sarcastic joke, and I have a feeling it'll take years for me to fully break down those walls she puts up. But this feels like progress. She usually balances levity with her more serious moments, but this time she doesn't.

So I set the coffee on the side table and tear into the bag of doughnuts.

"Oh, I was expecting the Diana special, a maple and a strawberry."

"I absolutely polished those off on the walk over here. I remember you saying you liked the chocolate doughnut holes, and you ... well, you eat a lot, so hopefully I got you enough."

I smile at her, and she doesn't turn away. "Thanks, Cuz."

"You have to promise me one thing, though," she says as I raise the first doughnut hole to my mouth.

"It's been two weeks, Heath. You have to say *something* to Reese, and you have to find a way to snap out of this. Give him a call. Something. *Anything*. If you don't, I'm taking back the doughnuts and I'm eating every single one in front of you."

"You're evil," I say.

She shrugs. "I'm not even hungry, but I'd do it just to punish you. That's how much I care."

I agree to her terms, and enjoy every last one of the doughnut holes, savoring my final moments of sulking. I don't know if I can actually commit to saying something to Reese, but it's worth trying. Diana and I talk about Cole, and how I hope things won't be awkward when we next see each other. I haven't seen him since the party, and at this point Diana must've told him about my feeling too sorry for myself to even hit the beach.

Diana leaves, and I put myself together. Shower, shave, and I even style my hair. I put on the tank top I got when I first showed up here, at the beach shop where Cole works, and just stare at myself in the mirror.

My hair's become a little lighter; my tan's deepened substantially—and this time without all the trademark baseball-practice tan lines. At first glance, I feel like a new human, but I also know I'm the same person. The only thing that's changed, the only thing that *matters*, is that I might have lost my best friend. And I can't let that happen.

I sit on the couch and start to draft the perfect text. Then I think a FaceTime might be better, but he probably wouldn't answer, so I think maybe we can go old-school with a lengthy email? Or maybe I can just shout "I LOVE YOU" in a voice message and turn off my phone until the embarrassment subsides or I have to move back to Ohio, whichever comes first.

"Heath!" Jeanie comes in with a giant iced sweet tea in her hands and takes a seat next to me. "You're up—you're human again! How are we feeling?"

"Did Diana tell you what happened?" I ask quietly.

"Some of it, though I don't think I got the whole story. She said you were upset about your mom finally moving out and your dad getting that apartment in your town. I talked to her recently, just to check in. Seems like she's happy."

"I wasn't upset about . . . ," I start, but I don't know if revealing to her what happened with Cole and Reese would do anything at this point.

But the more I think of it, the more I realize, yeah, it actually has hurt to see my mom leave our house, our hometown. To see Dad move out of our big farmhouse into that tiny apartment. It's been hard seeing pictures of moving boxes, FaceTiming with my dad as he set up my bed in the smaller bedroom.

Shit, Diana's not even lying to Jeanie. I *am* upset about it.

"It's hit me in weird ways," I finally say. "Like, I've had to be perky and normal with my dad, because it's hitting him really hard and I don't know how to deal with him being emotional. And I had a falling out, or something, with one of my friends. I think that kind of made the whole thing collapse."

"Yeah, I think Diana picked up on that. She's weirdly perceptive." She pauses. "I mean, a self-centered disaster at times, but sweet and perceptive too. I love that girl."

"She's great. You both are, really. I hate everything that's happening back in Ohio, but I'm glad I got to hang out with you and help with the arcade, even if I've burned a lot of corn dogs."

She pulls me into a hug, and I wrap my arm around her too. It feels like an invitation, like the ground is shifting beneath me. Before I even try to fix this mess with Reese, I need to accept my new reality. Holidays might look different, and our apartment might be small, and I might never stop missing that old house, but

I've also gained a lot too. My mom's in New Mexico, my dad's in Ohio, and my aunt and cousin are in Florida. I have family all over the country, and I think, with some work, I can learn to love and appreciate it for what it is: something special that only I have.

I tell Jeanie I'll be ready to work tonight, then say I'm going to take a walk to the beach. I've got no clue what'll happen once I get back to Ohio, but I feel hopeful. And it's been a long time since I could say that.

My mind drifts back to the beach party, standing next to Cole, watching the fire. The way he told me how he wanted to kiss me was so direct, so easy. Maybe it doesn't have to be so complicated with me and Reese. Maybe it doesn't have to be all quiet gestures or words with hidden meaning.

I pull out my phone and FaceTime Reese, and I pray that he'll pick up.

Please, pick up.

CHAPTER FIFTY-ONE

REESE

TODAY'S THE DAY WE turn in our final projects. The only issue? I haven't finished mine. I've already made my peace with the fact that I won't be having this dress produced for *any* runway. Objectively speaking, Philip's design deserves to be on, like, real runways. Right now.

Next week Professor Watts will present the designs to the class and we'll get our final critiques from her.

Also next week, my moms come for their visit, and thankfully Philip helped me put together this brilliant—his word, not mine—itinerary for their time in France. We'll hop to the UK after that, and they want me to pick the last location. Mom's draining all her saved airline points from her work travel over the years, so they're open to going wherever I want.

I'm excited for London, but I also want to go home. But it feels ungrateful to throw an opportunity like this away. I keep looking at flights, but the only ones that catch my eye are the ones that lead me back to America.

My journal this week is sparse, to say the least. I've barely had time to write in my daily schedule, let alone find inspirational quotes or sketch anything. Almost all my creative energy's gone into my final project. But right now, at least, I let my brain decompress as I pour myself into the page.

I start sketching my charm bracelet, but as my pencil shades in the charm itself, I realize I'm drawing in Heath's charm. The fire, the stack of wood. I'm feeling altogether homesick, and not just for Ohio, that's for sure.

After a while, I start back on my final project. Every edit I make improves the overall design, so I know it's worth it, but at the end of the day, what's the point? I've learned so much this summer, and the grades for this are mainly pass/fail and barely count. We can all put it on our college applications and feel accomplished or whatever, and life will move on.

I'm feeling a bit cynical about it all, but I do know that I learned a lot, so I hold on to that.

I'm a competitive person, but I also know when I'm beat. And that's okay. Philip and I have managed to salvage most of this summer, and I guess I feel okay with what happened with Heath and that guy. In fact, it's set me free in a way. I've been trapped in this pointless crush for so long, that I can finally . . .

My phone vibrates, and I lose my train of thought completely. It's him. *Shit.*

I realize that everything I've been telling myself was an entire lie as I scramble to the mirror and take a few deep breaths before answering the call. I can't avoid this anymore, can I? Maybe he's calling to check in. Maybe he's calling to tell me about his new boyfriend. I don't know. But whatever it is, I have to answer.

Right now.

His face lights up the screen, and I smile, despite myself. He's walking on the beach, wearing a tight-fitting tank top, and I can see his cheeks glistening with sweat. He smiles when he sees me, so sweetly, that it's almost like it was before. But I guess that makes sense, because to him, basically nothing has changed. I don't know if he even knows I saw what happened.

"Hey, Hea—" I start, but he launches in with, "I love you."

The world stops. He's said those words before, but he's so desperate this time that it almost sounds like . . .

"Reese, I'm sorry. I had a speech planned, and it wasn't supposed to start with that," he says, wiping the sweat—or is it tears?—from under his eyes. "I feel so stupid about what I did, and I hate that you had to see it. And honestly? I wanted to see what it was like, what Gabriel and Sal can do, something distracting and fun with no strings attached, but I don't want that. I want you, and I want complicated, and I want all the strings attached."

"Heath," I say. Memories of him kissing that guy flash in my mind, and I can't make them stop, but he's saying these words. To *me*. "I can't believe you're actually saying these things."

"I'm sorry, I keep cutting you off because I'm nervous, I don't mean to, but I wanted you to know how I feel. How I've felt this for so long, but I'd never let myself think about it because I didn't want to mess up our friendship. And then you were going to France, and I felt like I couldn't compete with that. And you have this huge family, while mine in small and fractured." He pauses, and I let him keep going because I still have *no clue what to say to all of this*. "I couldn't admit that I liked you. I couldn't . . . depend on you to be my family. I mean, you are, you all are my family, but I needed to be okay on my own before I even let myself realize how special you were to me. I know it's selfish, but I wasn't there earlier. I wasn't ready then. But I'm there now."

I feel tears slipping down my cheek, as wave after wave of homesickness hits me. I know now, I'm homesick for *him*. Maybe that image of him kissing that guy won't go away for a while, and yes, it hurt me, but like Philip told me, just because I was hurt doesn't mean what he did was wrong. But here he is apologizing anyway.

What he's saying now is so right. Everything I've wanted to hear from him for so long.

"This changes everything, doesn't it?" I say quietly. I want to tell him how I love him too, but I also need to think. "You don't know how long I've been waiting for you to say something like this. I care so much about you, Heath. I need some time to think about it, though. I forgive you, and you don't even have to apologize for any of it. I just need to get to a place where I can think of you and not have flashbacks to that moment. I don't judge you for doing it, but I need some time to think."

"Anything you need," he says. I know he means it, but I feel his voice deflate.

The red-colored pencil in my hand starts to tremble, and as I see his face, ideas for my design start coming to me.

"Thank you for calling me; you have . . . no idea how much this all means. And I really hate to say this, but I have to finish my project," I say. "It's actually inspired by fire. By you. How you've made me feel over the years. How I think of you. Can I send it to you once I'm done?"

"I'm honored. Yeah, send it to me please," he says, and I can tell it's improved his mood some.

"Thank you for saying all of that." I smile at him. "I miss every fucking thing about you right now. I just need some time."

I glance at my design as I hang up the phone. He was once such a gentle flame, the embers that cover my design. But he's a flamethrower now. A mix of warmth and desperation and passion like I've never seen. I look at the time and realize I have an hour to make some substantial edits, but I can see it.

For the first time in a while, I've found my inspiration.

MON
_____

TUES
_____

WED
_____

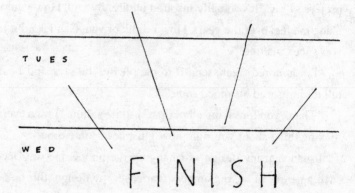

FINISH

THUR
_____

PROJECT !!

FRI
_____

SAT / SUN
_____

• PB Allergy •

GABRIEL + HEATH + SAL

Ok I may have screwed up our friend group for the rest of time, but I think it was worth it.

G ???

I..... told Reese I love him **H**

S You WHAT?

OH MY GOD HEATH!!!!!!

G You did it!!!!

How are you feeling?
What did he say? **S**

I'm feeling good. Relieved...
he said he needed some time
to process what I was saying...
idk, it's complicated.

Love usually is

CHAPTER FIFTY-TWO

REESE

THE REST OF MY time in Paris was a whirlwind. As soon as my parents landed, we snapped into tourist mode, seeing as many landmarks, museums, and restaurants as we could in our short time there.

But now, as our train pulls into King's Cross Station in London, it really hits me that I won't be back in Paris for a long time. Those weeks went slowly, but my time there was really just a blip on the radar. A couple months might be a small, insignificant amount of time, but it was majorly significant for me.

When I step off the train, I check my phone. An email's just popped up, so I click quickly to open it.

"It's here," I say.

"Oh! Your final project feedback?" Mamma asks. "Do you know which design was picked for the runway?"

I skim the email, which is fairly short, and see the answer

quickly. As expected, my design was not chosen. But Philip's was, and that makes me feel incredibly proud. I skim the notes, actually eager to dig into them for once. Professor Watts was thrilled with the new direction and the vibrancy of this fire design, and I'm excited to learn and grow from her feedback.

"They picked Philip," I say. "She liked my design, though. I'm going to call and congratulate him."

I find a somewhat quiet corner of the station, and almost as soon as I start the call, he answers.

"Reese!" he shouts. "I'm sorry you didn't get picked, mate."

"Oh please," I say. "This was yours to win, and you know it. You totally deserved it. I am so happy for you!"

"I can't believe something I designed is going to be on a real runway. It's . . . wow. I'm chuffed, truly." He sighs. "You make it into London?"

"Yep, I'm officially in your lovely country. We have reservations at all the places you and Emily suggested. It's going to be a blast."

I wish Philip were back in the UK so I could celebrate with him. Unfortunately, he's spending the last month of his summer in Paris with his girlfriend, and they're soaking up as much of the culture as they can.

And I'm going home too, finally, after one enormous pit stop.

"I've got to go," I say. "Promise me you'll send me hundreds of pictures when your dress hits the runway, okay?"

"Right. Goodbye, Reese." He hesitates. "I'll miss seeing you around every day."

"I'll miss you too. Now go celebrate—you deserve it!"

Once I hang up, I join my parents. I send the group chat a picture of King's Cross to let them know I'm okay, and the others reply right away with reactions and various utterings of jealousy. If there's one thing about this trip I do like, it's how much FOMO it's causing my friends. Bless their hearts.

Heath texts me on the side to tell me how excited he is for me to tear up London, then asks me where I'm going next. **Prague? Copenhagen? Berlin?** He keeps asking these in separate texts, so my phone won't stop vibrating.

"I wouldn't have added you onto our weeklong international phone plan if I knew you'd just be calling and texting your friends this whole time," Mamma says.

Mom nudges her. "Right, like you haven't been texting pictures to your sisters this whole time."

"Oh, that's different."

"Is it?" I ask, and she pauses.

"No, I guess it isn't. Fine, we'll *both* put our phones away. Deal?"

I agree, and Mamma leads us on a whirlwind sightseeing tour. It's been a while since she studied abroad here, but there's surprisingly a lot she still remembers. We see so many sides of the city—the supremely touristy regions, open markets bursting with food, shows in the West End at night, and we even see a cute guy playing the hell out of his oboe on the London Underground, which was a standout to me.

"Reese, one day you'll see that there's so much more to this world than we see in Ohio." Mamma puts her arm around me. "I hope you take more of these opportunities. I know they're scary, and you didn't have the easiest time, but you learned so much."

"I learned a lot this trip, so I believe you."

"And I have so many clothes I need you to alter and patch up once you get back," Mom says. "We're really going to get our money's worth of that sewing machine we got you."

"All this learning and culture aside," Mamma says, "I still don't get why you picked *Orlando* as your final stop on what was supposed to be an international tour."

I laugh. "I'm ready to get back to the states. And you've been promising me a Disney World trip for years, and we're basically out of summers to do it over."

Plus, it's only an hour and a half away from Heath.

Diana thinks she can get him to come up, and she's assured me that this will be the most epic surprise that's ever happened. Heath loves surprises, but I hope he appreciates this one.

Because, obviously, I do love him. So much. I just have to say that to his face. After all this time, after all we've been through as friends, I need to say it to his face. I need him to wrap me in the biggest hug of my life, so I can just melt into him and stay like that forever.

But one thing at a time. And the next thing on my list? Enjoying the hell out of London.

CHAPTER FIFTY-THREE

SAL

CONGRESSWOMAN BETTY CAUDILL IS a fully manifested fire. She never seems to run out of energy; she always knows her shit. She's able to recall names of people she's only met once or twice in passing, which I've seen on numerous occasions. Her scheduler and chief of staff act similarly to Meghan—overworked, overwhelmed, but intensely focused—but Betty picks things up way faster than the senator, and it's like she executes every movement with clear intention.

This also means she's never scared to turn back and talk to me while we're walking the halls. To stop when I'm not fully getting something, and to push me to ask questions rather than what I had to do a lot for Meghan—try to keep my head above water, do as I was told, and hope to god I didn't mess anything up.

I see April and Josh in the hall from time to time—I'm on the House side of the building now, which isn't too different in looks but captures a scrappier energy—and they're learning just as much in their experiences as I am. Finally. *Finally!*

"Dahlia, can you spend today talking with Sal about the campaign process? I want him to get a full idea of what it's like to work on a campaign, as I think he might like that side of things."

She nods. "Of course. Maybe we can break for a quick lunch, then I'll have our scheduler clear our boardroom for the next couple of hours."

I thank her and bid Betty good luck with her upcoming vote. And I'm on my own for the next hour. I quickly eat my lunch, which is just a boring ham and cheese sandwich, and then decide to take a walk. My strides here are shorter, slower than they were when I worked with Meghan, but I feel my heart race every time I walk these halls.

It's like a strange memory grips me and makes me feel like I'm late for something, or I'm screwing something up. I know now there are good work environments here as well as unhealthy ones. And I just found my way into one that was underprepared and over, overwhelmed.

When I make it to the Senate side, though, my pace quickens. I adjust my collar and my bow tie, and I confidently stride through Senator Wright's doors. Jenna notices me right away and throws me an awkward wave, then comes around to the front to see what I need. She ushers me back into the empty intern space where I spent so many hours. That back room with Meghan's office and the one round table. Meghan spots me, and she spins her chair around quickly.

"Hey," I say. "Hope you don't mind me dropping by."

"Of course not. How is it with Congresswoman Caudill?" If she's feeling awkward, she's definitely not showing it. "I hear she's got a great team."

"She does, she does. I'm learning a lot! How are you doing? Has it calmed down any?"

She laughs. "I don't think it ever calms down. I always tell myself that, like, after X happens, or after the Y meeting is over, that's when I'll be able to catch up. But I can't catch up. As you got to witness firsthand."

"Oh yeah, I picked up on that. I lost hope pretty early on, just thought I could put my head down and work through it." I take a seat and avoid eye contact. "I have to ask, Did you get in trouble? I feel bad."

This makes her shift uncomfortably, but she spins around fully and crosses her legs. She's got this casual look, but also one like she's got to defend herself.

"I did, sort of. Nothing formal—though I definitely would have if word would've gotten out anywhere beyond Betty. But I should have known what I was doing was wrong."

I nod, then tell her, "If it helps, I *did* learn a lot. And it was an experience I will definitely never forget."

"Well, I hope you keep learning with Betty." She shrugs coolly, and her gaze passes over all the college alumni paraphernalia on the walls. "For what it's worth, I think you'll figure out how to make a career out of this if college isn't your thing. It's not going to be easy, but from what I've learned about you, you're quick and determined. Just don't push yourself too hard. That breakdown you had? I think we've all been there. I'm trying to figure out a balance myself, because the only alternate is to transfer out of politics forever, and I don't want that."

I promise her I'll keep it in mind, and I begin to see a future without college standing in the way. Reese sends me a text as I walk back, and I jump when I see the notification.

Your mom is in the news, he says, and drops in a link to our local TV station's website. The article's title, "Gracemont High School Board Passes Motion to Require Anti-LGBTQ-Bullying Training for Teachers," strikes fear into my heart. When there are so few queer teens in our school, a news story like this might as well single us out. Unease washes over me, as I wonder exactly how my mom is involved in this.

I dive into the article, slowly picking up that the school board drafted and passed a measure that trains all staff on how to handle all anti-LGBTQ bullying, but also promises stronger punishments for bullies—including, in some cases, losing their right to walk for graduation. The measure was introduced and lobbied for by the vice principal. My mom.

When I reach the boardroom, I feel myself start to tear up. My mom and I have never had the sort of bond that Gabriel has with his, but so much of her energy has gone into preparing me for a life outside Gracemont. She just didn't realize that by only focusing on the future, she forgot to really pay attention to the present.

Right at one p.m., Dahlia steps into the office with a few bound handbooks. I look to each one, and their titles pop out to me: *Legislative Strategy, Allies and Coalitions, Media & Communications.*

I reach for the communications plan first, and Dahlia laughs.

"Thought you might want to look at that one," she says. "Your mom's the one who wrote it, after all."

CHAPTER FIFTY-FOUR

GABRIEL

THOUGH I'M SURE THIS is nothing like what Sal went through, working in the Save the Trees Foundation office has been *a lot*. It seemed like we had so many days leading up to the end-of-summer gala, but three weeks just evaporated in the blink of an eye.

Though she's a little high-strung, we're all basically obsessed with our new boss, Laura. She brings coffees in for us every day, and she leads with motivation and a more authentic energy than we're used to seeing around here. She's got this compassion that seems to resonate with donors based on how quickly she can secure big checks—I'm talking checks with a lot of zeros—but she also has this super-logistical side that she employs whenever she needs to flip into gala-event-planner mode.

We've all got different jobs, ones that are all a little more well suited to our strengths, and for that I am grateful. I would gladly work harder if it means escaping the awkward conversations on the streets.

"How are we going to fit another donor table in the ballroom?" Tiffany asks, partially to herself, partially to the rest of us in the little intern bay we've all been shoved into.

"Treat my clients well," Art says with a hint of satisfaction in their voice.

"Just because you guilted them into buying out another table doesn't make them your clients," she snaps back. "We have a partially open one in the back that we could move, but then your *dear clients* would be split across the room. We can't move this group, because they're all speakers. We can't move all of Deloitte back, because they're our biggest corporate sponsor. This is an impossible puzzle."

"We'll figure it out," Laura says calmly while putting her hand on Tiffany's shoulder. "Let's wait until we hear back from Matt's last two calls today. We might have to completely redraw this map, but it's a good problem to have, because that means we've gotten more donations than we had last year."

Art's taken over a few corporate calls. Though Laura's focusing on new leads herself, Art's proven that they are great at upselling, so she's having them go back to see if we can squeeze a few more pennies out of those accounts.

Tiffany's one request was that she didn't want to talk to people. Which is a hard job to find when we've essentially become a volunteer phone bank. But she's logical and extremely organized, which made her a perfect fit for her task: assisting the event planner to make sure the logistics of the gala go off without a hitch.

Matt, who was easily the best at getting people's attention—and their wallets—when canvassing on the street, gets to cold-call some potential donors. Which means he's basically calling up rich people every day. In a matter of minutes, he's able to match the donations we all got as a group over the past two months. When Laura heard Art say it made the grassroots stuff seem pointless, she explained that canvassing is as much about brand awareness and cause awareness as it is about getting donations.

But me? I have the best job of them all, though I think everyone feels a little bit sorry for me. Once a corporation or a donor comes through with a donation, I get to handwrite thank-you notes. Now, I might not have the design aesthetic that Reese does, but I can write a mean thank-you note. Each one is well researched, personal, and (I hope) sends a heartfelt message from the organization. No form letters here.

People keep donating to organizations when they feel personally connected to them, and I think that's something I can do well. Reaching people personally? Totally up my alley. Reaching strangers to shout at them about the trees? Not so much.

Before this is all over, I hope to talk to Laura more about non-profit fundraising, and I can see what she thinks about a career in it.

As we leave for the day, Matt and I link arms as we walk back to the dorms. Our time here is running short, but we haven't spoken about it just yet. We're back to where we were before . . . before I messed it all up.

"Why don't we go see another movie after dinner tonight?" I ask. "We can invite Tiffany and Art too."

"Only if we take a cab this time," Matt says with a laugh. "What are they showing this week? Something romantic?"

He gives me a goofy look, and I roll my eyes. "Very romantic. *Jaws*, I think."

"That park really has a brand. Spielberg movies featuring sharp teeth."

He walks me to my room, and I hesitate outside my door.

I lean in for a kiss and let my lips linger on his for a moment.

"Will you come in? I don't think the others will let us make out in front of them tonight, so I'd like to, um, get some of that time in now."

"Prudes," he scoffs, then pulls me in tightly for another kiss. "Absolutely."

As I lead him into the room and lead him onto the bed, I feel . . . right. I came here to become a new person, but all I really needed to do was find the person who was hiding inside me all along.

CHAPTER FIFTY-FIVE

HEATH

DIANA, COLE, AND I share a beach blanket, not unlike all those other days in my first month here, but with one substantial change: it's *awkward*. Diana told Cole about everything, and now I'm a little too embarrassed to look his way. But every once in a while, he'll do something sweet. Every time we hang out now, he'll bring an ice-cold Gatorade (blue, my favorite flavor) to the beach for us to share, and once, he got me a bag of souvenirs from the beach shop he works at that were being thrown out for being minorly chipped and unsellable, for my friends and family back home.

I don't need these things, but it reminds me why I felt so comfortable with him. When Diana runs to the arcade to use the bathroom, I take this opportunity to say something.

"Cole—"

"Hey, I wanted to—"

We both stop, then laugh at the awkward silence between us.

"You first," he says.

"I'm so sorry I ghosted you. I know Diana told you why, but it's kind of shitty to make out with someone, then fully ignore them for two weeks."

"Officially speaking, it is shitty. But I don't know, man, I get it. I was really bummed when you stopped coming to the beach, though. You're fun."

I blush at his direct compliment. Sure, I was able to bluntly tell Reese that I loved him, but I've got to get better about saying exactly what I mean. Something Cole *and* Diana are pros at.

"You're fun too, Cole," I say. It's a start.

"Also—and don't tell Diana I said this—I think you've made her a more thoughtful person," he says. "The other day, I forgot to bring down cash and she actually offered to split her pizza with me."

"She bought me doughnuts last week." I laugh. "I don't think it had anything to do with me, though. Aunt Jeanie has been talking about how much more helpful she's been all summer. Maybe she's just in a better mood lately?"

" *. . . because of you.* She finally has family around she can depend on who's not just her mom. Of all people, you must know what it's like." He sighs. "That boy you like? She's been texting with him a lot. She feels bad about the whole FaceTime thing, but she really wants to make you happy."

He scoots over and puts an arm around me. "We both do. I don't know how this would work, with you living in the middle of nowhere and me continuing my glamorous beach life, but I hope we can stay friends. This has been a fun summer."

I lean my head into his, and I savor this rare, platonic physical moment that for once isn't hinting at more.

"Okay, some ground rules: only *I* get to cuddle with Cole." Diana comes up behind us and forces us apart. "Did I witness some sort of makeup, though? Like, will things stop being weird?"

My gaze locks onto Cole's, and I smile.

"Yeah, we're done being weird."

• • •

While Diana and Jeanie take the night shift, I go to pick my truck up from the repair shop. A part of me feels sick for dropping six hundred dollars on a few fixes, but I still have a nice chunk of money in my savings to get me through the next school year.

As I pull out of the garage, I hit a speed bump going onto the main street and brace myself for the harsh impact, but my ancient truck just glides smoothly over it. I imagine Reese in the passenger seat and smile. It's about time I stopped throwing him into the roof.

I take a drive through Daytona, past Cole's beach shop, down side roads into the more residential areas, and back into the shopping districts. When I see a grocery store, a memory sparks, and I pull in. I start writing down a recipe in my phone, but I know I'm missing so many ingredients. I've been avoiding this moment, but I've finally thought of something I can do for Jeanie as a thank-you for this time here. I just need to get over myself and call Mom.

"Heath! How are you, baby?" Mom says, and my heart thrums at hearing her voice. It's hard not to blame her for all this—which, to be fair, is mostly her fault—but now that I've looked back on this experience as something that was surprisingly good for me, I can face her.

"I'm good," I say. "Just got the truck fixed and took it out for a spin. How's Santa Fe?"

"Oh!" she replies, and I wonder if me even asking about her well-being is surprising at this point. "Pat and I are all settled in. You'll love the place when you get to come visit. Maybe for one of your breaks next year. They have this baseball team here that I think you should look up. The whole league is independent, and they all play in high-altitude cities in the southwest. Ever heard of anything like that?"

"I haven't," I say. "But that sounds cool. I'll look it up. Hey, you always said Aunt Jeanie liked those family cabbage rolls we used to make, right?"

She pauses. "Oh yeah, Jeanie loved 'em but hated making them. She wouldn't touch raw meat to save her life. Probably still won't."

"I want to make them for her as, like, a thank-you. They won't be as good, but I'm hoping you can give me the recipe, if you have it. I'm at the store now."

"Oh, honey, I have that down by heart. Just go in the store and I'll walk you through it." She pauses. "You're right, it's the least we can do for Jeanie. I keep telling her she can't keep living off those corn dogs she makes at her restaurant, but you know she never listens to me."

I don't want to get into why they've been more or less estranged for my whole life, so I redirect the conversation back

348

to the cabbage rolls. It's an eastern European recipe that's been passed down by Jeanie and Mom's grandma. We have a small family that feels like it has no connection, but it's really nice to think that I have a shot at reclaiming one of our traditions.

The next day, I get up at four a.m. to start making the cabbage rolls, which is just after Diana and Jeanie have gone to sleep. I get out the necessary pans and remove my secret bag of groceries from the fridge. I chop and dice away according to Mom's instructions and try to remember how this works.

" . . . the fuck are you doing?" Diana asks. I turn and see her bleary eyes. The light smell of stale beer and deep-fat fryer oil clings to her as she joins me in the kitchen.

"It's a surprise for Aunt Jeanie," I say in a whisper. "Her grandma's—our great-grandma's—cabbage rolls. But they have to cook for hours."

"Oh! Mom's talked about these before," she says slowly, like she's trying to recall a buried memory. "I think one of the things she loved most about them was the parties the family would have. Granny would invite all her friends from that one Hungarian church she went to, and they'd spend all day making these rolls and bickering over the ingredients."

She washes her hands and takes over the dicing while I boil the cabbage leaves. We work in tandem, me telling her what to do based off a hair of a memory and Mom's not-so-detailed notes.

"Your truck's back," she says. "How's it running?"

"So great. I actually think I'll be able to get home at this rate. It almost exploded on the way here."

"I remember," she says with a laugh. "Hey, do you want to go for a little road trip next week? I scored us some tickets to Disney World and a few people will be meeting up there, but I have no car. Orlando's only about an hour away."

"Oh wow, sure!" I say. "I've always wanted to go. How'd you get the tickets?"

She shakes her head. "I've got my ways. I just hope you're ready—they call it the happiest place on earth for a reason."

Eventually, our conversation lulls, and we enjoy the silence. We work together, and as we stuff and roll the cabbage, fill up the pot with rolls, and cover the kitchen in paprika . . . I think that's something that our great-grandma would approve of. And for once, I feel actually, truly, connected to my family.

CHAPTER FIFTY-SIX

SAL

"SAL?" THE PRESS ASSISTANT for Congresswoman Caudill pops her head into the office I'm working in today. "Ready for the interview?"

I nod and stand. I've got a blazer on, but under it is the paisley shirt and gray bow tie I wore when I met Betty just before coming down here. It's an outfit I've never worn on the Hill, because truthfully it *is* a little loud for this office. Every once in a while, we'll see a congressman walking the halls in a linen or seersucker suit, but otherwise it's all dark suits, light shirts, maybe a funky tie if they're feeling wild.

I won't be leaving this internship experience with anymore clarity about my future than I had when I went into it, but I think it's still been good. I'm ready to get back to school, see the guys, and have one hell of a senior year. And since I won't have to worry about college applications, that gives me a little bit more time.

Though, of course, I'll have to actually tell my mom I'm not going to college. But I'm going to push that nightmare convo off as long as I can.

The press assistant walks me toward one of their interview rooms, and she gives me a cautious smile.

"Do you know what you're going to say?"

"Not exactly," I say with a smile. "But don't worry. Congresswoman Caudill has made this an enriching-enough experience that I can barely remember why we ended up making that little office change."

She smiles, then gestures for me to enter the room. I take a seat next to April and Josh, and the assistant lets us know the reporter from *The Hill* will be in shortly.

"Okay, who told?" Josh says, looking down the line at us.

A Republican colleague of Senator Wright's started rumors about the high school internship program that spread like fire on the internet, taking weird turns from valid concerns about the development of this program into questions of child abuse and child labor laws. To quell the rumors, or at least to get something on record, we agreed to talk about our experience with the press.

I laugh. "Not me."

"Me neither," April says. "But it wouldn't have been hard to put together. Senator Wright and his team screwed a lot of this up. The summer wasn't all bad. Maybe it was for Sal, though."

I shake my head. "Whatever. I don't want my name attached to any scandal. And I really do think they should keep this program going, now that Betty took the reins."

"It's settled, then," Josh says. "We lie."

April turns to me and says in a stage whisper, "Guess we know which one of us will end up being a politician."

We're still laughing by the time the reporter comes into the room.

GABRIEL

Our Lyft comes up to the entrance of the gala, and Art, Tiffany, Matt, and I all tumble out of the back seat. We're dressed immaculately in suits and dresses, and it feels a little like last year's prom. The biggest difference is that I have a date for this.

Matt and I hold hands as we walk up and into the gala. Allen, the insufferably chatty guy from our intern group, is helping Laura check people into the event, and within seconds he's talking Matt's ear off about something. Always the savior, Art steps in and grabs Matt by the arm and says, "Oh, I think I see our table!"

They pull us along until we're far enough away, and we all laugh.

"You've got to stop saving Matt like that," Tiffany says.

"I can't help it. He's so helpless. I'd save Laura if I could."

We do find our table—which is easy to do when you walk in

with the girl who designed the seating chart. The others go up to grab a soda and bring some back for us.

Tiffany leans over to me and Matt and whispers, "Two things. One, stop touching so much—you're gross. Two, I have a flask if you want to make this gala a little more interesting."

"What's in the flask?" Matt asks.

"Does it matter?" she replies, and we figure that it really doesn't matter much.

We each practice the art of smoothly pouring alcohol into our drinks and try not to think of what would happen if we got caught. We're volunteers, so they couldn't fire us, but they could kick us out of our own gala, which does seem like a harsh way to end this experience.

We take slow sips of our drink, and more people buzz into the place. The party feels alive, like the fanciest wedding I've ever been to.

I lean over to give Matt a kiss, and ignore Tiffany groaning beside me.

"They've—we've—only got a few days left here," Art says, and their voice is decidedly more somber than it usually is. "Let them kiss."

The buzz of the liquor hits me, just slightly, and I feel the reality of our timeline sinking into me with Art's words. Matt and I keep avoiding the conversation we know we need to have. Three days left, and then we'll be long distance. Or we'll be nothing, I guess.

Matt leans in to kiss me again, noticing my low mood. He says, in this perfect, reassuring voice, "You and me? We've got more than a few days left."

SAL

"The interview went well," I say. "Gotta go, Mom."

After I hang up, I feel a little better about everything. Betty saved my internship experience, and I've learned so much about how politics works. It's a complicated and bizarre arena, and it sounds like there's no one right way through, so I'm hopeful for the future.

It's my last day here, and it's a little late, so when I go back to Betty's office, most of the staff have already left. I return to my packed-up desk with a little thank-you card from the team for my experience here. I smile when I see Betty Caudill's name signed, and I want to ask if I can have a new fancy pen after this—one with her name instead of Senator Wright's.

I pack up my shoulder bag and check that I've got everything, and a sort of overwhelming sadness takes over. I might never make it back here, especially if I choose to not take the "normal" path after this. I might screw up my career even more that way. But I also don't know what I want to do. The only time that I really felt connected to the people during this whole internship is when I picked up the phone and talked to that constituent of Senator Wright's. I want to find a way to work with the people, and I hate that I'll be leaving this internship with more questions than answers.

But it was a successful experience. And I try to hold on to that.

"Sal, do you have a second? I want to have one last chat with you."

I turn to see Betty Caudill in the doorway. I drop my bag and say, "Sure, of course."

I follow her into the conference room and almost freeze when I see who's joined her. Senator Wright's team—Meghan, Pasquale, and the senator himself—all sit around the table.

Briefly, I feel like I'm in trouble, until Meghan gives me a cheery wave. I walk into the office, and Betty shuts the door. The senator clears his throat.

"Sal, it was great meeting you and working with you this summer. I wanted to say I really am sorry for everything that happened, and I was fully ready to take the blame at my interview with *The Hill* today."

"Not *everything*," Pasquale says, which makes the senator laugh.

"No, if I took the blame for everything I'm accused of on Twitter, we'd be here all day. But for overworking you and for taking advantage of your time and effort as an intern? For spearheading this program, then immediately delegating it to my overworked team? Absolutely. I did those things, and that's all on me."

He pauses and looks thoughtfully at me before saying, "However, they came in and explained that their story would downplay the egregious rumors, and that all three of you gave them a wonderful, empowering story about how much you learned over this experience."

"We did learn a lot," I say.

"You could have learned more," he replies firmly. "Anyway, I want you to know that I really do appreciate this. No doubt you've heard the other rumors floating around about me announcing my candidacy for president."

"I saw your name on a few possible lists, of course."

"Those rumors aren't exactly false, though nothing's set in stone yet. We still have a long time before any of this gets announced, and we won't be hitting the ground running and setting up a campaign for a while. But I want you to know that, if the stars align and everything works out, if you'd like to help out in the Ohio base—which will likely be managed by Betty—know you'll always have a spot open on my volunteer staff. Possibly a paid one as well once we get fundraising and talk this over more. I owe you that much."

"Thank you, sir," I say. "Thanks to all of you. I'll be in touch."

"Finish high school, Sal," Meghan says with a smile. "Enjoy the hell out of your senior year."

"I will," I say. "And then we'll make history."

GABRIEL

It was a million degrees at the gala, so it's a relief when the four of us are able to finally sneak out and dart into the fresh air. I loosen my tie and take in a deep breath. I decided to wear one of

Matt's bow ties, mostly so I could send a selfie to the group chat pretending to be Sal, but damn those things are restrictive. I don't know why he likes them so much.

We head into a nearby park and take a long, strolling walk around the dirt path. Matt's hand is clasped to mine, so tightly I think we might never pull apart. Tiffany and Art run to one of the outdoor gym areas for an impromptu pull-up competition (that Tiffany will absolutely crush Art in, but bless them for trying), so Matt and I savor the alone time.

"What did you mean back there, that we have more than a few days left? Are we running away together? Something cinematic like that?"

"Ha, I wish." He smirks. "Unfortunately we've got one more year of school before we can do any running away. But in the meantime, I've been thinking about how we can make this work."

"You have?" I ask, and a smile tugs at my cheek.

"You haven't? Geez."

"Shut up," I say. "I've been in denial about leaving here, so no."

He nods. "Fair enough. Let's think about it, though: I visit my family in Indiana twice a year, for a week at a time. Gracemont is a seven-hour drive from where I live in Jersey. We could handle that, right?"

"We could," I say. "I'd miss kissing you, but you're right, we could."

"And college, we do have a lot of overlap on the schools we want to apply to. I mean, I don't think we should really make this decision based on each other, but if we can do long distance for a year, maybe it's a conversation."

"It's a long shot," I say. "But it really feels doable, doesn't it? Like, we can really make this work."

"I want to try. But if you have hesitations, or if you want to fall back into . . . how things were for you before I was in the picture, I don't want to stop you. We both deserve the best senior years of all time. We shouldn't be adding more stress to it unless we're completely sure."

I look into his eyes and melt at how sincere and eager he is. I kiss him again, just to give my mind some more time to think about the perfect response. Something poetic and charming and perfect that we'll remember forever.

But sometimes these life-changing moments aren't poetic or perfect. Sometimes they're memorable just because they literally change your life. I want to remember this: the hope in his expression, the reflection of the lamppost in his eyes, the laughter of Art and Tiffany in the background.

"Let's make it work, then."

And we kiss, and we kiss, and we kiss like we've got no time left. But really, we have all the time in the world.

CHAPTER FIFTY-SEVEN

REESE

THE RILEY DESIGN SCHOOL sent out one last email to our class, including some early shots of Philip's dress in production. There's a rush of jealousy that hits me, even though I know it's a little immature when I *am* genuinely happy for the guy.

I can't believe it's finally happening! Philip says to me in a text. We've had a message chain going back and forth lazily, but that's not unexpected. We're not seeing each other every day, so it's hard to keep in touch. Especially as my parents just took me on one hell of a trip to London. But I want him to know I'm happy for him, so I respond with a quick, It's looking great so far! Your gran would be proud.

His "typing" dots appear, then disappear, then appear again, and when I think this text might never come through, it finally does.

Thanks, that means a lot. But I wasn't talking about me,

mate. You fly off to Orlando in a couple of hours, right? To profess your love, cinema shit like that?

I laugh, then tell him how nervous I am, and remind him that he shouldn't be thinking of my personal drama right now, not when one of his most exciting career dreams is coming true.

"We're in boarding group two," Mom says. "I can't believe you're actually going to do this."

"I can't believe he picked Florida over Spain," Mamma cuts in sarcastically.

"Don't be like that. It's sweet—he's choosing *love* over a week in the Spanish countryside. You'd have done the same, back when we first started dating."

Mamma pauses, then deflates a bit. "You're not wrong," she says.

"Please stop talking about my love life," I say. "It's really starting to freak me out."

"When you rob your poor old mothers of a Spanish vacation, this is what you get."

We all laugh at that, but shortly after, it's time to board. Diana promised me that Heath's going to be so excited to see me and not to worry at all, and he and I have had some really sweet moments in our calls, FaceTimes, and messages lately. That said, I still worry about what he'll say once he learns the "friends" Diana is meeting up with at Disney World is actually just me.

My mind spirals as I walk down the plane aisles and find my seat. *Will he be happy to see me? Will I be able to tell him that I love him? Can we actually have it all? A perfect friendship and a perfect love?*

I don't know the answers to any of these questions, but one thing's for sure . . . I'll be learning them soon.

HEATH

"Heath," Diana says as she reluctantly takes the last leftover cabbage roll from the fridge, "the next time we make cabbage rolls, can we make fewer than two hundred? They were great to start, but after eating these for a week, I've got to stop."

"Then let me have it," Jeanie says. She fishes in her pocket and pulls out a twenty. "Go get you and Heath some pizza for dinner and leave the good stuff to me. I can't believe I went twenty years without eating these."

I don't admit that the smell of cabbage is really starting to make me nauseous too, but I'm so grateful for the pizza money. We start to head out the door, but Jeanie wraps me in a hug first. "Thank you for making these. I know I've said it a hundred times, but it means the world to me. I called your mom yesterday as I was eating some and made her *so* jealous. It was perfect."

She laughs, and I feel like whatever rift they had before I came here might be healing. Even slightly. I might never know what happened between them, but I also don't care, as long as I can start to bring them together with my (admittedly shoddy) cooking.

Diana and I grab a few slices of pizza on the boardwalk along with sodas the size of my forearm. We snag a bench that faces the water, and the sounds of the boardwalk, the beach, and the ocean all settle into my core and make me feel like I'm home.

I may not have come here looking for family, but I think I came here *needing to find* it, and I did.

"So, the timeline for tomorrow," I say. "We head out around eight, get there by nine, then meet up with your friends around nine thirty?"

She chokes a bit on her pizza. "Yep, that works for me. And my friends."

"Great. Should be fun."

I notice that she avoids my eye contact, so I ask her if she's okay. She sighs.

"Okay, so. You know how I like to meddle in people's love lives?"

I roll my eyes. "I'm aware of that, yeah."

"We're not meeting friends tomorrow. Well, I guess *you* are. There's . . . someone special who will be there. For you."

I pull back, suspicious. One thing I'm not ready to do, weeks after I told Reese I loved him and didn't hear it back, is meet some other person.

"Oh god. Are you trying to set me up with one of your friends or something? I really appreciate the thought, but—"

"No. Heath, come on. I'm a better meddler than that," she says, and I look at her in pure confusion. "Reese will be there. He's coming to Orlando with his family. To see you." She pauses. "And Mickey Mouse, presumably."

I take a deep breath as her words hit me. It almost seems unreal that I might be seeing Reese tomorrow morning. And Reese wants to see me, which means . . .

"What does this mean?" I ask.

"It means he likes you, dummy. So much that he convinced his parents to take him to Disney World. I've been talking to him over the past few weeks. He really wanted it to be a surprise. Or maybe I convinced him that it would be more romantic as a surprise. Can't remember, doesn't matter. But he knew he couldn't wait for you two to get back to Ohio."

I stand up and drop the rest of my pizza into the trash can.

"I've got to go back," I say in a panic.

"What, why?"

"I need to do laundry." I start walking off. "What am I going to wear? This has to be perfect. Oh my god. Should I bring him his souvenirs now? Oh god, all my good tank tops are dirty, I need to do laundry . . ."

"Your *good* tank tops? Can you hear yourself right now?"

"Diana! I love him!"

"I know!"

"Then start freaking out with me!"

She laughs, then stands up in an exaggeratedly tense fashion, trying to mock my intensity. "Okay! Lead the way!"

REESE

"This is really happening, isn't it?" I ask my mom as our bus pulls into the park.

364

I try to ignore the fact that it is incredibly awkward to have your parents come along for something like this, especially when they *know* why we're here to see Heath. But he's family. My parents love him; my whole family does. And they know how special he is to me. So maybe it actually feels right that they're along for the ride.

Though by the cheeky jokes Mamma keeps throwing out, I'm wondering if this was a good idea at all.

We walk into the park, and its hugeness overwhelms me. This is someplace I've always wanted to go, that part wasn't a lie, and seeing the Cinderella Castle in the flesh is an awesome experience. But right now I don't have room for any emotion that's not sheer panic.

We get settled at a bench in the park, and I convince my parents to give us some alone time once Heath gets here. There's so much I want to say to Heath, but I can't say it if we're in a group.

But I'm here. I'm close to him—I can really feel it. Mom offers to grab me some food or soda, but I can't stomach anything right now. I just need to see him, and I need this to be real. Together, we count down the minutes.

"I love you," Mom says, and she pulls me into a hug. "And I'm excited for you."

"Don't be excited for me yet," I say, but even as I say it, I feel the falseness of what I'm saying. With Heath, I don't have to be cynical. I can trust him. But there's still this weird self-preservation instinct that kicks in every time I get my hopes up.

"He's here," I say, standing up. Heath and Diana walk through the gates and start panning the crowd to look for me. I wonder if he even knows what's happening—I should have never let Diana force me into this surprise.

My parents dash off stealthily, proving that they do in fact love me and will not be embarrassing me in this, my time of greatest vulnerability. He gets closer to me, and I count down the seconds until his eyes meet mine.

When they do, something releases inside me, and I feel the tears well up in my eyes.

He's here. He's here, and he's perfect.

HEATH

He's here.

He's really here. It almost seems unreal, after ten weeks apart, but here he is. He's wearing a button-up shirt (in Florida, in August) looking like a total goober amid entire throngs of people wearing Disney shirts or tank tops, but it's so perfectly him that it's taking all my resistance not to run to him.

Wait, why am I *not* running to him?

I see Diana step to the side as I jog in his direction. He's smiling so hard, and it must be matching my expression because my face already hurts. He walks up to me, and for once, in the crowd, it's just us. It's me with my hand on his shoulder in my truck bed as we look up to the stars. It's me with my arms wrapped around his body after I win a baseball game. It's me with my hands on his face in the quiet of my truck, pulling him toward me so quickly yet savoring every millisecond before our lips touch.

The taste of his spearmint gum gets passed between us as our lips pull against each other, again, and again. I put my forehead into his, and I'm no longer in the future, seeing the days, months, years that we have to come—I'm fully in the now.

"I love you," he says. "I've loved you so long, I thought I'd never be able to say it out loud."

I kiss him harder, and it starts to dawn on me that we're in public, and his parents and Diana are probably lingering in eyesight.

"I love you too," I say, with one last kiss, for now. "But . . . you already knew that."

EPILOGUE

SAL

THE FOUR OF US take our seats on the picnic blanket on the baseball diamond behind Gabriel's house. As per usual, Gabe's mom has shoved about eighteen pounds of food in our hands to carry out here, and as we spread it all out, I wonder if I'll ever be hungry again.

Reese was the first to get back, and his family instantly had a huge welcome party that none of us could attend. Not even Heath, which was pretty devastating to him, because (1) he loves Reese's family parties, and he was *sure* he'd get all the cousins' names right this time, and (2) it would've been his first chance to show up as Reese's boyfriend.

Reese asked me, once, why he couldn't have what Gabe and I had, and I found that to be an intensely silly question. Gabe and I didn't have anything but an addiction to each other, with years of complicated friendship being buried by habit and lust and, honestly, the need for real love.

I found love in what I do, of course. I'm not really interested in a boyfriend right now, even though I think it's wild that I was the only one who came back from this summer without one. I may not have a boyfriend, but thanks to the senator's secret bid for the presidency, I have some sort of plan to get me through the year. And for the first time in a while, I feel like my mom has my back too. And that's enough.

We've spread the blanket out like we did before, but the dynamic is different. For one, Heath won't stop wearing tacky air-brushed tank tops, which is a problem. But also, it's a little strange to have them sharing the same corner of the blanket, sneaking kisses when they think we're not looking.

Reese eventually showed us all his designs, and that was the moment I stopped thinking of this as some odd hobby and started thinking of it as his inevitable career. His illustrations have always been smart, but his designs are next level. It sounded like the feedback he got from his classmates all summer was impossibly frustrating, but it obviously did him some good.

Heath's back to practicing baseball eighty-five hours a day, but he's working hard for that Vanderbilt scholarship. He impressed the scouts a lot last year, and he'll be off to some training camps throughout the year that will hopefully secure him some sort of scholarship. He'll end up somewhere, but I don't want to be in the room when Reese realizes he's bound for New York and Heath is bound for Tennessee.

Heath's dad's apartment, though, is way better than he let on. It's not huge, but it's nice. And they don't have to mow their lawn, which is something I would literally kill for. I don't think he and his dad are perfectly happy, but they're talking more than they used to. And Heath has started cooking more? I don't know, suddenly he's embracing his eastern European heritage and their apartment smells only of cabbage, but I guess he was looking for family all along, and he found it. Diana is even coming up for a visit soon. She seems a little intense, based on her IG comments (I haven't followed her back yet, and she's pissed), but she cares a *lot* for our boy Heath, so she's good in my book.

. . . I should just follow her back.

Gabe and Matt are together, and they are so obnoxious about it that I think that's really all they got out of their volunteer experience. Or maybe I'm just a little jealous. My bed *is* a little chilly some nights. But it's for the best.

Because Gabe really is happy. He was such a mess when he left. I never expected him to fully reinvent himself—because, again, he just needed to figure out he was already awesome—but he did come back a different version of himself. He's excited about college, which his dad and sister are ecstatic about, and he finally knows he can make friends. Which we all knew, you know, *being his friends and all.* But sometimes it takes Gabe a little longer to get out of his head.

The sun passes briefly behind the clouds, and everything around us is encased in this soft glow. A lot has changed, but days like this? It's almost like they're a kind of perfect that'll never change.

So, yeah. We're good.

ACKNOWLEDGMENTS

I FULLY WROTE AND edited *Golden Boys* in the middle of the COVID-19 pandemic. While I was scared and isolated, I coped by writing a book packed with friendship and connection that held the message that, even if we're apart, we're all still there for each other in the end. I'm so proud of this story, but I couldn't have done it without so many of you. Some very big thank-yous are in order:

To my agent, Brent Taylor, for his constant work to make my dreams become a reality. I feel so lucky to have you in my corner for all the (many!) ups and downs of this career. Special thanks to the president of Triada US, Uwe Stender, for his additional support of this book.

To my incredible editor, Mary Kate Castellani, for helping me make this book stronger than I could've ever imagined. Also, to my entire team at Bloomsbury for all their work to put this book in the hands of readers all over the world: Lily Yengle, Ksenia Winn-icki, Phoebe Dyer, Erica Barmash, Beth Eller, Jasmine Miranda, Noella James, John Candell, Donna Mark, Diane Aronson, Laura Phillips, Nicholas Church, Pat McHugh, Liz Byer, Hannah Sand-ford, Bea Cross, Mattea Barnes, and Tobias Madden.

To Connie Gabbert, who designed and illustrated the US cover, and to Patrick Leger, who illustrated the UK cover. To Brett Wright for bringing Reese's character to life by perfectly illustrating his journal entries.

To Ryan La Sala, Claribel A. Ortega, Brigid Kemmerer, Adam Sass, Dahlia Adler, and the many other author friends who kept me going through the seemingly impossible task of publishing a book mid-pandemic!

To all my close friends, especially the few whose names I slipped into this book! To my Dayton2Daytona crew and to all my DC friends for the setting inspiration, it was so much fun revisit-ing these cities through Heath's and Sal's eyes.

To my parents, Karen and Phil Sr., my in-laws, Bruce and Andi, and to the rest of my incredibly supportive family for join-ing me on this amazing journey. I couldn't do this without you!

And finally, to Jonathan. Just when I thought we'd been through it all, a pandemic sweeps in and traps us in a tiny one-bedroom apartment for a year. Through all the puzzles, books, video games, TV shows, and Zoom parties, I'm so grateful to have had you by my side through it all.

FALL IN LOVE WITH MORE BOOKS
FROM PHIL STAMPER ...

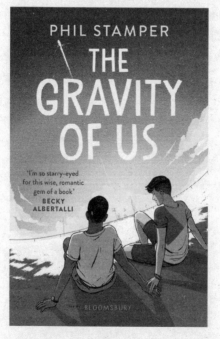

'I'm so starry-eyed for this wise, romantic gem of a book'

Becky Albertalli, bestselling author of
Simon vs. the Homo Sapiens Agenda

'A grounded romance that shapes into its own lovely constellation'

Adam Silvera, *New York Times* bestselling author of
They Both Die at the End

FALL IN LOVE WITH MORE BOOKS FROM PHIL STAMPER ...

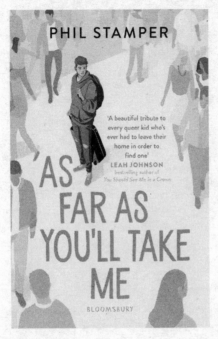

'A beautiful tribute to every queer kid who's ever
had to leave their home in order to find one'
Leah Johnson, bestselling author of
You Should See Me in a Crown